Praise for the *New York Times* Bestselling Orchard Mysteries

"Fun and entertaining . . . [A] well-written mystery with a wonderful cast of characters and a pleasant setting . . . Sheila Connolly's writing style brings the reader into the sights, scents, and sounds of a small town. You can almost smell the apples as they are picked off the tree. She draws the reader in and does not let go."　—Open Book Society

"Meg's determination to run an orchard on her own without any experience makes her an admirable character, as she faces each new challenge with good humor and a smidgeon of exasperation. A reliable cast of characters support Meg and make this a strong series that continues its streak of compelling plots."　—Kings River Life Magazine

"Sheila Connolly continues to include fascinating facts about apples and orchards within her stories . . . Not only will you get hooked on the mystery, but you will be racing to the kitchen to bake an apple treat!"
　—Cozy Mystery Book Reviews

"Fans will enjoy the heroine taking a bite out of crime in this fun regional cozy."　—Genre Go Round Reviews

"Really well written . . . I was constantly kept guessing. This series is in its stride, and I'm eagerly awaiting the next book in this series."　—Fresh Fiction

"Meg is a smart, savvy woman who's working hard to fit into her new community—just the kind of protagonist I look for in today's traditional mystery. I look forward to more trips to Granford, Massachusetts!"
　—Meritorious Mysteries

continued . . .

"An enjoyable and well-written book with some excellent apple recipes at the end."　　　　　　—Cozy Library

"[A] wonderful slice of life in a small town . . . The mystery is intelligent and has an interesting twist . . . *Rotten to the Core* is a fun, quick read with an enjoyable heroine, an interesting hook, and some yummy recipes at the end."
　　　　　　—The Mystery Reader (4 stars)

"Full of rich description, historical context, and mystery."
　　　　　　—The Romance Readers Connection

"Meg Corey is a very likable protagonist . . . [A] delightful new series."　　　　　　—Gumshoe Review

"An example of everything that is right with the cozy mystery . . . [A] likable heroine, an attractive small-town setting, a slimy victim, and fascinating side elements . . . There's depth to the characters in this book that isn't always found in crime fiction . . . Sheila Connolly has written a winner for cozy mystery fans."
　　　　　　—Lesa's Book Critiques

"[A] warm, very satisfying read."
　　　　　　—RT Book Reviews (4 stars)

"The premise and plot are solid, and Meg seems a perfect fit for her role."　　　　　　—Publishers Weekly

"Meg Corey is a fresh and appealing sleuth with a bushelful of entertaining problems . . . One crisp, delicious read."
　　　　　　—Claudia Bishop, bestselling author of
　　　　　　the Hemlock Falls Mysteries

"[A] delightful look at small-town New England, with an intriguing puzzle thrown in."
　　　　　　—JoAnna Carl, national bestselling author of
　　　　　　the Chocoholic Mysteries

A Late Frost

Sheila Connolly

BERKLEY PRIME CRIME
New York

BERKLEY PRIME CRIME
Published by Berkley
An imprint of Penguin Random House LLC
375 Hudson Street, New York, New York 10014

ISBN: 9780425275832

First Edition: November 2017

Printed in the United States of America
1   3   5   7   9   10   8   6   4   2

Cover art © MaryAnn Lasher
Book design by Laura K. Corless

To all the small farmers who believe in fresh healthy food grown locally, and who are inspiring a new generation of farmers' markets in towns all over New England and beyond.

Acknowledgments

After a honeymoon (and a murder) in New Jersey, Meg and Seth Chapin are back in Granford trying to figure out what comes next. Meg's longtime manager has taken off for an internship in Australia, so she's training a new person, recommended by her friend and ally Christopher—who is now courting Seth's mother, Lydia. Life goes on in the small New England town—and so does death.

Granford is based on a real town in western Massachusetts, and that moves on too. Since I started this series, they've added a wonderful new library, as well as a new police station. The town's offices are also hunting for new space. But the heart of the town remains the same. I thought the Yankee citizens of the town deserved some fun before farming season began again, so I gave them a new town festival, just when everyone is getting cabin fever.

I want to thank my editor, Tom Colgan at Berkley, and his able assistants for shepherding this series for so long, through a lot of turmoil in the publishing world. I also want to thank my agent, Jessica Faust of BookEnds, who has nudged and prodded this series all along the way. And as always, the support and professional insights provided by Sisters in Crime (and my local chapter, New England Sisters in Crime), the amazing SinC Guppies, and Mystery Writers of America have been essential. It is an ongoing pleasure to be part of the writers' community, which provides generous support and encouragement to all writers.

1

 "Did we celebrate Christmas this year?" Meg Corey Chapin asked her still-newish husband, Seth.

He turned from the stove in the kitchen, holding up a coffeepot. "More?"

"Please!" Meg told him.

Seth refilled her cup, topped off his, and sat down across from her at the kitchen table. His dog, Max, a solidly built Golden Retriever, laid a head on his foot and resumed his nap. "Christmas . . . yes, I believe we did. I seem to remember there was a tree, and boxes with paper and ribbons on them, and family members kept popping in. Why are you asking now?"

"Because it all seems like a blur. After the honeymoon, which wasn't exactly normal or typical—not that I'm complaining, and it wasn't our fault that we got stuck solving a murder—we came back and Bree told us she was taking another job and leaving in two weeks, and somehow I haven't gotten things together since. Thank goodness there's nothing that absolutely needs to be done right now in the orchard."

"It's too bad Bree had to leave," Seth agreed.

Bree had been Meg's orchard manager since she'd first arrived in Granford to find she owned an apple orchard and might actually need to make an income from it. When they'd first met, Bree had recently graduated from UMass in nearby Amherst, but she was young, untested, female, and born to Jamaican parents, any of which could have been an impediment to finding a job in agriculture. But she'd come highly recommended by a respected professor at UMass, Christopher Ramsdell, born in Australia, and Meg knew she needed someone to manage the orchard, since she was clueless about it, so she'd agreed to hire Bree. Christopher had been using the orchard as a sort of living demonstration for his students, so he knew it well. Meg had hoped that he had transferred most of that information to Bree, and it turned out that he had.

Meg couldn't afford to pay Bree much. She had thrown in free housing to sweeten the deal, so since her arrival Bree had been living in the Colonial house Meg had acquired along with the orchard. She'd proved to be a good roommate: she had kept to herself, done her share of the cooking and cleaning, and been invaluable to Meg in getting to know her orchard and learning what trees she had and how to harvest, store, and sell the apples. Bree's Achilles' heel was keeping financial records for the orchard, although she was good at tracking what had been done with which trees and what needed to be done from year to year. But Meg could more than compensate on the financial side since most of her professional experience had come from years of working in a Boston bank. They'd made a good team, even after Seth had started spending more and more time at the house, until they had finally married in December, almost two years after Meg had moved to Granford.

And then Bree had left for an internship in Australia, with Meg's blessing. She wanted Bree to succeed and be happy, but it had left her high and dry. Even after two years, there was still a lot she didn't know about growing apples.

"Tell me about it," Meg told Seth. "But Christopher said he had a good candidate to replace her."

"You think she'll come back here?"

"I really don't know. Selfishly I'd like that, but I want her to do well, so I can't exactly stand in her way. We'll have to see how the new person works out."

"You have anything major on your calendar?" Seth asked.

"Not until we need to prune, and that's not urgent—yet. You?"

"A few small clean-up projects, and I suppose I should start drumming up some new business for when the weather warms up."

"You like the old-house projects better?" Meg asked. Seth had been a plumber, running what had been his father's small company, when they'd first met, but his heart lay in house renovation and restoration, mainly for the older buildings in the area, and there were plenty of those.

"Better than what?" he replied. "There aren't a lot of major projects coming down the pike. Well, the town is still wrestling with what to do with the old library, now that the new one is open, but if they can't decide what that building should be, they can't exactly advertise for architects, much less contractors. And there might be a conflict of interest, since I'm a town selectman. You and I both know I'd give them a fair estimate, but we don't want anybody to challenge the process. I'm okay with that."

"And that's the only major project? That suits your particular skills, that is?"

"For now. Most people wait until winter's over to see what work their homes need, so I'm not worried. Besides, you can support me, right?"

"In your dreams! But we'll always have apples to eat. I can plant a garden, and maybe you can trap a muskrat or two in the swamp."

"There aren't a lot of muskrats in Massachusetts, and I think you need a permit to trap them. You want to make a fur coat? I'm not about to shoot anything. How do you feel about eating frogs?"

"I've tried them once, I think. Kinda like chicken? But not a lot of meat on them." Meg took another sip of her coffee. "So, the bottom line is, there's nothing either one of us has to do today?"

"Looks like it. You have any ideas?"

"I am at a total loss. I don't know what to do with spare time anymore. And I refuse to look at spreadsheets, though I know taxes are looming. Even if I was a financial professional."

"We should discuss our shared finances at some point, you know," Seth said.

"My head knows it, but right now I don't wanna. Very adult of me, isn't it?"

"We could schedule a time. You know, we've got two

unrelated businesses to consider, both of which are sole proprietorships, and the details are complicated."

"Seth, my love, you are depressing me. You think I don't know that? Let me ask you this: do we have money in the bank right now, after all the wedding and honeymoon hoo-hah?"

"So that was hoo-hah? Live and learn. Yes, we have some money, and we can cover our bills. But we may never be able to retire."

"That is the farthest thing from my mind at the moment."

Their banter was interrupted by an insistent banging on the front door. "What time is it?" Meg asked. "That much noise this early is seldom good news. And nobody who knows us uses that door."

"So you want me to go, right?" Seth said, smiling.

"If you will, please, sir. I've got your back."

Seth stood up and headed through the dining room and the living room to the front door. Meg didn't move. *Please, let it not be a crisis.* They'd had more than their share in recent months. She heard the creak of the door opening, and the rumble of male voices. All right, their unexpected caller was male. Salesman? State trooper? Religious fanatic? She couldn't begin to guess. Luckily Seth returned quickly, followed by a twentysomething guy wearing well-worn clothes and a heavy, shapeless coat. He was shorter than Seth—maybe about her height? He could use a haircut, but at least he didn't have one of the scruffy beards that seemed to be popular among his age group.

"Meg, this is Larry Bennett. He says Christopher sent him."

"Hey, hi," the guy said. "Sorry—Christopher said he'd

meet me here so we could do the introduction thing. He told me you needed an orchard manager?"

"Ah. Yes, we do," Meg said. "Please, sit down. You want some coffee?"

Larry sat. "Yeah, sure. Please," he added as an afterthought.

"Seth, can you do the honors with the coffee?" Meg asked. "I'm Meg Corey, uh, Chapin. Sorry, Seth, but I'm still getting used to it."

"No problem—I think my ego will survive." He set a mug of coffee in front of Larry and took a seat next to Meg.

"We just got married last month," Meg explained, feeling foolish. "I don't know how much Christopher has told you, but I'll give you the short version while we wait. I kind of inherited this place about two years ago, and when I decided to stay I realized I'd have to make a living from the orchard, if possible. But I had no experience, so Christopher suggested I hire Bree—Briona Stewart—who was one of his students. Did he explain all this?"

"Not a lot. So she's been working here for two years? Why's she leaving?"

"She was offered an internship in Australia, which would be a big plus on her résumé, and I told her she should take it. She left right after New Year's."

"So you need someone to manage the whole thing? What've you got?"

"'Bout fifteen acres of mature trees, and we put in another three acres of new trees last year, mostly heirlooms."

"What do you do for storage?"

"Seth built some refrigerated storage units in the barn when we started, but mostly I sell direct to local markets."

"So no big contracts?"

"No, and I'm not looking for any right now," Meg said,

reflecting that this Larry person wasn't exactly making nice with his new employer, although he was asking the right questions. A little rough around the social edges?

Larry turned to Seth. "You—Seth, is it?—you work in the orchard, too?"

"No, I'm a renovator, but I know plumbing. Separate operation, but I use the building next to the barn as my office space."

"Other employees?" Larry turned back to Meg, dismissing Seth abruptly.

"Bree set up a team of pickers for me who come in for the harvest."

"No automation?"

"Not for the picking. No, we pick by hand, and move the apples around with our tractor. When there's a drought, which we have had recently, there's a well that supplies the orchard, but we need to install a new pumping system."

"Expensive," Larry said.

"Yes, it will be." Meg decided it was time to take charge. After all, she was supposed to be interviewing him, not the other way around. "What's your background?"

"I've got a degree in plant sciences from Cornell. You know about their apple programs, right?"

"I've heard of them, but I haven't visited. It's on my wish list. When did you graduate?"

"A couple of years ago."

"And what have you been doing since?"

"I've taken a bunch of graduate-level agricultural courses at UMass—that's how I met Christopher. There was some grant funding for apple research projects, so I was working on those. I haven't made up my mind if I want to go for a grad degree, but I need a job."

"Have you worked in an orchard before?"

"My folks had one, but they're gone now, and so's the orchard."

"Why do you want this job? We're pretty small, and there's not a lot of room to grow. What can you learn here?"

"Look, I need a paycheck, all right? I know apples, and there are some good ideas I picked up, that I'd like to try out."

"Assuming I'm willing. You'd be working for me, and I need to be part of making any decisions."

Larry looked like he was swallowing a comment, but in the end he said, "Yeah, I get that. But I can bring new ideas to you, right?"

"Of course. I don't pretend to know everything, but I wanted to be clear from the start. I'm willing to listen to you."

Meg sat back and contemplated this Larry person. He was kind of abrasive. Defensive? Or just obnoxious? And young. Still, if he'd been raised with an orchard, he must have more experience than Bree had when she took on the job. And if Christopher vouched for him, he must have something going for him. Where the heck was Christopher, anyway? A knock at the back door answered that question. Meg got up to let Christopher in.

"So sorry I'm late, Meg, my dear. Seth. Ah, I see my young protégée has arrived. How've you been getting on, Larry?"

Larry shrugged. "Okay, I guess."

"Coffee, Christopher?" Seth asked.

"Oh, no, no, thank you. I've had my fill for this morning."

"Have you heard from Bree, Christopher?" Meg asked.

"My contact in Australia informs me that she arrived safely and is quick to learn. I don't expect to hear much more from her. And you?"

"No, but I assume she's busy." Not that Bree owed her any personal contact. They'd moved past an employer-employee relationship, but stopped somewhere short of friends.

"Has Larry seen your property yet?" Christopher changed the subject adroitly.

"Just from the road," Larry said. "We were talking about the job."

"Well, then, I suggest we take a look at the orchard and the relevant facilities," Christopher said, rubbing his hands together.

"I'll leave you to it," Seth said. "I've got some other chores to do."

"Seth, can you feed the goats, please?" Meg asked.

"Sure, no problem. And I'll give Max some exercise, too."

Meg stood up. "Well, then, let's take the tour." They gathered up their coats, and Meg led the way out the back door, followed by Christopher and Larry.

2

"Ask any questions you want, Larry," Meg said. They stood huddled together in the driveway, shivering in the January wind. Meg pointed. "That's Seth's office space, at the end of the driveway. The barn is obviously the barn. That's where the storage for the apples is."

"Can we take a look at that?" Larry asked.

"Sure." Meg led them to the front of the barn and hauled open one of the big double doors. Inside, she pointed to the apple storage units aligned along one wall. "That's what we've got, the ones Seth built."

"How full are they now?" Larry asked.

"About twenty-five percent, I think. The ones that ripened late or hold well."

"Where were the apples kept before you built these?"

"You'd do better to ask Christopher. I've got a pretty short history here."

Christopher spoke up. "We had no holding facilities here then. The university managed this as an experimental orchard, and while some of the apples were sold commercially, that was not a priority. Some went to the university kitchens, others to local shelters."

"So you were more interested in managing the trees than in optimizing the crop?" Larry asked.

"Yes. That's how I chose to define my mandate," Christopher said. "The sale and marketing aspects were handled by others. In your opinion, young Mr. Bennett, would this division of labor have had an impact on the crop?"

"Maybe. If you'd been interested in producing more apples, or modifying size or resistance, you might have made different choices."

"A valid point. One which you and Meg might choose to explore at some point."

"We should get moving before our fingers freeze, Christopher," Meg interrupted him. "I'll take you up to the main part of the orchard." She marched up the hill behind the house, followed by the two men, and she explained along the way, "The boundaries are the road that runs in front of the house, up to the one that runs along the crest of the road at the top of the hill—about fifteen acres total, as I told you, plus the new acreage to the north. As you can see, the trees are aligned with the top road."

"North-south?" Larry asked. "Why?"

"I have no idea. Christopher, you have any thoughts?"

"There's been an orchard here since long before my time. But a north-south alignment is generally recommended."

"You could plant more densely now," Larry pointed out. "Close spacing."

"We've tried that for the new plantings, but we haven't seen the results yet. That's the wellhead there, in the center. I'm going to have to run the numbers for this past season before I know whether we can afford a more efficient irrigation system."

"You used it much?" Larry asked.

"A few times, in dry spells."

"How've you been distributing the water?"

"We've used a water tank pulled by our tractor."

"So essentially you've been hand-watering the whole orchard? That's a lot of work."

"Yes, it is. But I had priorities more important than replacing the irrigation."

"What kind of production did you get this past year?" Larry asked, and Meg launched into an accounting of bushels harvested, for each apple variety and in total, and timing of the harvest, and handling, and any number of arcane items Meg hoped she had an accurate handle on.

Finally Larry seemed satisfied. "You said you put in some new trees last year?"

"Yes. Technically they're planted on Seth's property, which adjoins mine, but I lease the land from him, so it's part of my business." When all that had happened, they'd had no thoughts of marriage, and Meg had wanted to keep a clear boundary between business and personal issues. But Larry didn't need to know that. She and Seth had arrived at a different agreement regarding his use of the office space on her property, although she'd had no other use for it, so it was standing empty anyway. It didn't hurt that he'd improved the space, adding storm windows and dependable heating to what had been a ramshackle out-building.

Meg dragged her attention back to Larry when he asked, "Equipment?"

"An elderly tractor, with a trailer for collecting the harvested apples. Some hand-carried sprayers. I practice integrated pest management here, so I don't use pesticides, or only biologicals."

"Got it. What did you plant?" After Meg had listed the choices she had made, Larry said, "These new trees you put in—they're not the most productive varieties."

"I know that. But I wanted to preserve some of the heirloom varieties, and I've found a niche market for them locally."

"So you're not all about making money from this orchard?"

Meg was getting tired of Larry's abrupt attitude. "No. As I told you, I inherited the house and property, and I knew nothing about raising apples at that time, although I have a financial background. I've spent two years learning the business and trying to see where I fit. *If* I fit. I've enjoyed it, and I'm committed for the near term. But I respect the old ways of doing things, and I don't want to sink any profits I make into fancy new machinery. It's a small orchard. If that doesn't work for you, you don't have to work here."

Larry looked down at his feet, suddenly appearing younger. "Sorry," he mumbled. "I was just trying to get a feel for what you wanted. I'm not against small, but I do think that efficiency matters, and trying to optimize your yield. I know there's a trade-off between mechanizing the operation to produce more and staying small—boutique, even—and enjoying the process more."

"Exactly. Have you seen enough?"

"Yeah, I think so. Nothing else to see?"

"No, that's the whole operation."

"Why don't we go back down the hill now?" Christopher suggested. "I for one am a bit chilled."

They filed down the hill in silence. Meg was fuming internally. What did Christopher see in this rude young man? Why on earth did he think that Larry would be a good fit for her admittedly small orchard operation? There must be more to the story.

Back in the driveway once again, Larry said abruptly, "Look, I've gotta meet a guy in Amherst. Thanks for showing me around, Meg. Christopher, I'll call you." He turned on his heel and loped toward his battered far-from-new car before either Meg or Christopher could respond. They watched as he pulled out of the driveway.

"What was that all about?" Meg asked.

"He doesn't make a very good first impression, does he?" Christopher said ruefully. "If you'll invite me in, I'll try to explain."

Back in the kitchen, Seth was seated at the table reading the paper. "Chicken—is that the work you just had to get done?" Meg said.

"Forgive me, Christopher, but that kid kind of rubs me the wrong way," Seth said. "Whatever made you suggest him?"

"He was just about to explain that to me," Meg told him. "I felt pretty much the way you did, Seth. Can I get you something, Christopher?"

"Could you manage a cup of tea? The wind's a bit cutting."

"Of course." Meg set about boiling water, locating the

teapot, and scrounging up some tea bags. At least they were imported, not generic. She listened with half an ear to what Seth and Christopher were saying.

"I've been meaning to have a chat with you, Seth, but you were gone for a time, and . . . well, the appropriate opportunity has not arisen until now."

Seth help up a hand. "Christopher, I think I know what you're talking about. I don't need the details. But you and my mother are both adults, and if she's happy, I'm happy. I'm not going to ask if your intentions are honorable. By the way, Mom hasn't said anything. Are we okay?"

"And here I thought we'd been so discreet. How did you know?"

"Well, we saw you together at the wedding," Seth told him, "and if we noticed in our state of newly wedded bliss, I'd say it had to be pretty obvious."

"Bree noticed, too," Meg said as she set the full teapot on the table. "And she's not particularly sensitive to human beings' emotional states." Which, Meg had to admit, was sort of like Larry. She went back to retrieve mugs, spoons, sugar, and milk.

"So I have your blessing?" Christopher asked, helping himself to the tea.

"Of course you do," Meg said firmly. "You're grown-ups. Gee, Seth, so are we now. We're an old married couple."

"I hope so. Grown-up, that is—not old," Seth said. "But definitely married."

Meg turned her attention back to Christopher. "So now that's settled, what's the story with Larry? Does he even want the job here, or did he come here today just to keep you happy?"

"Let me say first, I do hope Bree returns, although I'll

concede coming back to work here might not be the best career choice she could make for herself. But I'd like to leave that door open."

"So you think Larry would be a short-term placeholder, until Bree decides what she wants to do?" Meg asked.

"Something along those lines. Let me be frank with you. Larry Bennett is clearly lacking in some fundamental social skills, but he is a talented orchardist. He mentioned he had grown up with orchards?"

"He said that, yes."

"It was not an easy life. The orchard itself was played out—it had been neglected for too long, and his family was in no position to bring it back, nor did they care to. Larry was an only child, and apparently his father was allergic to hard work. So Larry did what he could do, and kept it going until he reached college age. Then he told his father and mother that he was done, and if they wanted to keep the farm, they could take over. They sold it within months. Larry attended Cornell on scholarship, combined with part-time jobs and student loans. He came to UMass, and I found some grant funding for him. He is, if nothing else, a hard worker. But he never had the opportunity to socialize with his peer group, and it shows."

"I hope you don't think I'm supposed to fix that, Christopher," Meg said.

"No. You would be his employer, not a surrogate mother."

"I have another question, which might be more relevant to his working here," Meg said slowly.

"And that would be?" Christopher asked.

"Several of his comments seemed to me to suggest that he was displeased with the way Bree and I chose to manage things. Like, we should be getting higher production from our trees. We should have made upgrading the irrigation a higher priority. We should have chosen different trees for the new section—that heirlooms were a waste of time." Meg stopped, wondering what her question was, exactly.

"I understand what you're saying, Meg, and it's a valid concern," Christopher said. "He sees running an orchard as a business and no more. In contrast, I'm going to guess that you harbor a slightly more romantic notion of it?"

"Romantic?" Meg sputtered. "You've got to be kidding."

"Hear me out. You have a familial attachment to this place. The old house, the ranks of trees, the barn—all of this is the quintessential New England to many Americans, and New England is the psychological icon of your country. In addition, you value hard work, even overcoming hardship, and to some degree you have chosen that as your lifestyle. You could simply have walked away when you first saw the place, could you not?"

"I guess," Meg admitted. "I had no better idea at the time, and I guess I thought hard work might distract me from my own lack of plan or direction. I suppose I see why you might call it romantic. It certainly wasn't practical on my part. But what's your point, as it applies to Larry?"

"Larry is the antithesis of a romantic. As was Bree, in her own way. She came to you with a chip on her shoulder, as if daring you to find fault. Larry doesn't feel he has something to prove, but he believes he's right in his ideas. In a way, he is, from a practical viewpoint."

"Can you see us working together? Or rather, him working for me, with my so-called romantic, impractical ideas?"

"Let me put it this way: he will do what he believes is best for the orchard. If you disagree with him, for what he sees as frivolous reasons, then you will have to justify those reasons to him. But clearly those decisions are yours to make. Not his. That he has to learn."

Meg nodded. "I see your point. Do I have to decide right this minute?"

"I'd say you have a week or two. I don't know that he's talked to any other places around here. As you've noted, he doesn't present himself well."

"Then let me think about it for a few days, all right?" And discuss it with Seth, who'd have to live with Larry, too.

"Of course, my dear. Now you must tell me about your honeymoon. I've never had the opportunity to visit Jefferson's orchards, although I've read about them. Are they all they're said to be?"

And the talk turned to more pleasant matters.

3

After Christopher had left, Meg settled back at the table with Seth. As she had told him, having free time left her unsettled. She had a long list of household projects she could be working on, and there was always the looming accounting for the orchard waiting for her, with taxes following hard on its heels. As a result, she had to force herself to sit still and enjoy the moment. Unfortunately she couldn't turn her mind off, and it kept churning away, popping out new *Things to be Done* at intervals.

"We should talk about Larry," Meg told Seth.

Seth neatly folded the newspaper he had finished. "Yes. How much input do you want me to have in this decision about a manager?"

"It seems to me that you have to—well, not exactly live with him, but share space with him, see him regularly—so you should have some say. But as I think you're suggesting, this is my business, so I should be making the decisions. And I have no intention of meddling in your business affairs, unless I think you've taken on more than you can possibly handle and you're wearing yourself out. So, back to the question. Can you see Larry working here, with me?"

"I'm trying, but it's not easy. If I hadn't heard Christopher's explanation, I probably would have said no way. But if you do hire him, I wouldn't expect him to change, or at least, not quickly. He appears to have strong opinions about orchards. Can you handle that?"

"Seth, almost anybody around here knows more about orchards than I do."

"Meg, you've learned a lot in the past couple of years, and you've done well, all things considered. Bree played a part in that, but you paid attention to what she did, and you listened to her. The question now is, can you stand your ground if Larry has very different ideas?"

"I don't really know. Christopher says I'm a romantic when it comes to the orchard, and that may mean that I sacrifice some money-making potential. I'm going to have to think about that."

"I think you have two major criteria: one, you have to make enough money to support yourself, and two, you have to enjoy what you do. It's up to you to balance those two. Can Larry help? Maybe. He seems to have the right expertise. But can you enjoy working with him? That's not as clear."

"A tidy summary, Mr. Chapin. I guess I don't have to decide today. Maybe I'll sleep on it. I still feel a bit, well, kind of jet-lagged, after the wedding and the honeymoon and what happened at my parents', and then coming back and diving right into Christmas. I feel kind of disoriented."

"Then we're lucky to have some downtime. Enjoy it."

Meg was startled when their landline rang. Nobody ever called, preferring either their cell phones or bypassing a phone altogether and e-mailing them. Seth stood up. "I'll get it." He walked over to the old wall phone and picked up the receiver, then walked around the corner into the dining room for some privacy. He was gone for a few minutes, and when he returned to the kitchen, he resumed his seat. "The real world is catching up to us again."

"What do you mean?"

"That was Tom Moody."

"Who?"

"Head of the Granford Board of Selectmen, remember? He reminded me that we have a meeting tonight—not a regular meeting, but one that kind of cropped up at the last minute, about something that needs immediate attention."

Meg shut her eyes and feigned intense concentration. "Okay, you're still a Granford selectman. Check. When do you run again? Or do you even want to?"

"To answer your questions, in order: yes, in the fall, maybe. In any case, the only item on the agenda is planning for the WinterFare."

"The what?"

"Okay, I'll have to take a step back and explain. A few months ago, a woman who had recently moved to Granford with her husband got in touch with Tom and said she'd love to volunteer her time and act as what I guess amounts to a booster for the town. Raise our profile, find ways to make tourists stop here rather than just pass through on their way to Amherst or Northampton. Not a bad idea, in principle, but as you've no doubt noticed, we don't have a lot of things to drag people in."

"There's Gran's," Meg protested.

"Yes, but it's still young, and it hasn't quite reached 'must-see' restaurant status. That's not to say it won't, but it's not there yet. And apart from that, there's the Historical Society, which is small, with a mainly local collection. As I told you, it's possible we may end up doing something with the old library, but that's still a ways off. But to cut to the chase, we agreed to talk with this woman—"

"Does she have a name?"

"Yes, it's Monica Whitman. Her husband's name is Douglas. They're in their late fifties, maybe early sixties. Anyway, there was a meeting in December that I missed, but Tom told me the details about them. He thinks Monica has some good ideas—and of course she's not charging us—but the most immediate one was to hold a WinterFare. That's F-A-R-E, not F-A-I-R. She thinks we could hold a food and crafts fair next month, in the high school gymnasium, and offer whatever crops we have in storage plus winter-based crafts, like knitting. Or things like wood carving, pottery. You get the drift."

"I suppose. Why February?"

"Because it's the slowest time of the year. It's dark and cold, and there's not much that can be done outside, for the farmers. People are getting antsy by then, and they've been cooped up for a couple of months. I think I agree with Monica—it would be nice to get everybody out of their houses for a fun event, and the timing makes sense."

"I can see that. Of course I'd contribute some apples— wait, is this a fundraiser?"

"I'm not sure we've decided, but that's not essential. Except we need to get it planned, recruit vendors, sort out refreshments and publicize it—all in about three weeks."

"Yikes! You all don't ask much. You think it can be done?"

"Between the Internet and word of mouth, I think we can pull it off. But we shouldn't expect too much—this is kind of a test. If there seems to be support for the idea, we'll start working to make it bigger and better next year. If it falls flat, we'll have shared a pleasant winter afternoon with our neighbors. We're not asking anybody to churn out twenty-five knit scarves in three weeks. You've already got apples in storage, and other people have other vegetables. Maybe grass-fed beef. Baked goods."

"That sounds nice. I assume you've already counted me in. So what's the meeting about?"

"Planning. Getting the high school on board, since we'll need their gym for it—we've already checked the sports schedule and that's clear. Talk to Nicky and Brian about food. Check what permits we might need, but it should be pretty much like the Harvest Festival, so they or we may be covered already. Maybe find somebody to provide music. We'll have a general meeting for all the participants later in the month."

"Have you met Monica?"

"Not yet—I only know what Tom told me. But she seems really eager to get involved in the community."

"I should have thought of that when I moved here—my life would have been a lot simpler if I'd introduced myself. But I didn't expect to stay."

"And yet, here you are. Are you sorry?"

"Of course not."

They smiled at each other across the table. "Uh, you want to . . ." Meg said.

"Definitely."

After lunch Meg wandered out to chat with the goats, Dorcas and Isabel. They were undemanding creatures: fairly quiet, not messy, and always curious. Meg had rescued them when they were headed for a local Greek restaurant, destined for dinner, but she hadn't made any further plans for them. Breed them? They were both female, but then she'd have to find a male, and worry about birthing baby goats. Kids. No, she had enough else to worry about. Shear them for their wool? Even to her inexperienced eye, she wasn't sure she'd want to wear anything made from their coats. Make goat cheese? But if she remembered her biology correctly, the goat would have to be pregnant and produce a kid before she made any milk. Rent them out to clear other people's fields of poison ivy? She'd read somewhere that the nasty weed didn't bother them, and they could offset the cost of their feed. But that would take organization, and again, she didn't want to add another task to her to-do list. So mostly they remained a decorative addition to her otherwise unused field. They didn't seem to mind. As she leaned on the fence, they stared at her with their weird eyes, and when no treats were forthcoming, they went back to grazing on the frozen grass.

She was surprised to see Larry's car pull into the driveway. She leaned back against the fence and waited for him to approach.

He spoke first, in a rush. "Look, I know I was pushy

and, well, kind of rude before. I guess I was showing off, telling you how much I know. I'm not good with people."

"Christopher told me a bit about your history. I'm surprised you wanted to go into agriculture at all."

"It was all I knew. And it's easy to manage trees and plants—they don't argue with you. Look, I'm out of cash and I really need a job. I don't want you to hire me because you feel sorry for me—I can do the work, and I think I can help you make your orchard better."

"You don't think I'm silly to want a few old-fashioned trees?"

"Not if you accept you're giving up some yield. But I figure you're not in it for the money, right?"

"I already told you that. I want enough, not a lot—I don't expect to get rich doing this. I like this town. I like the work, not that I'm looking for a bigger orchard, after that last addition. I don't much like big machines, but I know I've got to upgrade the ones I've got, if the money's there. I'd be willing to listen to your ideas because I know you know a lot more about all this than I do. But it's still my place, and I don't like arguments."

"I don't, either. So, you want me or not?"

Meg sighed. "Larry, you've got to polish up your people skills if you're going to survive. Do you want to work for me?"

Larry swallowed. "Yes. I'd like that."

"I can't pay much. I pay the pickers market rate, and a lot of them have been working around here for a long time. Can you work with them? Most of them are older than you, and they've got a lot of experience. I'd hate to lose them. But I can only pay so much." Meg named a figure and watched for Larry's response. He didn't seem horrified. Was he really scraping the bottom of the barrel? Because he hadn't found a job for a while, or because he'd lost the ones he'd found?

"Where've you been living?" Meg asked.

"Here and there." He looked away, and Meg wondered if he'd been sleeping in his car—not good weather for that.

"Bree lived in the house here, which was part of the deal we made. Seth came along later. But since we're married now, we'd kind of like more privacy—nothing personal. But there are some other options. You want me to ask around?"

"Yeah, that'd be good. You pay cash? Check?"

"This is a business, and I keep good records. I'd prefer a check, but if I pay cash, I'm going to declare it all, and I'm going to give you a tax form at the end of the year. I won't pay you off the books."

"That's fair. So, we got a deal?"

"I think so. Let's try it for a while and see how it goes. What's the next thing we've got to do?"

"Did you fertilize in the fall?"

"Yes. Bree saw to that, and she left the reports."

"Pruning, then, in the next month. And look into that irrigation system, before you need it and it craps out on you. Look for a secondhand tractor, too—that one you've got is pretty old. Nothing fancy, just sturdy."

"That's about what I was thinking. So, anything you need to work out or take care of before you start?"

"Nope. Thank you, Meg." He stuck out his hand, and Meg shook it. "I'll come back tomorrow, if that's okay."

"No rush—this is about the only downtime I get. I'll pull together the tree records and we can go over them later."

"Great. See you tomorrow." Larry turned and strode toward his car with a noticeable bounce to his step.

He'd just pulled out of the driveway when Seth emerged from his office. "Was that Larry?"

"It was."

"What did he want?"

"The job. By the way, he apologized for being rude and pushy."

"Did you hire him?"

"I did, at least until I see how well we work together. I think he needs a place to stay, and I don't think Bree's old room will work out for him. Any ideas?"

"I'll think about it. Can we do an early dinner? That meeting tonight's at seven."

"Fine by me."

4

Seth came back from his meeting around ten, looking troubled. Meg was tucked up in bed, trying to read a book, although she kept nodding off every few pages. But she was determined to stay awake until her husband—husband!—came home. "How'd it go?" she asked.

"I'm not sure. You'll have to meet Monica. She is a bundle of energy." He didn't sound exactly happy about it.

"Has she done this kind of organizing before?"

"It sounds to me like she's been an uber-volunteer most of her adult life. She said she'd give us references from her last community if we wanted."

"Do you think she knows what she's doing?"

Seth threw himself down on the bed after kicking his shoes off. "I think so. We've done enough of this kind of event here ourselves, and she seems to have touched all the bases. If there's one rule in management, even on the most basic local level, it's 'never turn away a volunteer.' And I think she's got a grip on reality—she doesn't expect the moon from this. She sees it as a trial run. Maybe all she really wants is to get to know some of the people in Granford. This is a great way to get a lot of them together, under happy circumstances."

"Was her husband there?"

"No."

"Where do they live?"

"They bought the old Keyser place, on the road to Amherst. Not far from here, actually."

"That tumble-down old farm? Are they planning to farm it?"

"No, I don't think so. The outbuildings are pretty far gone anyway. I may try to talk to her about working on the house, which is in decent shape considering it's been empty for a while."

"Small-town networking—gotta love it. Who else has signed on for the event?"

"Nicky and Brian were there, and they're enthusiastic. This time of year is slow for them, so they're happy to show off what they can do."

"But not meals as such, right? More like munchies, sandwiches, that kind of thing?"

"I think so. And plenty of coffee, and hot cocoa for the kids."

"Sounds nice. Should I plan for a table? Large? Small? Are you charging a rental fee for space? Does the town expect a cut of the profits?"

"Slow down. We're trying to keep things simple this year. We may implement some of the things you just mentioned next year, if this works out. As for your own table, you won't be the only person with apples, so don't go overboard."

"Who else has apples?" Meg asked.

"A few families—I don't know if you know them. Most of them have a range of crops, and just a few apples, but more than they can use themselves and not enough to sell. But there's one organic farm that I don't know much about."

"I didn't know there was one in Granford. Where is it?"

"At the foot of the mountain, north of here. There's been an orchard there for a long time, but it wasn't managed well, and the last owners kind of let it go. These people bought it maybe three years ago, but they've been working to get the trees back in shape, and clear out the weeds and junk. It's taken them this long to produce even a small crop, which is probably why you haven't been aware of it, but they're eager to show it off. That and the fact that they haven't had a lot of time for socializing."

"Are they registered as organic?"

"Yes. They take it seriously. Or at least, the wife does—she came to the meeting without her husband, said he was home watching the kids. But all their registrations are in place, so they can officially call themselves organic."

"That's not easy to do—lots of paperwork, and lots of restrictions. Bree and I talked about it at some point, remember? It seemed too complicated to deal with then. I'll look forward to meeting them. What's their name?"

"Virginia—Ginny Morris. I think he's Alden on paper, but Ginny called him Al."

"How about the alpaca ladies? Are they in?"

"Oh, yes—they're really excited. They've got a good website business going, but they think they'll sell more if people can actually handle the wool products. They mostly do socks, mittens, hats—that kind of thing. Too bad they can't bring the alpacas into the gym—the kids love 'em."

"Sounds good. Looks like it's coming together, despite the short notice."

"I think it is. I'm going to grab a shower."

"Before you get wet, any ideas about a place for Larry?"

"Sorry, haven't had time to think about it."

"You know, Bree once said something about turning the old chicken coop into a tiny house. Would that make sense?"

"You're asking me to do it?"

"No, because you're supposed to be earning money, right? But maybe Larry could handle the conversion, with a little guidance from you. If he's interested, that is."

"What about lighting? Heating? Plumbing?"

"Hey, I didn't say I'd worked out the details. I'm just putting the idea on the table. You could let him use your house, if you'd rather. That's one of those things you and I need to talk about for the long term. It shouldn't just sit empty." Seth's house was a true Colonial much like her own, but over the past year Seth had been spending more and more time in hers, leaving his own orphaned. Meg understood why he didn't want to sell it, since that house, as well as his mother's next door, had been built by Chapin ancestors a couple of centuries earlier. But leaving it unoccupied was not a good option, and Seth hadn't explored the idea of renting it out. Not that Larry would be a good candidate: it was too big for one person, but he didn't seem like the kind of person who wanted multiple roommates. Something to think about.

"I know. It's on my list. Let me sleep on both ideas, okay?"

"Go right ahead."

The next morning Meg was awakened by an insistent rapping at the back door. Seth wasn't in the bed, so she assumed he was already downstairs, a guess that was confirmed when she heard the sound of the door opening and a piercing female voice greeting Seth.

"Oh, good, it's you, Seth. I'm so glad I got the right house. I'm not too early, am I? I'm always up with the birds, and sometimes I forget that other people like to sleep a little later. What a wonderful house this is! You just got married, didn't you? What's your wife's name? Meg, is it? That's so nice. I hope you'll be very happy together."

As far as Meg could tell, the woman hadn't yet taken a breath, nor had she given Seth time to say anything. She had a picture of him wrapping his hands around her neck, just to stop the gush of words.

At last he managed to get a word in. "Monica. Good to see you. Come on in—it's freezing out there. Can I get you a cup of coffee? Have you had breakfast?"

Meg deduced that it was the eager new resident of Granford, Monica Whitman, not that it was hard. She might as well face the music and go downstairs. In bare feet, Meg padded across the floor to the bathroom, did what was necessary, then pulled on a pair of fleece pants and a matching sweatshirt—the height of elegance for this hour of the morning in her own home. At least they were the same color. She ran a brush through her hair, found slip-on shoes, and descended to the first floor and made her entrance into the kitchen.

"Here she is now," Seth said, stating the obvious. "Meg, this is Monica Whitman—I told you about her."

Meg held out her hand to Monica, who proved to be an older woman slightly shorter than Meg, with more curves. Her hair was silver, cut in a short and practical style. Her outfit was calculatedly casual—nice jeans, a turtleneck, and a colorful sweater over it. "Indeed he did. So you're the woman behind the WinterFare?"

Monica shook her hand vigorously. "I wouldn't go that far. I thought it would be a nice idea to do something at the most miserable part of winter—you know, just get folks together with some good food and things to look at and music. People have told me that you all do a Harvest Festival in the fall, but that's not really the same thing, now, is it? And I'll confess, I really wanted a chance to meet the other people in town. We've only been here a couple of months, and everybody's been so busy. Seth here tells me you grow apples?"

When Monica finally paused to breathe, Meg jumped in. "Yes, I do. I inherited this house and an orchard a couple of years ago, and I've been trying to make a go of it."

When Meg paused, Monica plunged right in again. "Oh, that's so brave of you! I wouldn't know where to start. I haven't had a paid job in years, but I love to help out with projects and events. Are you going to bring apples to our fair? The ones that you grew here? That's wonderful—so New England. What do you think of our name? Did you get the pun? Fare F-A-R-E, like food, for the fair F-A-I-R?"

"Oh. I hadn't seen it written out, but it's a cute idea. I'd be happy to bring apples. Who else have you talked with so far?"

"Well, those lovely young people at the restaurant. Douglas—that's my husband—and I have eaten there a couple of times, and the food is wonderful. And all locally sourced, they told us. Isn't that nice? Do they use your apples there? Because if they do, we've probably already had some. And then there are other farmers in town who would love to show something, and those ladies with the—alpacas, is it? I keep thinking they're llamas, but that's something else, isn't it?"

"Yes," Seth said firmly—and more loudly than he usually spoke. "Have you looked for a band yet?" Meg guessed he was trying to stop Monica's flow of words.

"No, I thought I'd start that today. What kind of music do you think people would like? Modern? Country? Old-timey? It's only background, but I thought it might sound nice. Do you know any musicians?"

"Can't say that I do. Between my work and my town responsibilities, I don't have a lot of spare time. And no musical talent, either. But ask around—I'm sure there's somebody local who'd like the visibility."

"I knew you were the right person to ask!" Monica beamed at him. "I just love this town! It's so, so historical."

"How did you and your husband decide to move here?" Meg managed to ask.

"He's, uh, retired, a couple of years ago. We wanted a place in the country—you know, quiet, pretty."

"Where were you living before?"

"Outside of Chicago. And we've lived other places, too—we went where Doug's job took us! We've lived in a lot of different states, but we never made it to New England. This is the first chance we've had. Well, I won't keep you—I just wanted to stop by and say hello, and to meet you, Meg. Seth, we're going to have another meeting, with all the participants, in a week or two, right? And you'll be there too, Meg?"

"Just as soon as we can put together a list and send out notices," Seth replied. "Can you handle e-mail?"

Monica smiled again. "Well, of course I can! That's how I keep in touch with all my friends from all those places we've lived. I know—we could put together a quick Facebook page for this event. I know Granford has its own website, but I think we can reach out to people more quickly through social media. Don't you?"

Seth commented patiently, "Again, I don't really have time for it. Plus, I grew up in this town, and went to college near here, so most of my friends are pretty close by. Our town staff is small—you'd have to talk to them about updating the website and such."

"Isn't that wonderful! And I'll talk to the people at town hall. Well, I'll let you two eat your breakfast, but I'll be in touch. Does the board of selectmen have an e-mail list? Or does anybody else have one I can borrow?"

"I don't know, but I'll check," Seth said, trying hard to be patient. "I have your number, so I'll let you know when I find out anything. And when we have that meeting scheduled. Thanks for stopping by." Somehow Seth managed to herd Monica out the door without being rude, although Meg wasn't sure Monica would have noticed.

When he came back into the kitchen, Seth all but fell into a chair. "That woman is exhausting! Do you think that's her natural personality, or is she on uppers?"

"Maybe she's just nervous, and wants to make a good impression. Coffee made?"

"It is. I'd volunteer to get it for you, but I haven't got the energy."

"I think I can manage. Did you walk Max?"

"Before I made the coffee. I think he's in the front room, napping."

Meg's cat, Lolly, jumped down from her favorite perch, the top of the refrigerator, and demanded her breakfast, so Meg dished that up, and the sound of popping a can top brought Max running, demanding his own meal, so it was five minutes before Meg managed to fill two coffee mugs and sit down herself. "Larry said he'll be back today. We need to sit down together and figure out what needs to be done. And I need to price irrigation systems. Think we'll have another drought this year?"

"I am not the person to ask, believe me. And if you stop to think, in my business drought is a plus—I can get more outside work done."

"Oh, dear—a major conflict of interest. Do you know anybody around here who handles agricultural water systems?"

"Not offhand, but I can ask around."

"One of the pluses of having spent all your life here. I hope Monica doesn't latch on to you like a limpet to borrow your friends list."

"I may have to hide when I see her coming. Do we sound petty? She's not a bad person, just . . . overeager, I guess."

"I know. Maybe she'll calm down once she gets settled. And makes more friends. It must be hard, getting uprooted every few years. Wonder what her husband's like?"

"Want me to return the favor and drop in on them to find out?"

"And I can come along with a plate of cookies to welcome them to the town. Just like in an old sit-com!"

Seth struggled to suppress a smile. "I don't think we need to go that far. Let's wait and see how the WinterFare goes—maybe Monica will burn off some steam with that."

"Men!"

5

Meg was sitting at the dining room table with her laptop, orchard records, and spreadsheets covering most of the table, when she heard a car pull into the driveway. She knew Seth was out back. *Please, let it not be Monica!* She sent up a silent prayer. She didn't have the energy to deal with another dose of the woman. That was hardly a charitable attitude toward a woman who was new to the town and probably lonely, but Meg did have things she needed to get done.

She stood up and went to the window overlooking the driveway: Larry. He was following through on what he had promised the day before. Since he was here, maybe he could help her with the statistical details of her own orchard. She had plenty of experience with financial documents, but she wasn't even sure what constituted a good result for a working orchard. What kind of profit margin should she be looking for? What could she write off? Lump sum or amortized over time? Had any of his courses at Cornell covered issues like that?

Larry knocked on the back door, and Meg went quickly to let him in. "Come in!" she said when she pulled the door open. Lolly opened one eye, then went back to sleep. "I was just going over my numbers. Did you have something specific you wanted to talk about, or should we simply discuss general plans?"

"The second one, I guess. You have drawings or a map of your place?"

"Not one that shows the orchard details. But there's always Google Earth, and they're pretty much up-to-date with their aerial images. Oh, do you know how to handle a computer?"

"Of course. You can't get through school without one."

"Do you have one of your own?"

Larry looked away. "A crappy one. I haven't been able to afford to replace it."

"Surely there's a market in secondhand ones, with all the colleges around here. Unless you don't think you need one?" Meg found that idea hard to imagine—record keeping even for her small orchard would be a nightmare if she had to do it all by hand.

"I'll look. You want to get started?"

"Sure. Oh, one other thing, about your housing situation?"

"Yeah. What?" he asked cautiously.

"This may sound odd, but Bree made a suggestion before she left about converting what used to be a chicken coop in the back into what I guess is officially called a tiny house these days. There's even a television show about them. You know—everything you need packed into an impossibly small space? It sounds like it could work for one person without a lot of baggage. Have you heard of those?"

Larry shrugged. "No, but I don't watch television shows. Might be some RVs or campers around I could use, at least until the summer vacation season when everybody clears out. Better than a chicken coop."

"Yes, but it would be a real house once it was converted—you know, electric light, indoor plumbing. Just an idea. You know much about construction?"

"I kept things going on the family farm. I hear this state is pretty tough about regulations for things like wiring and plumbing, though, and I pretty much stayed away from those."

"Seth could handle that end. Look, I just thought I'd put it out there. I have the feeling you aren't the frat-jock type who'd be happy with a bunch of drunken roommates."

Larry gave her a crooked smile, and Meg realized she hadn't even seen it before. "You got that right. Be handy to live onsite here—save on gas and stuff."

"You don't have to decide today. Let's take a look at the orchard figures."

While Larry wasn't particularly articulate in ordinary conversation, he was surprisingly up to speed with orchard statistics and related information. Meg let him take the lead, because she'd exhausted her own knowledge early and also because she wanted to hear what he had to say. When he wasn't forced to talk about himself or his life, he spoke much more openly and enthusiastically. She started taking notes halfway through their discussion. And she refrained from commenting when Lolly made her way to his lap: he didn't comment, but stroked her absently as he went on talking. Points for him: he liked cats.

After an hour or so, Larry leaned back in his chair and said, "Okay, in a nutshell you've got fifteen acres in one parcel, mostly older trees, about half on a slope, right? Plus that three acres you've just planted but they aren't bearing yet. You've been running it with two people—yourself and a manager—plus seasonal pickers. Any chance for expanding?"

"What, acquire more land and plant it? As you just said, it would be years before they produced anything. Seth might own a few more acres to the north of the main orchard, but that place hasn't been a farm for a long time and it would take work to prepare it. There's the goats' pen, but that's tiny. And what's beyond and behind that is boggy, so that's no good. You see that as a problem?"

"Not necessarily—I'm just figuring out your options. So, say you can't add land. I don't know your current trees well, but some are probably past their prime. Thing is, you can't put in more compact planting—closer tree spacing— without taking out a *lot* of trees, not just one or two here and there."

"I get that, Larry. I wasn't planning to expand. I feel comfortable managing the amount I have, with some help. And I know I'll have to replace some trees and wait for them to grow up. But I know I can handle what I've got right now, and I like that. Does that make sense to you?"

"Yeah, you're a control freak." Once again there was a brief flash of a smile. So the guy had a sense of humor? "We talked about that before. With what you've got, you're limited in what money you can bring in. If that's okay with you, fine. I'm just saying. Your call."

"Look, I may change my mind in a year or two, or beyond, assuming I'm still here. But this works for me for now."

"Great. So that means we have to look at how to get the best yield from the trees you've got." And Larry launched into a detailed discussion of pruning, spraying, watering, and several things Meg had never even heard of.

When he finally slowed down, Meg said, "It's clear that you know what you're talking about. Can you make me a timeline or a spreadsheet for what we have to do now, and in what order? Or maybe two—one if we just keep doing what we've been doing, and one if we start implementing the changes you've suggested?"

"Sure, no problem. Except that second one won't look much different from the first one, at least for the first couple of years."

"Okay, I get it. What's next on the calendar?"

"Like I told you, pruning. Clean-up. I can test the soil in different parts of the orchard to see what nutrients you need to add. Check for insect damage. That kind of thing."

"Fine. Give me a list, and tell me when we start."

Larry was gone when Seth's mother, Lydia, dropped by in the late afternoon, rapping at the back door after walking across the fields between their houses. "Am I welcome?" she asked when Meg opened the door.

"Of course you are! Why do you even ask?" Meg held the door open for her to come in, then gave her a quick hug.

"Well, I haven't seen much of either of you since you got back from your honeymoon," Lydia said, unwrapping her scarf and hanging it on the wall rack next to the door. "From what little Seth has said, it was rather . . . unusual."

Meg laughed. "To say the least! Solving a murder that took place in my parents' backyard was not on the schedule. But up until then it was lovely."

"A trial by fire, so to speak. If Seth can survive being cooped up with your parents while solving a murder, you two can weather anything. Not to mention how many hours on the road going and coming back."

"Yes, he's a keeper. Would you like tea? Coffee? Something stronger, since you're not driving? I'd offer you cookies, but I haven't gotten around to baking any yet. Or you could stay for dinner, if you don't have other plans."

"A glass of wine would be welcome. And as for dinner . . . I have plans."

"With Christopher, I assume?" Meg said as she retrieved the bottle of wine from the refrigerator and found two clean glasses.

Lydia sighed. "So everyone knows?"

"Of course we do. I kind of expected you to bring him for Christmas dinner."

"I considered it, but I thought we all could use some family time."

"That was nice of you. But as for you and Christopher, it was obvious at the wedding, although you'll have to tell me how long it was going on before then. And I think it's great. Christopher is a lovely man, and I don't know if I would have survived my first year here without his help."

"Good—I'm relieved. Is Seth okay with it, too? He's a man, and men don't talk about things like that much."

"Yes, he's fine. He told Christopher as much yesterday. All is good in our little Granford world."

"And you're bringing in a new manager to replace Bree?"

Meg filled two glasses with wine, then sat down, leaving

the bottle on the table. "We are. I'm not sure 'replace' is the right word, but Christopher recommended someone who has a different skill set, and he's already started, sort of. This is our slowest time of year, you know, so we've been talking about what needs to be done over the course of the next year or two. I'll introduce you at some point, but I warn you—he's kind of rough around the edges. Apparently he had a difficult childhood and he comes across as kind of defensive at first. But he's smart and he knows his stuff. I'm hoping things work out."

Meg took a sip of wine and let it trickle down her throat. Was she supposed to be cooking dinner? What did they have in the house that could be made to resemble a meal? "Did Seth tell you about the WinterFare event?"

"He mentioned it briefly. I gather there's a new woman in town and she wants to make her mark?"

"That's about it. But I think it is a good idea, and she's willing to put in the work to make it happen. Winter's hard on everybody, and a little human contact and fun would be welcome. You have any ideas? It's open to everyone."

"Is anybody doing a jumble sale?"

"You mean, like all those items from the attic that people want to get rid of?"

"Yes, that—although most people usually end up going home with as much as they brought. It brings in a little money, and people are happy to think their possessions are going to a good home rather than a Dumpster. Is there any fundraising involved? A worthy cause to donate to?"

"I haven't heard, but it's likely. As for the jumble thing, mention it to Seth—I like the idea."

Seth came stomping in the back door. "Oh, hi, Mom. Mention what?"

"Lydia has an idea for WinterFare," Meg told him. "Want some wine?"

"Let me warm up first. What's your idea, Mom?"

"A jumble sale, sort of an indoor yard sale, or known to some as a junk sale. Do you have one lined up?"

"Not that I've heard, although we're letting Monica Whitman run with the ball. You could call her, but be prepared to have your ear talked off."

"The poor woman is probably lonely and looking for a way to keep busy."

Seth and Meg exchanged a glance. "That's what we keep telling ourselves. She does seem nice. I'll hunt up her number for you." He settled in the third chair at the table. "Making space in your house for some reason?" he asked slyly.

Lydia didn't bite. "Meg says you know all about Christopher and me. And no, we haven't made any plans in that direction. But the possibility is open."

"That's fine by me, Mom. He's a great guy."

"I think so. Meg's been telling me about the new orchard manager. What's your take on him?"

"I haven't talked to him much—Meg's spent more time with him, and it's up to her."

"Seth Chapin, are you avoiding the question?" his mother asked.

"No. He's young, and he's got a chip on his shoulder, kind of."

"So did Bree when she started, if you recall," Meg reminded him.

"This is a different kind of chip, but I think he does feel the need to prove himself. My guess is he was hoping for a larger playing field here, to show what he could do. He seemed disappointed that this orchard is so small."

"I think he is. But that doesn't mean he won't do a good job for me. And nobody stays around forever. In a year or two, I'll know more about apples and the orchard will be in better shape, and he can move on with my blessing. Okay?"

"Great," Seth said—then changed the subject. "How's Rachel? And the baby?"

"Your sister is wondering why you haven't bothered to call her since Christmas—and there wasn't time to talk then and she was busy with the kids. The baby and everyone else in the family is fine, thank you."

"Why don't we have everybody over for dinner on Sunday?" Meg said suddenly. "I'll never have more free time to cook than I have now, and there won't be all the pressure of the holiday, and the kids won't be completely wired. We can just hang out and eat ourselves silly and have a good time."

"I like it. You want me to call?" Lydia said.

"I can do it. And invite Christopher, will you?"

"I'd be happy to."

6

After a couple more weeks, Meg's life had finally settled into a sort of routine. It wouldn't last, she knew, but she'd found ways to enjoy the downtime, especially since Seth was available for much of the same time. In a way, the bubble of January time was more of a honeymoon than the official one had been. They went their own ways when they had business to attend to; came back together for meals; visited with friends and family. It was almost boringly normal, not that Meg wanted anything different. She had even managed to finish reading a couple of books, something she rarely had time for during apple season (or could stay awake long enough to do).

"Don't forget the all-hands meeting for the WinterFare tonight," Seth reminded her at breakfast.

"Oh, that's tonight? I'll have to check to see if my

calendar is clear." Meg spread the last of the homemade apple jelly on her toast.

"Very funny. It's the only chance we'll have to get all the people involved together before the event, and make sure we iron out any wrinkles."

"Are there any guidelines for displays? Like, does everyone have the same size table? Table covers or not? I assume there's no wiring laid in, so things won't get too fancy, and there's overhead lighting in the gym. How are Nicky and Brian handling the food?"

"A, there won't be a lot of hot stuff, and they'll have room for a couple of sterno warmers. B, they're going to bring it in shifts, not all at once, so it won't clog up the area. They'll be serving on paper plates—oh, remind me to make sure we have enough trash barrels, including one or two next to their tables. We promised the school we'd leave the place in good shape, so it would help to keep ahead of the mess as we go along."

"Is there room for all the vendors?"

"I think we'll be fine. Oh, and another reminder: the school is lending us folding chairs, but we have to set them up and break them down after."

"That's your department, not mine. How's Monica holding up?"

"She's been far better organized than I expected—I guess she wasn't kidding about having done plenty of these before. I'll admit I was worried that she was all talk and no action, but she's stayed on top of things, and even looked like she was enjoying it all."

"Will she have any sort of table or booth, or will she just wander around making sure everything is working?"

"Probably the latter. She said she didn't have the knack for crafts or cooking."

"So this meeting is just the final polish on the plans?"

"I hope so."

The conference room in the town hall was crowded when Meg and Seth arrived at six that evening. Meg estimated that there had to be at least thirty people around the big table and the chairs along the walls, although some of them were probably couples, so there would most likely be fewer than thirty booths, which would fit in the gym—it would look well filled without being crowded. Meg spotted Nicky and Brian at the far end of the room and waved, but there were no seats available near them. Seth joined the other selectmen in the middle of the long side of the table; Monica was seated next to them, looking excited. Meg hoped the meeting would be short, because most people would want to get home for dinner or to oversee kids. This was just a final check, right? With time allowed for fixing problems.

When the room was filled, Tom Moody stood up. Seeing him again after a few months, now Meg recognized him—a cheerful, stocky man with a lush head of brown hair. She tried to remember if he'd been at the wedding, and failed. Tom said loudly, "Settle, people! This is not a town meeting, but an informal get-together to make sure we're ready for the first Granford WinterFare just two weeks away. Thank you all for volunteering to take part and support Granford. I've got only one instruction for you: have fun!" Several people around the table clapped.

Tom went on, "The school is ready for us, and there's a packet at your seats that outlines what they expect from us for setup and breakdown, and other useful information about things like where the restrooms are, in case you haven't been inside the gym for a few years, and where the other important utilities can be found. Oh, and you'll notice the lower parts of the bleachers on the far side will be opened, so if you're sampling some of the great food we'll have, you can sit down over there. And that's all I've got! I'll turn the rest of the meeting over to Monica Whitman, who's done an amazing job in a very short time. Monica, take it away!" Tom sat down, looking relieved that his part was over.

Monica stood up, smiling broadly. "I can't believe how kind you've all been—most of you said yes the first time I asked you!" That brought a quick laugh from the crowd. "There are twenty vendors lined up. I've included additional information in that packet that Tom gave you, showing you the layout of the space. I've tried to distribute the tables so that the food is spread out, not all clumped in a corner—except for you, Nicky, Brian—you can have all the space you want, and plenty of room for people to get to your tables. But we want people to wander around and mingle, and maybe buy a thing or two. But this isn't about making money, although we hope to do a little of that. It's about brightening a dark time of year and, like Tom said, having fun! Read the materials, and if you have any questions or need to make any changes, I've put my cell phone number at the bottom of the sheet. Does anyone have questions now?"

Someone Meg didn't know raised a hand. "How've you publicized the event?"

Monica answered promptly. "Through the town's web-site and social media pages and local papers. I've put up posters in local libraries in adjacent towns and other town halls when they've permitted it. I've talked to selectmen in the towns closest to Granford and asked them to include us in any publicity they'll be doing over the next couple of weeks. Some even have closed-circuit television that they use for announcements. If you have any other suggestions, I'm happy to hear them. Oh, and word of mouth is always good!"

Meg felt tired just listening to Monica, and that was only a short portion of the list of things she'd accomplished. She scanned the room to see who she recognized, in addition to Nicky and Brian: one of the alpaca ladies; Gail from the Historical Society; a couple of the people who ran the farmers' market near her house, although they were closed in the winter. She had met or at least seen maybe as many as half of the people. Lydia wasn't there, and Meg wondered if she'd abandoned her jumble sale idea, although for some odd reason people loved buying tacky old things, hoping to pick up treasures for a low price. Meg had to admit she'd been guilty of indulging on more than one occasion, filling in the gaps in her house with gently used furniture. The general mood was happy, and nobody voiced any complaints. Maybe this would actually be fun. Meg hoped so, for the sake of the town.

The meeting broke up well before seven, but a number of people lingered to chat. Brian waved as he headed out the door, back to the restaurant at the top of the hill, but Nicky waited to greet Meg.

"Have I told you how great your wedding food was?" Meg asked as Nicky came near.

"Only about twelve times. It really was a nice wedding, and I think it may have given some other people some ideas. We'll see how it goes. So, how's married life treating you?"

"You heard about our so-called honeymoon?" When Nicky nodded, Meg went on, "Well, it's gotten better since then. Sometimes it feels like the wedding never happened, and then I realize I actually have a husband and he's not going anywhere. It's a slow time of year, so we're still getting used to it. And we've hired an orchard manager."

"Yeah, I heard Bree had moved on. How's the new one working out?"

"So far, so good. Mostly we've been planning, since there's not much to do in the orchard at the moment."

"You're selling apples at the WinterFare?"

"The ones I have. I'll probably spend a lot of time at the table explaining to people that no, they're not imported from South America, and yes, some varieties of apples last well when refrigerated. Some even improve in flavor. You've seen that yourself."

"I have indeed. Maybe we should whip up a WinterPie together?"

"That could be fun. You have any issues with serving food at the WinterFare?"

"Brian and I have done plenty of catering, and we can handle it. We're not planning anything exotic or tricky, just good New England food. And our permits cover the food preparation at the restaurant—we won't be cooking anything at the school."

"Have you talked to Monica much?" Meg asked cautiously.

Nicky leaned forward. "You mean, have I *listened* to Monica much? Some. I don't want to run her down, but she's got so much enthusiasm, it can be hard to take. Still, she and her husband have become regulars at the restaurant, so I want to stay on her good side."

"What's he like? I haven't met him yet."

"Quiet," Nicky told her. She laughed.

"Does he have a choice?" Meg said, joining her laughter.

"I doubt it. Maybe we can all get together for dinner when the fuss dies down and get to know each other."

"Nice idea. She really seems to want to make friends here, and who can blame her? It's hard being the new kid, as we both know."

"You're right. Well, I'd better get back to the restaurant. See you soon, I hope?"

"Of course."

Seth took a few more minutes to disentangle himself from Tom Moody and the other member of the select board, then came over to Meg. "Ready to go?"

"I am. No problems?"

"Nothing important. I have to give Monica credit for what she's done, and the town has really stepped up. This should be a good event."

As they walked back to the car, Meg asked, "Did your mother decide not to take a table?"

"Yeah. I guess she found she had less junk to get rid of than she thought, and she didn't feel like calling everyone in town to ask for more. That would mean a lot of driving around and collecting stuff, then making it reasonably clean, then pricing it, and . . . well, you get the drift."

"I do indeed. She's still got a day job, and then there's Christopher. Maybe she can think about doing it at the Harvest Festival, and I doubt the town's junk is going anywhere."

"I don't think I'll even ask about how Christopher figures into whether or not my mother can collect the town's junk. Let's just say she's busy, all right?"

"Of course. Any thoughts about dinner?"

"Pizza? We're going right by the place on the way home."

"You've convinced me."

Food ordered, picked up, and consumed, pets fed and walked as needed, Meg and Seth made their way upstairs. "It's been nice, hasn't it? Not being rushed off our feet and running in opposite directions, but actually getting to spend some quality time together?" Meg said.

"It has. Isn't that what everyone hopes for?"

"Yes, but they don't always get it. And you and I both know it can't last—we're going to get busy again pretty soon. Should I pencil in 'get to know my husband again' for November?"

"I suppose we could swap roles now and then. I'll learn to pick apples, which I assume is less simple than it sounds, and you can learn basic carpentry. Then we can work together."

"Might be fun. I think any woman should know the basics of carpentry, plumbing, and the like. I can't stand helpless women. But you're right—if you don't pick apples right, you lose some of your crop, and that means you lose income."

They got ready for bed and crawled under the covers. "I've been thinking about that tiny house idea," Seth said.

"Oh? Larry didn't seem very excited, but maybe he's always like that—you know, cautious? Why are you thinking about it?"

"Because a lot of people these days want a private space, somewhere to escape to," he told her. "They might not think about moving into a little place full-time, but it could make a great office space if you wanted to write a book or work on something delicate like ship models. I bet kids would love it as a playhouse. It could be a guest room, for one flexible person. Heck, with all the online options these days, you might even be able to rent it out for short-term stays. Or put one or two of the pickers in it."

Meg reared up on one elbow and looked at Seth. "Wow, you have been thinking about this! How much work would it take?"

"Hard to say. I think the foundation is strong enough to support a full building, and the framing is good, but that still leaves a lot to make it livable. But it's fun to imagine."

"Well, you go right on thinking about it. Maybe we could install a goatherd there. Or put in a loom for making stuff from goat yarn . . ." Meg said, warming to the topic.

But Seth was already asleep.

7

Meg had pulled together three bushel baskets of late apples, and she drafted Larry to help her polish them. He helped her load them into the car, and then backed off. "You aren't coming?" Meg asked, surprised. She thought he'd become a bit more sociable over the past couple of weeks.

"Nah. Not my thing. You gonna be okay carrying the baskets in?"

She almost laughed. "I do it all the time, you know. Seth and I will be back later in the afternoon, and we've both got our cell phones if you need anything."

"What would I need?" Larry said.

Good question. He wasn't a child, and there wasn't anything in progress that he might need help with. Why was she feeling oddly protective of him? "See you later!" she said as she started the car.

The weather had cooperated: no snow or ice. The sky was uniformly gray but the forecast was reassuring. Meg arrived at the high school after a five-minute drive, and was pleased to see the parking lot was already half-filled. She parked at the far end to leave plenty of space for non-vendors, retrieved the first basket of apples, and started her trek to the gym. In her shoulder bag she'd brought a length of brightly colored oilcloth to cover her table, plus a bundle of paper bags for apples if people didn't come with their own bags, and an envelope with small bills to make change. She had drawn the line at accepting credit cards—one complication she didn't need. She'd even printed out labels for each of the three kinds of apples she was bringing, with a brief description of what they tasted like and what they were best used for.

Once inside the building, she stopped for a moment to take in the scene. The tables were set up in a large rectangle around the perimeter of the gym, and she was standing at one of the short ends. Nicky and Brian were stationed at the far end, and Nicky waved when she saw Meg. From Monica's floor plan Meg knew her table would be somewhere in the middle of the side to her right. About half the tables were already occupied, and people had opted for bright colors for their decorations, which in some cases were fairly elaborate. She was going to look like a plain Jane in comparison, so she'd have to let her pretty apples in their vintage baskets speak for her.

Seth popped up beside her: he'd come early to help with the physical setup. "Need any help?"

"There are two more baskets of apples in the car, if you really need something to do. It's looking great so far. How long until you open the doors officially?"

"Half an hour? I'll go collect one basket—where's your car?"

"The far end of the lot. It's not locked."

"You're a trusting soul," Seth told her.

"Hey, this is Granford."

After Seth had left, Meg carried her basket over to her designated table and set it on the floor. She pulled out the table cover and smoothed it out over the tabletop. It was a nice simple pattern, so she had brought a quilted runner with an apple motif to lay down the center of the table. She'd been at a loss about how to display the apples, because the harvest baskets were simply too big and bulky. She'd finally decided on smaller replicas of those baskets, purchased at a party store, and she'd have to keep replenishing them. She laid out the mini-baskets filled with apples, stepped back to assess their placement, then tweaked one. Then she retrieved her labels and taped them to the oilcloth in front of each basket. And that was that.

Seth arrived with one more basket, trailed by someone else Meg didn't recognize, carrying the last one. "Hey, it looks good. Simple but effective."

"You don't think it's too plain?" Meg asked anxiously.

"No. The apples will sell themselves."

"Who else is selling apples today?"

"A couple of people have included apples along with other winter produce. There's only one who's selling just apples. That organic farmer I told you about—Ginny Morris."

"Oh, right. I still haven't met that family."

"Maybe now's a good time, since you look like you've finished here."

"Okay. Where are they?"

"Across and up two tables." Seth pointed. Meg saw a

slender woman about her own age spreading a gingham tablecloth over her table. There were a few baskets of apples clustered around her feet.

"Got it. Maybe I can offer to help. We're all in this together, aren't we? It's not like we're competing."

"You're just being neighborly. You've got about half an hour, so go for it."

As Seth headed off to help someone else, Meg took a last look at her display and then walked across the space between the tables until she reached the other woman's table. Up close, she looked older than Meg had guessed, and wiry rather than thin. Or maybe she was just worn down. When the woman glanced up, Meg said, "Hi! I'm Meg Corey, uh, Chapin. I'm surprised we haven't met before now."

The woman straightened up and pushed her hair off her face. "I know who you are—you grow apples, on the south side of town, right? I'm Virginia Morris—Ginny." She extended her hand, and Meg shook it. She almost laughed, since Ginny's hand felt much like her own: calloused and strong.

"I do. Not organic, though. I'd love to see what you're doing at your place. Is it an older orchard?"

"Yeah. We bought it three years ago, but it was a mess—it had been neglected for years. Last fall was the first time we had any sort of crop worth selling. What about you?"

"I inherited the orchard, through some relatives on my mother's side of the family. It's not a new orchard, but I was lucky—the university had been managing it as kind of a teaching tool for several years, so it wasn't in bad shape. Is your whole family involved?"

"My husband is—the kids are still kind of young."

"Will he be here later?"

Ginny shrugged. "If he can. You married?"

"As of about two months ago, yes."

"Oh, right—you married Seth Chapin. You had the wedding up at Gran's."

"We did. Do you know Nicky and Brian?"

"Yeah, I introduced myself. They told me they used some of your apples. I was hoping they'd take some of mine."

"I'm sure Nicky would be happy to. Maybe we can compare lists of our varietals and see where you could fit. You know, I'd love to talk to you sometime about how the whole organic classification works. I was so clueless when I took over my orchard, I couldn't even think about dealing with a lot of regulations. But you should have a good market for your apples around here."

"I think so, once I start getting a big enough crop."

Meg glanced around: most of the tables were ready for business. "Well, I should let you finish getting set up. Good to meet you, Ginny. Let's get together before the orchard season gets busy."

"Sounds good. Thanks for stopping by." Ginny bent down and picked up another basket of apples and started arranging them on her table, effectively turning her back on Meg. Meg meandered back to her own spot.

She wondered if she'd regret not insisting that Larry take a shift at the table—it would be a good opportunity for him to get to know people in the town. But he'd turned her down fast when Meg had suggested the idea, and she had to admit he wasn't exactly a crowd kind of person. Maybe Seth could cover for half an hour or so while she browsed the other tables. Not that she needed any more stuff at home, but there might be some good food products, and it would be nice to support her neighbors. And she should say hello to people, and introduce herself to the ones she didn't know.

Without any fanfare, the double doors at one end of the gym were thrown open, and people started streaming in. WinterFare had begun.

The people kept coming throughout the day. Meg smiled until her face hurt, selling apples, making change. She made a mental note that if this event was repeated, she should bring some recipe cards along as well. She kept an eye on her supply of apples, hoping it would last until the end of the day, not that she'd mind if she sold out early. Nicky and Brian had been smart to bring in new food in shifts. Meg wasn't sure if each of their loads included different recipes—she'd hate to miss anything that Nicky made, because she was a terrific cook. They both looked happy as well as busy.

At one point she looked up from counting the apples under the table to see Art Preston, Granford's chief of police, standing in front of the table, grinning. "Hi, Art!" she greeted him enthusiastically. "I don't think we've seen you since the wedding!"

"You'd be right—the missus and I decided to take a winter vacation since the weather kind of discourages crime around here."

"Where'd you go?"

"North Carolina. Pretty beaches, not too many people. Very peaceful. I hear your honeymoon got a little complicated."

"Did Seth tell you? Yes, my father had some problems

that kind of grew out of a case he handled a long time ago. Funny how the past keeps intruding. And, yes, there was a body. And Seth and I are still married. Want some apples?"

"Sure. I'm not here in any official capacity—I just thought I'd see how things were going."

"Have you met Monica yet?"

"I have not had that pleasure, since I left before all this WinterFare stuff came up. But I'm sure she'll find me. What's your take on her?"

"Energetic! But look around—she gets things done. She's made all this happen, and in a short time. And that's about all I can tell you. Any particular apples you prefer?"

"Nah, you can pick."

Meg filled a bag with two of each variety and handed it to Art. "There you go."

"Thank you, ma'am. Or am I supposed to call you 'missus' now? What do I owe you?"

"Meg will do fine. And it's on the house."

Art drew himself up. "Are you attempting to bribe an officer of the law?"

Meg grinned at him. "Maybe. Is it working?"

"I'll take it under consideration. Good to see you, Meg!"

She watched as Art strolled off, looking relaxed, and then she spied Monica making the rounds: she'd worn an all-red outfit, which made her easy to find. She looked bouncy and bubbly and . . . Meg was running out of adjectives. How did she do it? She never seemed to slow down. Monica had started along the left side of the rectangle, so it was a while before she arrived at Meg's table.

"Oh, this looks so pretty!" Monica said when she greeted

Meg. "I'm not sure I've heard of all these varieties—what can you tell me about them?"

Monica actually held still and paid attention while Meg explained about ripening schedules and heirloom varieties. Then Monica said, "And you didn't know any of this when you arrived in Granford? I'm so impressed. And that husband of yours is wonderful. Sometimes he seems to know what I need before I even ask him. And he knows everybody! I don't think all this could have happened without him. You are a lucky woman!"

"I think so," Meg said, smiling. "Everything seems to be going really well! Is your husband here? I don't think I've met him yet."

Monica waved her hand. "Douglas. He doesn't like crowds. He's perfectly happy at home with a book. But I'm sure you'll meet him sometime soon. Save me a couple of those apples, will you?" Monica pointed at the Northern Spy variety. "I'll pick 'em up later."

"Good choice. I'll do that." Meg watched as Monica moved on to the next table, then placed half a dozen apples in a bag and stuck it under the table, out of the way.

When she stood up, Seth was standing in front of her table. "You need a break?" he asked.

"I won't say no. I'd like to see what everyone else is doing. By the way, Monica said nice things about you."

"It's nice that she's appreciative. You go take a walk. How're you pricing these?" He waved at the baskets of apples on the table.

"Two bucks for a bag of six, all varieties at the same price. There are more under the table—but don't sell the ones in the paper bag because Monica asked me to save those for her. Here's the envelope with the change. I promise I won't be long."

"Take your time," Seth said, then turned to a family with a small child as they approached the table.

Meg enjoyed the opportunity to stretch her legs. She started out going counterclockwise, because she realized she was hungry, and stopped in front of the Gran's restaurant table. "You look like you're doing a booming business," she said during a brief lull.

"Oh, we are. It's great. You want something to eat?"

"What've you got?"

"There's this incredible carrot soup, and it's really good with corn bread. Interested? If you don't think you can juggle both while standing up, you can go sit on the bleachers to eat."

"It's a deal." Nicky handed her a cylindrical container of soup, a spoon, a piece of corn bread wrapped in a napkin, along with a few extra napkins. Meg balanced them carefully as she walked over to the partially open bleachers and sat down, only then realizing she'd been standing for the last three hours. She carefully pulled the lid off the heavy paper container of soup and almost burst out laughing. Carrots were still orange, weren't they? Well, this carrot soup was a flaming scarlet—and tasted wonderful, once she dug into it. Definitely a keeper recipe, and great for winter.

She finished the soup and started on the corn bread as she looked around the room. Everybody looked happy. How rare was that? Ages ranged from babies through octogenarians, and most of the people old enough to hold something were carrying bags filled with one thing or another. She waved to the alpaca ladies at their table, almost regretting that none of their herd had escaped lately and wandered onto her property. She'd gotten kind of fond of the alpacas.

After throwing away her trash (neatly, in the recycling container), Meg continued her circuit around the rectangle of tables until she arrived back at her own. Seth had been keeping busy, and the apple supply was dwindling fast. "Did you get lunch?" Seth asked.

"I did. I can definitely recommend Nicky's soup. How much longer will this go on?"

"Until three. We figured it would be getting dark not long after that, and a lot of us will be exhausted."

"Two more hours, then. I hope the apples hold out. It's really gone well, hasn't it?"

"It has," Seth said. "I haven't heard any complaints, except that people wanted more. Great idea, well carried out."

"And it was Monica's inspiration. Isn't it great when things like this happen?"

"It is. Look, I'd better get back to my own chores. Let me know if you need help breaking down your stuff."

"Seth, I think I can handle a couple of empty baskets. If I don't see you again, I'll see you at home. Do I need to take anything with me?"

"Nope, we're good. See you later!" He gave her a quick kiss and took off across the gym.

Meg stayed until all her apples were gone, and then stacked the empty baskets. Granford was a nice town, and after two years she was truly beginning to feel at home there. And to think it had happened more or less by accident. If her septic tank hadn't backed up when it did, she might never have met Seth. She might have sold the house and headed back to Boston, where she'd worked before, or maybe chosen someplace entirely new. Or traveled for a bit. So many choices, and yet, here she was—and she was happy about it.

The empty baskets were light, so she waved to Seth before she picked them up, and pointed toward the door. He nodded: message received. Then she headed home.

8

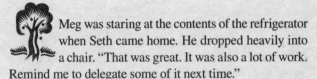 Meg was staring at the contents of the refrigerator when Seth came home. He dropped heavily into a chair. "That was great. It was also a lot of work. Remind me to delegate some of it next time."

"Will there be a next time?" Meg asked, opening a plastic container of something that had turned green a while ago.

"I don't see why not. February is a pretty dull month for most people, even if they're not farmers. This was a nice break."

"What, you don't take Groundhog Day seriously?" Meg joked.

"I'll leave that to Pennsylvania. And much as I admire Washington and Lincoln, it's hard to party on their behalf, plus a lot of people take the long weekend off to go skiing or something. Have I missed anything?"

"Not that I can remember. Oh, but there's always Saint Brigid's day—she's the female equivalent of Saint Patrick for Ireland, but her day is earlier than his, not that anyone notices. What do you want to eat?"

"Surprise me."

"Don't say that—you might end up with freezer-burned chicken coated with raspberry jam and cookie crumbs, or whatever spice I grab out of a dark cabinet."

"Have I complained about anything you've set in front of me?"

"No. You are a hero. And you're not a bad cook yourself. I will miss some of Bree's Jamaican dishes, though. At least she left her spices behind, so maybe I'll experiment."

"Can we take the easy route and have breakfast for dinner?"

"You mean bacon and eggs? Sure, why not? We don't have to tell our mothers."

They'd almost finished their sketchy dinner when Seth's cell phone rang. He'd left it in the dining room, so he rose stiffly from his chair and went to retrieve it. *Who calls on Saturday night?* Meg wondered idly, as she ate the last of her toast. *Note to self: make a bunch of muffins and freeze some for nights like this.*

Seth was back in less than a minute, but his expression was grim. "That was Tom Moody. Monica is in the hospital with severe gastroenteritis. They think it may be food poisoning."

"Oh no!" Meg said. "How awful. Does anyone else seem to have it?"

"Tom didn't say, or maybe he doesn't know."

"Is someone official supposed to do something?" Meg asked.

"Not with just one case, and that diagnosis isn't firm. But if more people show signs, then the health department has to get involved."

"It can't be Nicky's fault—she's careful, and she's had all the inspections. Her kitchen is certified."

"I know—I rebuilt the kitchen there, remember? But if there's an official investigation, they'll have to look at her food."

"I had the soup, and I'm fine. What did you have?"

"Some kind of wrap thing. I'm fine, too. But food poisoning can be tricky, and sometimes it takes a while to show up. I guess we just wait and see."

"Poor Monica. After all her hard work, this has to happen."

"I know—she didn't get much of a chance to enjoy her success. Hey, I'll do the dishes if you'll walk Max."

"Deal. But you're getting off light—there's only a skillet and a couple of plates."

Meg put on a warm jacket and jingled the dog's leash, which brought Max running. "Come on, Max—fresh air! Exercise!"

Outside it was very dark, with the only light coming from the kitchen window. She and Seth had talked about installing outside lights, but she'd been reluctant because either they'd never be on when they needed them and they'd have to stumble around in the dark to turn them on, or if they installed the kind with automatic sensors, Meg worried that every passing squirrel or raccoon would trigger them. Which was why she kept a flashlight in her jacket pocket, in case she needed one.

Max clearly had more energy than she did at the moment. He strained at the leash, wanting to go out into the fields and check out all those interesting smells. Meg wasn't in the mood to chase after him, and wasn't sure he'd come back to her if he got distracted, but she picked up her pace to accommodate him. She was startled when a dark figure emerged from the barn; she hadn't realized a door was open, but it must have been one of the side ones. The figure resolved into Larry, which she should have realized when Max didn't react to the sight of him.

"Hey, what're you doing here?" she called out.

"I was dropping off some supplies I picked up today. How'd your thing today go?"

"It was great." At least until she'd heard about Monica, but she saw no need to tell Larry about that until they knew more, and he hadn't even been there. "I sold all of the apples. And I met Ginny Morris—you know, the one with the organic orchard? Have you met her?"

"Yeah, Christopher sent me over to talk to her a while back. She hadn't been there very long."

"Then you probably know her better than I do. I'd like to know more about what distinguishes an organic farm and why it's worth the effort. Remind me to call her sometime this week and see if we can find a time to get together."

"You want me there, too?" Larry appeared surprised.

"Only if you want to be there. You've probably studied organic farming anyway. I haven't." Max tugged at the leash again, whining. "Anything critical we need to do this next week?"

"I'll let you know on Monday. Okay?"

"Fine." Meg watched as Larry disappeared into the darkness as quietly as he had come earlier. She was relieved when she heard his car start up—so he wasn't wandering around in the dark on foot. Maybe he'd just parked behind the barn to make it easier to unload his supplies.

"Okay, Max, let's get things done. It's cold out here!" Max must have agreed, because he finished his business quickly and loped back to the kitchen door, tugging Meg along. Meg let herself in and hung up her coat. Seth wasn't in the kitchen, so she assumed he'd gone upstairs.

In the bedroom she found him sound asleep. Poor baby, he'd worked hard today. He really did care about Granford, and he felt responsible for what went on in the town. She slid into bed next to him and was asleep in a minute.

In the morning Meg awoke slowly to realize that Seth had already gone downstairs to answer his cell phone, whose ring had entered her dream with some rather odd results. She checked the clock: it was barely seven, and the sky outside was a murky gray. So much for sleeping in. But now she was awake, so she might as well get up and start her day. She pulled on grubby sweats and went down the stairs to find Seth sitting at the kitchen table staring into space. He barely noticed her arrival. "What's up?" Meg asked.

He dragged his attention back to the present. "That was Art. Monica didn't make it. There are a few more possible cases, including some kids."

"Oh God, that's awful. So what happens now? The officials come in and investigate?"

"That's the law."

"I hate to sound petty, but are all food vendors going to be investigated?"

"Are you worried about your apples? You didn't use any chemical pesticides or preservatives or whatever on them. They haven't left this property since they were picked. But

I suppose somebody will have to test a few, just to be sure. They aren't going to take my word for it."

"I understand. Is it likely that more people will get sick? You said the timing for food poisoning could vary."

"It hasn't been even twenty-four hours yet, so I can't say we're in the clear."

"What do we need to do?"

"I need to go into town and talk with Tom and Art and figure out who's going to speak for Granford, and who we need to call in."

"The town has a lawyer, doesn't it?"

"Yes. You met him a while back—Fred Weatherly. But there's no reason to bring him in yet. We looked carefully at the regulations for events—we've got them all on file for the Harvest Festival. The restaurant permits are all current, and they've had no problems there. Maybe Monica went home and ate something she shouldn't have. Someone will have to ask her husband."

"That wouldn't explain the other cases," Meg said.

"No, it wouldn't, unless she was handing out tainted candy to kids. Which seems absurd, but we don't know her well. Maybe she's a serial killer, living here under an assumed name."

"Seth! You don't believe that," Meg protested.

"No, I don't. And I shouldn't joke about it. I think she was a good person and she didn't deserve this." He stood up abruptly. "I'm going to take Max out." At the sound of his name, Max, who had been sitting under the table watching his master, jumped out, tail wagging.

"Should I answer the phone if it rings?"

"Maybe it's better if you don't, if it's town business. I won't be long."

"I'll make coffee." Again. Her primary purpose in life these days: to make coffee. She waited until it was ready and poured herself a cup, then sat down at the table again. Lolly came and jumped on her lap and went to sleep, but Meg was glad of the soft furry creature keeping her company.

Seth was still out when his phone, which he'd left on the table, rang, but Meg recognized Lydia's number, so she answered it. "Hey, Lydia," she began.

Lydia spoke immediately. "Have you heard?"

"About Monica? Yes. Seth got the call. Terrible, isn't it?"

"Where is Seth?"

"Out walking Max. I think he needed the fresh air as much as Max did."

"It's such a shame . . . How was the event before . . . this?"

"I thought it was great. Everybody seemed to have a good time. I sold all of my apples, which is good because there weren't enough of all those varietals to sell to a market right now. Are you sorry you missed it?"

"Yes and no. I just couldn't get psyched up for sorting through cast-offs, mine or anyone else's. Amazing how much junk we all end up with without even noticing."

"True. We were in my parents' attic recently and found my father had kept documents for cases that go back decades. Of course he's a lawyer, so maybe he had a reason for that. At least his boxes were labeled."

"Did your new manager go to the fair?" Lydia asked.

"No. I invited him to tag along, but he didn't want to. He's not a people person, and he knows it. Which is okay when it comes to our division of labor: I'm the face for the orchard, and the marketer and promoter, and he keeps the apples healthy and growing. I handle the books. In theory, he's going to manage the pickers, which should be interesting. At least I know them now and I can run interference if necessary. Which I hope it won't be. We've got a few months to work out the kinks."

"Well, I won't keep you," Lydia said. "Tell Seth I called, but he doesn't have to call back."

"Will do. Talk soon!"

She'd hardly hung up when Seth came back with Max galloping before him. Before he could ask, Meg said, "That was your mother. You don't have to call her back."

"Good. Sorry, I'm not good company right now."

"Why are you supposed to be? A person is dead. I hope that we and anyone we care about had nothing to do with it, but you have every right to mourn for her. She became part of this community very quickly, and then suddenly she's gone. I wonder if her husband has any friends around here, that he can call on?"

"I still haven't met him. Poor guy. They didn't have kids, did they?"

"I don't think so—nobody's mentioned any. Or maybe they're grown and don't live around here. He's retired, so he doesn't have any colleagues he can lean on. Still, I doubt he'd want strangers like us barging in on him right now. Sad."

They sat in silence for a few moments. Then Meg said, "Coffee's made. You want breakfast?"

"Something simple is fine."

"No problem. You have any projects for today?"

"I was thinking about the tiny house idea again. It's kind of growing on me, no matter what use it's put to when it's done."

"What can you fit into a space like that?" Meg wasn't

wedded to the idea, but it would be better if Seth had a distraction to occupy his mind since there was nothing he could do for Douglas Whitman. "Is there room for a bathroom?"

"You'd be surprised. But one of the first things I have to look at is running pipes out there—and they've got to be buried deep enough to avoid freezing. Wiring's not a problem. Mostly I need a template so I can move things around and see what fits."

"Is there software for that?"

"Of course. There's software for everything these days. The problem with programs like that is that they're too much fun to play with—they're distracting. I'm still thinking about it."

As Meg made her way over to the refrigerator, she stopped to kiss Seth on the top of his head. He reached back to squeeze her hand. "I know what you're doing—you want to distract me. But thanks."

"Anytime."

9

After a breakfast that he consumed with little interest, Seth escaped to his office, in theory to work on plans for the tiny house, but in reality to be alone, Meg suspected. She didn't mind. A death in the community should bring forth an emotional response, and she'd seen her fair share of them, at least after the fact. She hadn't known Monica well, but from what she'd learned of her, Meg thought that she would have been a good addition to Granford. Poor Douglas—he was still a stranger to the town, and now his wife was gone in the blink of an eye. Meg wondered if he would stay in town now or go back to wherever they'd lived before Granford—Chicago, was it? He'd seen so little of the town that Monica's passing would have imposed no bad associations with the place, so he could go either way. But Meg thought he'd be lonely wherever he went.

Meg was finishing up her second cup of coffee when there was a knock at the back door. She looked out to find Rachel, along with baby Maggie, bundled up like a snowman. Snow person. Whatever. Meg opened the door quickly.

"Hi, Rachel. What brings you two over this morning? We didn't have anything planned, did we? Because things are a bit jumbled today."

"I know—Mom told me about, uh, Monica, was it? How awful. Please don't think me ghoulish to come over to get the whole story, but Noah said he'd keep an eye on the big kids, so I bundled up Maggie and here we are. Want to hold her?" Rachel thrust the baby at Meg without waiting for an answer.

"Sure. How about I hang on to her while you take off all the outside clothes?" Rachel was still riding high on baby hormones, Meg guessed. Did she have an agenda for Meg?

"Great."

Meg took three-month-old Maggie—her namesake!—rubbed noses with her briefly, then turned her so she faced her mom so Rachel could unzip, unbutton, un-Velcro, or whatever else needed doing. It seemed to take a long time because there were a lot of layers. When Rachel had added the last sweater to the pile of clothes, Meg turned Maggie around to greet her properly. "Hey, baby girl, how've you been? I swear, you're bigger than the last time I saw you, and that was only like a week ago."

"She probably is—we haven't been to the pediatrician for a couple of weeks. You look like an old pro with her."

"Don't get any ideas, Rachel. Seth and I haven't even started dancing around that subject."

"Clock is ticking, my friend."

"You're worse than my mother!" Meg told her, although she had to admit she enjoyed Maggie, who looked surprisingly intelligent for such a young child.

Rachel was still smiling. "Where's my brother?"

"Out in the barn."

"Hiding?"

"Not exactly. I think mostly keeping himself busy so he doesn't have to think about . . . Monica."

"Did you know her well?"

"I met her a couple of times, in connection with the WinterFare, but I think Seth had met her more often, on behalf of the town."

"What was she like?"

"Energetic! Tireless. Detail-oriented. As a person, it's harder to say. She really wanted to fit into the community here, and she had some really good ideas. What a waste!"

"They're still saying it's food poisoning?" Rachel asked.

Who is "they" in this case? Meg wondered. "As far as I know, but we only heard this morning. There may be other cases, apparently. Want some coffee?"

"No, I'm still nursing. Any herbal tea?"

"No caffeine?" Meg asked, opening a cupboard and surveying the choices.

"Nope, which is too bad, because with the two kids and a baby I kind of run out of steam by late afternoon."

"Cocoa?"

Rachel shook her head again. "Caffeine again. Plus it gives Maggie the hiccups."

"Really?" Meg asked.

"Really. Always did, even before she was born. Might be a mild allergy that she'll outgrow, but for now it's better to stay away from it. The other no-no's are fish and fatty meats and some dairy. But all the crunchy people are still saying that natural is better, at least for a few more months."

"Well, that leaves us with hot milk or hot water."

"Maybe hot milk with some vanilla added?"

"That I can do." Meg set about finding a clean mug, wondering where she'd last seen her vanilla extract. She filled a mug with milk, then stuck it in the microwave on low for a couple of minutes while she hunted down her vanilla extract. Which reminded her that she hadn't baked anything lately, and with no doubt there would be people dropping by to talk to Seth about the death . . . "How long do you plan to keep this up?" she asked, watching the timer on the microwave.

"Until one or both of us get tired of it. The other kids lost interest after about six months. So, enough baby stuff! Unless you're planning to make an announcement soon?" Rachel said, trying to keep her voice neutral.

"Nope, not now. But I promise when and if that changes, you'll be one of the first to know."

"Got it. So talk to me about adult stuff. I've been talking mainly to children for what seems like forever. And this one"—Rachel nodded toward Maggie, now asleep on her lap—"doesn't answer. You've given us the honeymoon story, unless you held back a few juicy tidbits?"

"Not really. The biggest surprise—outside of the body—was that it was the past that set the whole thing off. That and running into an old high school classmate very unexpectedly, and for some weird reason he turned out to have the key to the whole thing. Maybe Seth and I have some sort of karma that attracts murders."

Rachel shook her head. "That's on you. Seth got through all of his life without tripping over a body, until you arrived in town."

"I apologize, to Seth, to Granford, and to the universe in general. I would be happy to have it stop."

"Meg, do you think there's any possibility that this Monica's death was . . . not natural?"

Meg delayed answering by retrieving the mug of milk then adding a dash of the vanilla extract. For herself she poured the last of the coffee into a mug and decided it wasn't worth nuking—cold would do, but she started a fresh pot because no doubt someone else would drop by shortly. She slid Rachel's milk across the table to her. "The thought had crossed my mind, mainly because of my history here, but I rejected it pretty quickly. For one thing, Monica hasn't been here very long, certainly not long enough to make enemies who would want to kill her."

"Maybe she lived here before, thirty years ago, under an assumed name, and had done someone wrong?"

"Well, if that's true, I don't know about it. And I didn't get an evil vibe from her."

"What about the husband?"

"I haven't met him. Seth hasn't met him. He didn't come to the WinterFare. So maybe he doesn't exist, or he's a cripple, or he finally got fed up with Monica's incessant scurrying around and killed her to get some peace. Sorry, that sounds very shallow, and she was a nice person from what little I saw. So let's shelve the husband for now."

"Huh. She didn't have any other relatives around here?"

"Not that I know of."

"Then why was she here?"

"She told us that her husband retired and they were looking for someplace new and they'd never tried New England."

"Do you buy that? I mean, to make a big life change like moving without doing their homework?"

"Well, what other reasons are there? Lower property costs? Their place couldn't have been very expensive—Seth will tell you it needs work, but they were kind of past the age for do-it-yourself. Rachel, I don't know! You're asking good questions, but I don't have any answers. I know you're bored, but do you really need to create a crime where none exists?"

"Sorry," Rachel said, although Meg didn't think she looked very sorry. "But this is *you* I'm talking to. And you do have a rather unusual track record in this department."

Meg was relieved when Seth chose that moment to appear. "Hey, I thought I recognized that car. What brings you here?" He leaned over to kiss Rachel on the cheek, and then to peel back the blanket partially covering Maggie's face with a careful finger. Meg watched the tenderness in his touch and felt a pang: did they need to talk about children sooner rather than later? They'd been careful to avoid that talk so far, but they were married now, and both approaching a fortieth birthday . . .

"I got bored watching this one sleep"—Rachel nodded at Maggie—"so I thought we could go for a ride. And here's where I ended up. You want me to leave?" Rachel grinned.

"Of course not. You talked to Mom much lately?"

"Nope, although she looks, uh, glowing every time I see her. Christopher?"

"Seems like it. I don't pry."

"You're no fun. You okay with that?"

"Of course I am. I want her to be happy. How's Noah?"

"Same as always. He's great with the kids, though—he really enjoys their company. Maggie's a bit young for intelligent conversation. I was just asking Meg about the death this weekend. She said you both knew the woman, but not well."

"We never had the chance to get to know her well, although she was a bit older than we are. And I don't know if Mom met her at all. It sounds terrible, but I'm hoping it was simply food poisoning, for everyone's sake."

"That means there'll be a problem for someone else—most likely one of our friends or colleagues," Meg pointed out.

Seth shrugged. "Food poisoning happens, sometimes even when you're careful."

"Didn't I hear that there were other people with symptoms?" Rachel asked.

"Well, yes, but they could have purchased food anywhere. It's not like everyone came down with this thing all at once. Why are you so interested?"

"Just curious," Rachel said. "Or maybe I'm just hyperaware of it these days because of Maggie. I've seen a lot of poop and spit-up lately, and I've learned all over again how to interpret them. I feel lucky that I'm the one feeding her—I know I'd feel terrible if I gave her something I'd bought and it made her sick."

"Well, let's hope that it's the simplest possible case, and no one else is badly affected."

"Amen, brother!" Rachel told Seth.

Maggie began wriggling and opened her eyes. At the same time, Rachel said, "Oopsies, somebody needs a new diaper. I'd better head home, rather than burden you two with the fun parts."

"You can drop in any time, you know," Meg told her.

"I know. Besides, I haven't even met this mysterious new handyman of yours."

"Orchard manager. Don't imagine someone mysterious, dark, and brooding. He's pretty much a kid from a hard background, but Christopher says he knows what he's doing with apples, and I need the help right now."

"And now Meg is pressuring me to build him a tiny house," Seth added, "if 'house' isn't too grand a word for it."

"I am not!" Meg protested. "Well, maybe a little. But only if you want to do it."

"Cool," Rachel said. "I've seen that show. Don't tell my kids or they'll start bugging you for a playhouse."

"I'll remember that. Let me see you out."

"Thanks. Here, hold Maggie while I put on her winter gear. And my winter gear. And by then it may be spring." She thrust Maggie, now more or less awake, into Seth's arms, and the two of them stared at each other. Then Maggie reached out one tiny hand and tried to make a grab for his nose, but missed and her hand landed on his mouth, and Seth made a silly noise into it, and Maggie looked delighted. By then Rachel had her coat on and was ready to start outfitting Maggie. But first she winked at Meg. "Look at them! Aren't they great together?"

Meg wanted to glare at Rachel, but she had to admit she was right. *Worry about one thing at a time, Meg!*

10

Seth hadn't had time to retreat to his office when yet another vehicle pulled into their driveway, and Meg recognized the car as belonging to Art Preston. "I suppose there's no hope of hiding in the basement and pretending like we're not here?" Meg asked wistfully.

Seth quirked an eyebrow at her. "I thought you liked Art."

"I do. He's a great guy and a good friend. But since we had a nice chat yesterday, and he's just back from vacation, I have to assume his presence here means that something is wrong. And it won't take three guesses to figure out what it is."

"I'm afraid you're right. You want to hide while I deal with him?" Seth asked.

"Of course not. I'll let him in."

Reluctantly Meg went to the door and opened it. "Hi, Art," she said with little enthusiasm.

"That's the best you can do?" Art said, walking through the door and shrugging off his winter coat.

"You're the police officer. How would you interpret my not-so-cheerful greeting?" Meg asked.

"Well, either you two lovebirds are in the middle of a major fight, which I find unlikely, or you're already pretty sure that this isn't just a social visit."

"Door number two. Come into the kitchen and let us have it. Oh, you want coffee? Or does that constitute a bribe of a law enforcement official?"

"I will be delighted to have a cup of coffee. Hi, Seth."

"Art." Seth nodded.

"Wow!" Art said. "Both of you ticked off at me?" He pulled out a chair at the kitchen table and sat.

Meg slid a mug of coffee in front of him and resumed her seat. "Okay, why are you here? As if we can't guess?"

"Monica Whitman died of food poisoning, but she was the only one who ate at the fair and was affected, which looks kind of suspicious. So for now I'm calling it a murder, at least between us."

Meg felt stunned. "Wait—didn't you tell us that there were other cases?"

Art nodded. "I said there were other cases of stomach troubles, but it turns out they were just kids who ate too much junk food and ran around a lot, with predictable results."

"Oh," Meg replied. "How do you know it's murder, though? And so fast? I thought all those tests took time."

"The doctors at the hospital called this morning. There's no toxicology done yet, but the pattern looked wrong to them, and so did how fast she went downhill, so they decided to take a harder look before they released . . . her body."

"I thought they'd agreed it was accidental food poisoning? Not that I'm cheering for that idea, given that it might implicate someone at the WinterFare," Meg said. But then she realized that if Monica had been deliberately poisoned, someone had to be implicated.

"I know. Anyway, when she first got sick, she presented with the classic symptoms of gastroenteritis. Well, more like stomach flu, which is not quite the same thing. Anyway, you know the symptoms—watery diarrhea, vomiting, dehydration, and so on. Gastroenteritis is more serious, since it's usually due to bacteria or a virus, and it can be spread from person to person."

"And why do we need to know this?" Seth asked.

"As I said, at the start—last night after the fair was over—it looked like ordinary gastroenteritis, a serious case, and that's what they treated her for. It was bad enough then that they decided to keep her overnight rather than send her home. But then things went south really fast—too fast for a simple virus. So the doctors took a different approach and realized that her kidneys were shutting down big-time after less than twenty-four hours. That's not the normal pattern for gastroenteritis."

"So what do they think the problem is? Was?" Meg asked.

"She was given some substance that killed her."

"Poisoned? Why? Who? How?" Meg said.

"All good questions, Meg, and we don't have any answers yet. The lab people are running tests, but if you watch any of those detective shows on TV, you know they don't test for everything. They've got a basic set of things they look for, and if they don't find those, then they go on to another list of less likely candidates. But it's kind of one list at a time. You don't see a person dying like this and automatically assume the person was poisoned by the venom of a snake that lives only on the top of Mount Everest. They look for things that are easily available to ordinary people first."

"That makes sense," Seth said. "And that's where things stand right now? The people in white coats are looking for the simple answers first, and if that doesn't pan out, they'll look for complicated answers?"

"That's about the size of it. Let me say now: this is not yet an official investigation. I'm the only one who's brought up the M-word. It may be that when the wonks figure out the substance she took, they'll find a big bottle of it sitting on Monica's kitchen table."

"And if they don't?" Meg asked.

"Then we take it to the next level. And then, as you know, it's out of my hands—I have to turn it over to Marcus."

"Oh, joy," Meg said bitterly. She'd had some difficult confrontations with Detective William Marcus of the state police, the agency that investigated homicides in the area. She had hoped that they were on track toward more amicable relations, but another suspicious death in her backyard was not going to help.

"So what do you do now, Art?" Seth asked.

"I'm kinda caught in the middle. It's not officially a crime—yet—so I can't investigate officially. But when and if it becomes a crime, I'm not sure if I'll have a chance to help with the investigation. Can we just go over between us who provided food or drink or anything that the woman might have put in her mouth at the WinterFare?"

"Sure," Seth said quickly. "I keep forgetting that you weren't around for the planning process. Nicky and Brian were the main food providers, and they said they'd done really well at the fair. Which might suggest that their food was fine, because a lot of people ate it and didn't have a problem."

"Just those kids we talked about, Meg," Art said, "and they bounced back fast. Of course we'll have to check them out, talk to the parents and see what they ate. Who else, Meg?"

"The fruit and vegetable vendors. For apples, that's me, Ginny Morris—who runs the organic farm on the other side of town—and a whole bunch of other people who sold some apples along with a variety of winter vegetables."

"Okay. I'll have to find out what 'organic' actually means. You don't qualify with your orchard, right?"

"Right. Too many regulations. I'm not against it in principle, but I haven't been ready to do all the paperwork. Apparently Ginny's got that done."

"But you don't use chemicals or any additives to your trees?" Art asked.

"Only widely used and approved natural agents. You know, biological things that eat other things. No chemical sprays or anything like that."

"Okay. But don't be surprised if whoever ends up investigating this asks those questions and possibly even tests whatever apples you have," Art told her.

"That's okay with me—I have nothing to hide. Although I'm not sure if I have any samples left of all the apples I was selling yesterday."

Art turned to Seth. "You don't have any toxic furniture finishes and the like that might have seeped into the apples?"

"Of course not. And I keep anything potentially toxic, like mineral spirits or turpentine, in a separate part of the building anyway. Meg, what about the craft vendors—didn't some of them sell jams and jellies?"

"I think they did. Did they have to apply for a license?"

Seth looked troubled. "We've never worried about individuals selling to other individuals, or we'd never have a bake sale in town again. It's not the same if it's a commercial operation or a bulk distributor. But people have been selling jelly at the Harvest Festival for years and nobody's had a problem."

Art didn't look too happy. Had he hoped for a quick and simple answer? "Seth, you'll have a list of who was selling what, right?" When Seth nodded, Art added, "Make sure you have it available, if somebody asks for it. And make sure all the town's official paperwork is in order."

"Of course," Seth said.

Seth didn't look happy, either. It appeared to Meg that both men were anticipating trouble. Great. But there couldn't be anything harmful in the food that was sold—could there? People knew children would be eating it, among others. "Guys, do you think this was just a general thing, or did somebody have a beef with Monica?"

"I don't think we can guess right now," Art said. "Of course I'm going to go talk to Douglas Whitman, see if he remembers what Monica ate, or if there are any scraps left around their house. He may not remember much about his meals over the last day or two—some days I have trouble remembering what I ate for breakfast, much less what my wife did."

"Do you want me to come along with you, to see Doug?" Meg volunteered.

Art didn't answer immediately, thinking it over. "Do you know the man?"

"No, I've never even seen him. And I didn't spend enough time with Monica to learn much about him, or their history together."

Art seemed to come to a decision. "The heck with it. Yes, Meg, I'd appreciate it if you would come with me. If Seth can spare you, that is. This is not yet an official investigation, although that might be no more than an hour or two away. But the man must be hurting, and it would be good to have a woman along. Plus you might see things that I'd miss."

"No women on your force, eh, Art?" Seth said, but at least his tone was joking.

"Only behind a desk." Art held up his hands. "I know, I know—we're working on the problem. And I agree—we need to add a couple of women. Remember that when our budget comes up for a vote again, okay?"

"You know I will. How long do you think you'll be?"

"I can't imagine it would be more than a couple of hours, and he lives maybe two miles from here, right? Why? Can't be apart from your blushing bride for long?"

"Well, there's that, but mostly I want to know what time we've got available to get anything done before dark."

"You have something in mind, Seth?" Meg asked, bewildered. He hadn't mentioned anything.

"I'd like to talk to Larry and see if he's had any further thought about the tiny house idea. But I'd also like to take him over to my house—maybe I'm not being fair to him to assume he wouldn't want to stay there."

"What're you charging if you're going to rent the place, Seth?" Art asked.

"I really haven't decided. I want to cover my own expenses—utilities and taxes and the like. And it might make sense to have someone in the house just to keep an eye on things. I don't like having it standing empty, so close to Mom's house. But I'm not looking to make a lot of money. You have somebody in mind?"

"I can keep my ears open, if somebody's looking. You going to sell it or keep it?" Art asked.

"Why, are you interested? Let's say I'm not planning to sell it, but I'll entertain ideas for it."

"Got it. Meg, you want to go over to the Whitman house now?"

"I guess so." What had she gotten herself into? She was sorry that Monica had died, and so unpleasantly, but in addition she had a personal stake in figuring out what had happened: if her apples were suspected, she needed to clear that up quickly, because her orchard was her livelihood. She knew she hadn't used anything on them that was toxic, but she didn't want her orchard practices to be tied up while this death—accidental?—was investigated. Better to find a solution quickly. "Let me grab my coat. Seth, I've got my cell if you need me. Are you cooking tonight?"

"Sure, I'll take care of it. See you later."

Meg pulled on her coat and followed Art out to his car. Once they were settled inside with the heater going full blast, Meg asked, "Is this legal?"

"Mostly. Look, I know as well as anyone that you've got a difficult relationship with Marcus, and I don't want to make things any worse. But nobody has called this a murder yet, and if it was accidental, and we can figure out how it happened, it'll make things easier for everyone."

"Including me. But I agree. Don't borrow trouble, right?"

"Exactly. Keep it simple."

It took less than five minutes to arrive at the house that Monica had lived in. Meg had known of it by the name of the last owners, who hadn't lived in it for over ten years. She'd always been saddened by its gradual decay as she had driven past it over the past two years. Now it looked greatly improved: the trim had been reattached, and a coat of fresh paint had transformed the house. A decade of weeds had been cleared from the lawn immediately around it. Monica and her husband had done a nice job.

Art pulled into the driveway, where there was another car parked. "Ready?" he asked her.

"I suppose. Will you take the lead? This is your case, so to speak."

"Sure." Art waited for Meg to get out of the car, then he walked purposefully toward the front door and pushed the button for the doorbell. Meg, close behind him, heard a "ding-dong" from somewhere inside the house.

At first nothing happened, and then finally she heard the slow shuffle of feet, and a few moments later the door opened to reveal a man who looked closer to seventy than sixty. His clothes were rumpled and his hair hadn't been combed recently, nor had he shaved that day. "Can I help you?"

"I hope so. Are you Douglas Whitman?"

"Yes, I am. Who are you?"

"I'm Arthur Preston, chief of police for Granford. May we come in?"

The man didn't move. "I didn't call for any police."

"I know that, Mr. Whitman. This is about your wife."

"Monica? She's not home right now. I'm not sure where she is, but she didn't make my breakfast."

Meg glanced at Art with dismay. Clearly something was not right with Douglas Whitman, but Monica had never mentioned anything about any problems her husband might have. But then, she hadn't said much at all about her home life, as far as Meg knew. "Would you like me to make you some breakfast? We can wait for your wife inside."

"Why, thank you, my dear. That's very nice of you. I'm sure she'll be back soon." Douglas took a step back and gestured them into the central hallway of the house. "The kitchen is in the back. I'll show you."

As Douglas led the way down the dark hallway, Art said, "I think we may have a problem."

"I think you're right, Art."

11

"What now?" Art said in a quiet voice.

Meg felt out of her depth, but they were here and Douglas was hurting. "We have to talk to him to get a sense of what his problem is, although I'd be willing to guess it's Alzheimer's or dementia—I don't know enough about either to tell them apart. And the fact that he doesn't seem to remember that his wife is dead suggests that this isn't new. Unless the news gave him some sort of short-term amnesia." In which case, Meg decided, she didn't want to be around when he came to his senses and realized Monica was gone. Did that make her a shallow and uncaring person? She hoped not, but she wasn't responsible for Douglas Whitman's well-being.

When they reached the door to the kitchen, both Meg and Art stopped in their tracks. The room was a mess, with most horizontal surfaces covered with plates of half-eaten food, some of which looked as though they dated back for more than one day. Despite the fact that it was midwinter, a few flies hopped from plate to plate. The smell was appalling, and Meg quickly saw that the trash had not been emptied in some time. How could energetic, organized Monica have let things get into this state?

"I apologize for the mess," Douglas said. "My wife usually takes care of the dishes. I cook," he added proudly.

"Why don't you let me take care of those dishes, Mr. Whitman?" Meg asked. "May I call you Douglas? Can I get you some coffee? Tea?" Assuming she could find the fixings somewhere in this mess.

"Coffee would be wonderful, thank you. I think Monica keeps the coffee in one of those cupboards." Douglas waved vaguely at the cabinets over the stove.

"It won't take me long at all," Meg told him. "Art, why don't the two of you chat while I make the coffee?"

"Uh, sure, I guess." Art turned back to Douglas. "So, tell me, Douglas, how long have you and Monica been married?"

Meg turned her back on them and tried to decide where to start. Coffee: she'd promised coffee. If she could find something to boil water in, and the coffee—instant?—it would be one small step forward. She started opening cupboards until she found a jar of coffee, then rinsed out the cleanest pot she could see, filled it with water, and set in on a stove burner, flinching at the film of grease. She turned the burner on and went back to the larger issue of the dirty dishes.

She had to remove stacked dirty dishes from the sink to find dish soap and fill the sink with water. Then she started shifting the piles of dishes and pots. As she worked, she thought, *Monica was home—here!—yesterday morning.* She'd been hospitalized yesterday evening, and had died early this morning. That was a pretty tight timeline. But looking at the rotting remains in the kitchen, Meg wondered if she might have contracted whatever it was well before the fair—there had to be enough bacteria in the kitchen to fell an ox. Were there rubber gloves anywhere in the kitchen? she wondered. She was reluctant to immerse her hands in the scummy water and greasy pans, but in the end she had no choice.

Meg tried to keep the noise down so she could listen to Art talk quietly with Douglas. She had to admit that Art was handling the poor man with sensitivity. Not that she'd doubted Art had it in him, but this hardly seemed his "policeman" side. Douglas seemed to be replying courteously and coherently, with the glaring exception that he didn't acknowledge that his wife was dead. Had Monica told anybody of his problems? Meg seemed to remember Monica saying that she had told the town assemblymen that her husband had retired before the move to Granford. Monica had been so eager to make friends in her new town, to fit in. How long could she have kept Douglas's problems a secret? And wouldn't she want or need the community's help in taking care of him?

Why was she dead? Meg had finished washing the plates and cups, and started in on the greasy pots and pans. The state of the kitchen raised a new possibility—that she'd died because of some nasty bacterium in her own kitchen. But Monica had always appeared neat and well dressed when Meg had seen her. How could she have let her home reach this state? And if this bacterium had struck her down so quickly, why wasn't Douglas showing any

effects? He looked to be a solidly built man, with no out-
ward appearance of poor health, apart from the normal
signs of age. Meg felt vaguely ashamed of her earlier
thought, that maybe husband Douglas had poisoned his
wife to get rid of her and her endless chatter. Unless Douglas was an amazing actor, that seemed highly unlikely.

Another ten minutes and the dishes were done. Meg
wiped down the countertops, then the sink. The water had
boiled, so she spooned coffee crystals into clean mugs,
and returned with them to join the two men. "All done,"
Meg said brightly, in a tone that sounded false even to her.
Douglas didn't seem to notice. "Douglas, do you and
Monica have any children?"

Art quirked an eyebrow at her but didn't comment.
Douglas answered with what seemed like an oft-repeated
line. "No, we weren't blessed with children, although we
would have loved to have some. It wasn't meant to be, it
seems." He paused, looking around in confusion. "Where
is my wife? Have you seen her?"

Meg looked at Art. "What now?" she mouthed.

Art shrugged. "Douglas, do you know if your wife had
seen a doctor lately around here?"

"No, she hasn't gotten around to that yet. She keeps
saying she means to do it, but she's been so busy. She really
likes it here, you know."

"Does she take any medicines?" Art pressed.

"Yes, a few, and some vitamins. We aren't as young as
we used to be. I take some, too. We muddle along together,
just like we always have."

"You said you did most of the cooking?" Meg asked.

"Well, it's more like we share it, kind of. We have our
own favorite dishes that we like to make. She's a good

cook—she says that natural food is the best thing to put in your natural body."

"It must be working—she certainly has a lot of energy," Meg said.

"She does indeed! I'm a lucky man." Douglas sat back and smiled cheerfully at them.

Meg hated to burst his happy bubble, but it was unavoidable. "Art, we have to do this."

Art sighed. "I know. I hate this part of the job." He turned to face Douglas. "Do you remember going to the hospital last night?"

Douglas looked bewildered. "I'm not sick. Why would I go to the hospital?"

"It was your wife, Monica, who had to go. She got very sick to her stomach last night."

"I . . ." Douglas began, then he looked down at his mug. "Oh. I remember. I went with her—I don't drive anymore—Monica does all the driving now—but she wasn't well, so she called for an ambulance and they let me stay in it with her."

Meg tried to convey a silent message: *Take it slow, Art.*

"Do you remember what happened when you got there, Douglas?" Art prompted gently.

"They took her away on a—what do you call it? That bed thing on wheels—it's got a funny name. They wouldn't let me stay with her while the doctors were looking at her."

"What then?"

"After a while somebody came out and said that Monica would have to stay overnight at the hospital. Somebody arranged to bring me home here. Oh, and they asked me to look for some insurance papers. Monica usually handles all that."

"Did anyone come to talk to you this morning?"

"You mean, here? Uh, maybe. But it could have been yesterday. When will Monica be home?"

Meg's heart ached for the poor man, but he needed to know—if he could process the information. "Douglas, Monica won't be coming home. She died at the hospital."

Douglas shut his eyes, and for a moment his expression seemed to show that he understood what Meg had just told him. But when he opened them his expression shifted to childlike confusion. "But she has to make my lunch."

Meg looked quickly at Art. "What do we do now?"

"It's pretty clear we can't leave him alone here, and there doesn't seem to be anyone nearby to look after him, and no kids to call. I'm going to have to call in a service of some kind—I'll have to check with my office and see who we're using these days."

"We'll need to stay here until you get that sorted out."

"That's my responsibility, Meg—you've done enough."

Would it be wrong of her to admit she was relieved that Art felt that way? "I can stay for a while. And I can call Seth to come pick me up here."

"Okay. You stay with Doug while I make a couple of calls." Art fished out his cell phone and walked back toward the front of the house to call.

"How did you and Monica meet?" Meg asked Douglas.

He smiled fondly. "We met all the way back in high school, in Ohio, and we were a couple right away. Oh, we went to different colleges—we figured we needed to see more of the world before settling down. But there was never any doubt that we'd end up together. She lit up a room just by walking into it."

"When did you get married?"

"In 1984, I think it was. It was a nice small wedding. And since then we've lived all over the place. That was for my job, you see. Monica worked sometimes—she was a teacher, or maybe it was a classroom assistant in a school, for a while. But I made enough money to keep us, so she didn't really need to."

"When was your last job?"

Douglas looked blank. "I . . . uh, right before we moved here?"

Meg wondered if his medical insurance had lapsed if he wasn't working anymore. Meg hoped that efficient Monica had taken care of it somehow. "How did you choose Granford? Did you have family here?"

"Monica picked it. We'd always wanted to live in New England, and she was looking for a place that was kind of in the country, and where we could make new friends. She loves to meet people."

Meg noted that Douglas had consistently used the present tense to talk about Monica. Maybe his deep denial was a good thing, for now. Maybe his subconscious brain knew that he needed time to process such a shattering event.

Art reappeared and said tersely, "Someone's coming over. You might want to get out of here while you can—my office is on half-staff today, but somebody took a message from the state police, and you can probably guess what that means."

"I'm afraid so. I'll give Seth a call."

Like Art before her, Meg left the kitchen to make her call. Seth didn't pick up, on either his cell or the landline, but she left a brief message, saying mainly "I need a ride home." She'd just hung up when there was a heavy rapping at the front door. She wasn't sure what she was supposed to do—after all, it wasn't her house—and she was relieved when Art came out and opened the door.

Damn. State Police Detective William Marcus, her not-favorite person, stood on the other side, looking very official, albeit surprised to see Meg at the house. "Preston," he said curtly. "What're you doing here?"

"I was concerned about Mr. Whitman's well-being, so I thought I'd come by and check on him."

"And Meg here had the same idea?" the detective said.

"No, I asked her to accompany me here. I thought a woman's presence might be a good idea."

Marcus made a "humph" sound that stayed barely on the side of polite. "The man is here?"

"He is. But I think you need to know that he appears to be suffering from some form of dementia. He doesn't seem to recall that his wife is dead. What're *you* doing here?"

Marcus stood up straighter than before. "Monica Whitman's death has been declared a homicide. I'm here to interview Mr. Whitman, and to examine a potential crime scene."

"How'd you decide it was a homicide?" Art asked. "Have you identified the cause of death?"

"I'll tell you, as a professional courtesy, but I ask that neither of you spreads this information around. You understand?"

Meg and Art nodded obediently.

"We have reason to believe that the woman was poisoned, and we've narrowed down the substance to a particular type, although we don't have a final answer."

"It looked a lot like food poisoning," Art said. "What made you change your mind? And who called you in?"

"The coroner. The initial symptoms were consistent with gastroenteritis or a virus, but the total collapse of the kidneys and liver in such a short period pointed to something else. Our forensic team is on their way over now."

Alarm bells went off in Meg's head, but she knew she had to say something. "Uh, detective? When we arrived, the kitchen was a mess, full of rotting food. I washed the dishes and cleaned up a bit."

Marcus's expression turned even colder, something Meg would not have thought possible. "You tampered with a crime scene?"

"It wasn't a crime scene then," Art pointed out. "The place was unsanitary and potentially dangerous to Mr. Whitman. Look, you'd better talk to Douglas yourself. He has a kind of shaky grasp on reality right now, and he seems to be waiting for his wife to come home and fix his lunch. I can't see him killing anyone, much less the woman who manages his life for him."

"That's for me to decide. You two might as well go home. If I have any questions, in particular about what you cleaned up, I'll be in touch. Did you remove any garbage from the house?"

"No, it's still in the kitchen," Meg said.

"Oh, one more thing: do either of you have a prior relationship with either of the Whitmans?"

"No," Meg spoke first. "Today was the first time I met him. I spoke with Monica a few times, and saw her yesterday at the fair. That's all."

"Same here," Art added.

"Then you may go."

Art said quickly, "One more thing—someone from social services will be arriving shortly to assess Doug's condition and make arrangements for him for tonight, at least. He shouldn't stay here alone."

"I'll be the judge of that. Thank you for your efforts on his behalf." Marcus turned his back on them and strode toward the kitchen: they were dismissed.

12

 When Meg and Art walked out the front door of the Whitman house, they found Seth waiting in the driveway.

"I saw Marcus's car and I was trying to make up my mind whether to stay out here or come in and rescue you. You okay, Meg?"

"I'll survive. I'll tell you in the car. Art, are you leaving?"

"I think I'll hang around until social services arrives— I'm worried about Douglas, and our favorite detective is somewhat lacking in sensitivity."

"Carefully put," Meg told him. "Okay, let me know if you need anything else from me, or if I should flee the country."

"Will do. Thanks for your help, Meg."

"I'm glad I could help, and I hope you can get Douglas sorted out—and keep him out of jail."

"My thoughts exactly. Bye, lovebirds."

Meg climbed into Seth's car and buckled herself in. Seth slid into his seat and did the same, then turned on the engine. "Home?" he asked.

"Please."

"I gather there's a story? I didn't expect to see Marcus."

"Of course there's a story. Marcus was there because based on the physical evidence the coroner observed, Monica's death has been declared a homicide. Talking to the husband is the obvious first step, but I don't think Marcus was ready for what he found."

"Which is?" Seth asked.

"Let's wait until we get home. It's complicated, and I don't have any idea what to do, or what the best outcome would be. And Marcus isn't exactly happy with me."

The ride was short, and they were back in the kitchen in minutes. Meg went straight to the kettle and filled it for hot water: she wanted tea. Something comforting. Cookies might be good, too, but she couldn't remember if they had any.

Seth sat down and waited patiently while she went through the process of making the tea.

"You want a cup?" she asked him.

"Sure. I've already had enough coffee for the day."

Meg searched out two clean mugs, and filled a small pitcher with milk. She set everything on the kitchen table, then brought over the teapot, bundled in a cozy, and set it down. "There." She sat.

Seth was watching her with a slightly amused expression. "Are you ready to talk now?"

"I guess. I'm sad and mad and confused. I hope talking about it will help."

"Go for it."

"Let me start at the back end: Marcus is ticked off at me because I messed up a crime scene. Although it wasn't officially a crime scene when I messed it up."

"You're going to have to explain that."

So Meg did, starting from her arrival at the Whitman house with Art, and the discovery that Douglas Whitman was not competent to care for himself, at least at the moment, through her need to clean up the kitchen so Douglas wouldn't inadvertently make himself sick with spoiled food. It had never occurred to her that she might be destroying evidence. Her main concern had been to protect poor Doug. Marcus was right: the crime scene was irreversibly changed. But he should be able to understand why she had done it, with only good intentions.

"And Art called social services or something, because no way should Douglas be left by himself. I don't know how Marcus is going to react to that."

"He may not be the world's warmest person, but if what you say about Douglas is true, he should see it pretty quickly."

"I hope so. The idea of Marcus dragging Douglas off to Northampton and browbeating him about who could have killed his wife makes me feel sick. Of course being taken somewhere unfamiliar by someone he doesn't know isn't much better."

"I agree. But what are we supposed to do about it?"

"Douglas's welfare is now in the hands of Art or Marcus. But, Seth, you haven't stated the obvious. If Marcus is correct, and Monica was poisoned, and Douglas didn't do it—which I don't think is remotely possible, given what I've seen of his mental state—then someone else killed her. Who?"

"I have no idea," Seth said. "For once we're on the same playing field as anybody else investigating this death. Monica and Douglas had lived here only a couple of months. They apparently have no history with Granford. So you and I can't conveniently point to a grudge that dates back to a fourth-great-grandfather. We don't know these people. We know only what Monica told us, and that might not be true. Douglas can't tell us much, or maybe he doesn't want to, for some reason. Maybe they were in witness protection, or fleeing from some evil foreign group. But right now, as far as I can see, there is no way that Monica should be dead. Nobody here knew her, and nobody I know had a motive to kill her. I'm stumped."

"So am I. But it's hard to say 'not my problem' and just walk away."

"I agree. And since I represent the town of Granford, I have an even stronger reason to be involved and concerned. No offense meant."

"I know. We may have ancestors here going back to seventeen-whatever, but in the modern world I've been here barely longer than Monica. By the way, Douglas said she never had a career, and her only paid jobs were as a teacher or classroom aide. He also said they met in Ohio, in high school. So—if he's telling the truth or at least remembers correctly—there's no big scandal or embezzlement lurking in her past." Meg paused to take a sip of her tea. "Monica told people that Douglas was retired, but she never said why. Do you think he was offered no choice?"

"We can't know right now. It must be hard to introduce yourself to an entire new community and say, oh, you won't see much of my husband—he has an Incurable Disease that will only get worse with time."

"We asked Douglas, why Granford? He said it was Monica's idea. Since it's pretty clear it wasn't because she knew people or had family here, then maybe she wanted a place where nobody knew them, and she could make up whatever story she wanted. Maybe she was embarrassed by what was happening to her husband. Damn, it's all so sad! So what happens now?"

"If it's homicide, then Art won't be involved, unless Marcus invites him in. Marcus may not even look for a local angle, since the Whitmans were new to Granford. Presumably the lab will figure out what the poison was, how hard it was to obtain, who could get hold of it."

"And how they administered it to Monica without poisoning half the town, which could have been tricky if it happened at the fair. From the glimpses I saw of Monica yesterday, she was sampling just about everything. I even sold her apples. That's a lot of legwork for the police. But she seemed fine the last time I saw her, mid-afternoon. Does that help with the timeline?"

"Until the lab comes through with results, you don't know how long it would take for his poison to take effect," Seth pointed out. "It could still prove to be a simple bacterial thing, from food in the house, if it's as bad as you said. Although you'd think Douglas would be sick if that was the case."

"He did say they both took medication of some sort, but that Monica hadn't gotten around to finding a new doctor for either of them, according to Doug. So if either of them happened to have a preexisting medical issue, it can't have been too urgent."

"Still, prescriptions do run out, and they aren't automatically renewed. Maybe she was seeing a doctor without telling Douglas."

"But no doctor would prescribe for Douglas without examining him first, would they?" Meg asked. "Of course he might have seen one or more but he simply doesn't remember it."

"I hope not. And it seems unlikely that he could have been seeing one on the sly himself. I don't think he can drive anymore, and he's not familiar with the roads around here."

"He said he didn't drive now. So if there was a medication involved in Monica's illness, it had to have come with them, or Monica must have gotten it since she arrived. Oh, Seth, I don't want to think that Monica did that to herself. And I can't see Douglas harming her—he seems to have cared for her. Plus he depends—depended—on her."

"Maybe somebody gave it to him and told him it would boost Monica's energy? Or calm her down?"

"But who? Nobody knew him. The only place I've heard that he went outside of the house was to Gran's for dinner, and Monica was always with him there."

Seth shook his head. "Meg, I don't have any answers. I'm just throwing ideas out there. Let Marcus do his digging and see what he turns up before you get yourself tied up in knots."

"I hate being sensible," she muttered. "Is there anything else on our to-do list for today? And please don't tell me housework, because I am so not in the mood."

"Go see Mom? Ask Mom to come over and consult on the tiny house?"

"You really are serious about that?" Meg asked. "The house, I mean?"

"I like the idea—it's challenging. A space like that would not be for everyone, but it could be perfect for the right person. And like you, I need the distraction right now. I can make all sorts of plans, but that doesn't mean I have to build it."

"Fine. Let's go out and pace off your tiny house. Make me visualize it. Tell me how it will work. I need the fresh air."

"Done!" Seth stood up and held out a hand to Meg, who took it happily, then leaned into him.

"I'm sorry," she said.

"For what?"

"Everything. That Monica is dead—she didn't deserve to die. That she left a helpless husband behind and nobody knows yet what will happen to him. That this whole mess kind of wrecked the WinterFare, which was a good idea and was fun. I know—you're going to say it's not my fault. I know it isn't. I just feel bad. Is that wrong?"

"Of course not. You're a good person, and you care. And that's one of the reasons that I love you. I'd be the last person to tell you to shake it off and get on with your life."

"Thank you. So let's go outside and poke at your tiny plot before we lose the sun."

The fresh air did help, Meg realized. She didn't like emotional confrontations—not that any normal person did—but she wanted to help, to do the right thing, because people had helped her when she had found herself in Granford with no friends and a murder accusation hanging over her. That's what community was all about—helping each other.

When they reached what little remained of the former chicken house foundation, Meg asked, "What's the footprint?"

"About twenty by twenty-five feet. Five hundred square feet all in."

"You aiming to do it on one floor?"

"That's easiest, although a sleeping loft is always a possibility."

"What rooms do you think you'll want? Or isn't there room for more than one? Five hundred square feet sounds so small."

"I can work—I've seen plans. Bedroom, living slash eating room, kitchen, bath."

"You want to dress it up?"

"What do you mean?" Seth asked.

"Fancy roof? What kind of windows? A front porch?"

"Lady, you're getting way ahead of me. And some of that can be added later, like the porch."

"True. Modern materials? I mean, no salvage?"

"Probably, although I wouldn't say no if I found something interesting."

"You never do—you've filled a lot of the barn with your treasures. What kind of heat?"

"Probably electric. I know, it's not the most efficient, but it's the most manageable under the circumstances. A coal-burning stove could work, but it might be a fire hazard."

"Does the town put any restrictions on this kind of building?"

"Things like this are not exactly spelled out in our by-laws, but of course I'd look into it before I started anything. There was a case in Hadley not long ago, so it's something people are looking at more seriously."

Of course you will, Meg thought. *And you'd never think of asking for any kind of special consideration just*

*because you're an assemblyman. But people would be
happy to give you an exception because they like you and
they know you'd be fair about it.* "As of right now we're
just kicking around ideas, right?"

"Exactly. What do you think?"

"I think the idea is growing on me. You can go ahead
and ask the town planners about approvals anyway. If they
say no, then we'll move on."

"You think Larry would like it?"

"I don't exactly know him well yet, but I think he'd
appreciate having his own space, no matter what size it is.
And he'd have a really short commute."

Seth laughed. "That's certainly true. Are you going to
charge him rent?"

"I hadn't really thought about it. I gave Bree free housing because I couldn't pay her as much salary as she deserved, plus it was her first job. I'm paying Larry a little
more, because he has more experience, but it's still not a
lot. How would I calculate it? By square footage? By the
local rate for one-bedroom apartments?"

"I have no idea. That's your business. Building it would
be mine. When would you, or he, need this to happen?"

"I don't really know where he's living right now, but I
know it's only temporary. Once the apple season gets under
way, he's going to need to be here on-site. How fast can you
build?"

"A couple of weeks? The foundation's in place, and
framing would be easy. Think he'd be willing to help out
with the construction?"

"I don't know. We can only ask, but it's not part of the
job description. You getting cold yet?" The sun was approaching the horizon—winter days were short.

"Maybe. You're cooking?"

"I guess so. Remind me to do some shopping soon—we're running out of things."

"And we do like to eat. Tomorrow? I don't have anything scheduled."

"Works for me."

13

Seth got an emergency plumbing call early Monday morning, so Meg went to the supermarket alone. But when she arrived she realized that she'd conveniently forgotten that the market was information central for the town of Granford, and she couldn't walk ten feet without running into someone she knew, and of course that person wanted to know what Meg knew about Monica Whitman's death and was itching to share what information he or she had collected, which was often wrong. Meg felt obligated to correct most of the misconceptions, but she didn't want to say too much in case it got back to Detective Marcus.

Yes, she'd met Monica's husband, Douglas. (She omitted the part about his diminished capacity or whatever the term should be.) Yes, she'd heard that Monica's death had been declared a homicide, but no one was sure—or had said publicly—how she'd died. No, she didn't know if anyone had been arrested. Yes, she thought there would be a number of possible suspects, and yes, she might be among them since she'd sold food to people, including to Monica. No, she had no idea what was going to happen next, and Detective Marcus hadn't shared any information with her. (Why would anyone in Granford assume he would, after their interactions in the past?) She thought it was likely that anyone who had sold or consumed food at the Winter-Fare would be contacted by the state police. Unfortunately that number included at least half the population of Granford, and who knew how many people from adjoining towns. No, she didn't think terrorists were behind it. (She had to work hard not to smile at that question, although the person who asked was a querulous old woman who might well believe it was possible.) And that was all she knew—or all she felt free to say.

It was exhausting. She threw the bare essentials into her shopping cart and raced for the checkout line, then hurried to her car. She and Seth could eat cereal for dinner until the furor died down—they'd survive. But as long as Monica's death remained unexplained, the curiosity, and then the anxiety, would linger. She checked the time: not even ten. Meg decided to go see if Nicky was in the kitchen at Gran's, although the restaurant didn't open until lunchtime. Surely the police had come and gone there, since Nicky and Brian had provided the lion's share of the food. She drove the few miles and pulled into the near-empty parking lot at the restaurant.

She knocked at the front door, then knocked again—she could hear people moving around in the kitchen, clanging pots. Finally somebody stomped across the front room and grabbed open the door. It was Brian, looking harried. "We're not open yet— Oh, hi, Meg. Come on in."

"Hi, Brian. Can I hide out here? The market is buzzing and I had to get out of there. How are you and Nicky doing?"

"About as well as can be expected. The police were here, asking questions and taking samples of the food. You have any idea what they're thinking?"

"Not really. I was at Monica's house when Detective Marcus showed up, and we really got off on the wrong foot." *Again,* she added to herself. "I'd cleaned up the kitchen for Douglas, because I'm pretty sure it was a health hazard, and Marcus accused me of tampering with a crime scene. Of course I hadn't known it was or would be a crime scene—I was only trying to keep Douglas from getting sick. Is Nicky here? I don't want to repeat all this twice, but I know you're setting up for lunch and I don't want to be in the way."

"Don't worry about it—come on back." Brian led her through the dining room of what had once been an elegant older house, and into the kitchen. Nicky looked up from whatever she was sautéing and said, "Meg! We need to talk. Give me two more minutes on the mirepoix here and we can sit down. Brian, get her some coffee or something stronger."

"Coffee's fine," Meg said quickly as she followed Brian back to the end of the dining room nearest the kitchen. "How was business yesterday?"

"The good citizens of Granford did not stay away, I can safely say. We were full, which I took as the best possible vote of confidence in our cooking. In any case, the police won't find anything here that could be a problem. We run a clean kitchen."

"I know you do. But I guess they have to do their job."

Nicky came out of the kitchen then, wiping her hands on her stained chef's apron. "Okay, that much is done. What's the scoop?"

Meg sketched out the timeline for the day before, from when she arrived at the Whitman house with Art until they were more or less thrown out by Marcus after he'd accused her of tampering with evidence. Both Brian and Nicky made comforting noises. When she'd wrapped up, Meg asked, "How well do you know Douglas Whitman?"

"He and Monica ate here a number of times," Brian said. "He was always quiet, polite. He seemed to enjoy the food. Monica did most of the talking. Why do you ask?"

"Please don't spread this around, but I do trust you two to be discreet. When Art and I arrived yesterday, he seemed to think that Monica was out on an errand and would be back any minute. He apparently didn't know that she was dead, although I know he was told officially. I wondered if there was something wrong with him. I mean, it could have been shock, after hearing his wife had died unexpectedly. But he seemed oddly cheerful, or at least, not upset. I was thinking Alzheimer's or dementia, however they define the two these days. Did you ever notice anything like that?"

"I was the one who talked with him, since I handle the front of the house," Brian said, "but that was mainly to take their orders and ask if they'd enjoyed the meal. As I think back, it was usually Monica who told me what they wanted, and I think she paid the bill, too. I just figured she was the talker of the family, and Douglas sat there and smiled and nodded and let her do it. I've seen that before in older couples, and it doesn't mean one partner is ill."

"I've probably seen it, too, Brian, and I didn't think twice," Meg told him. "Art said he was going to contact some social service agencies to check on Douglas because I don't think he has any family in the area, or anywhere at all, for that matter. But then Marcus came charging in and more or less ordered us out because it had become a potential crime scene—and he jumped all over me for washing the dishes. I'm worried about how he'll handle Douglas. If he'll wonder if Douglas is faking or trying to cover up something. I mean, Douglas is the obvious suspect if Monica was poisoned—although from what I saw at the house, it's just as likely to be rotting food that was the underlying cause, and it's hard to say whose fault that was. But I'm not sure Marcus will see Douglas as a sick man who's just had a major psychological shock and who isn't in any shape to be questioned in a murder investigation. And I have no idea what will happen to him if he is taken in. Marcus might easily decide Douglas was just being stubborn and obstructive, and who knows how Douglas will react to that?"

"Douglas is the most logical suspect," Nicky said carefully. "But as you say, it could have been an accident due to careless food handling. If not Douglas—who you're saying isn't capable of planning much of anything—who else could have wanted Monica dead? And how did they do it?"

"None of this makes sense," Meg said. "He didn't know anyone here. Monica might have been a bit, uh, overwhelming to get along with, but people are seldom killed for that. And her heart was in the right place. I'm not sure anyone gains from her death. So what's the motive?"

"I have no clue," Nicky said. "Maybe somebody who

wanted to give Granford a bad name? Maybe it didn't matter who died, as long as the headlines read 'Unexplained death in Granford.'"

"You're not helping, Nicky. That could be any of a lot of people, going back years." They sat in silence for a few moments.

Then Nicky said, "I'm concerned that there were other people who were affected."

"Weren't there some kids, too?" Meg asked.

Nicky waved a hand dismissively. "There are always kids getting sick at this kind of event—they eat too much, and run around and get too worked up. Then if they hear that someone else has—excuse me—puked, they decide they're feeling sick, too. Psychosomatic, right?"

"Maybe." Meg sighed. "Of course the state police are going to want to check out my apples, not that I'm worried about that. Oh, speaking of apples—you've met Ginny Morris, right?"

"Briefly, a few months ago. Why?"

"I'm embarrassed to say that I just met her at the fair. Kind of silly, since we're in the same business and we live pretty close to each other, but we've both been busy."

"I gather she's been working her buns off trying to get the old orchard back in shape and get it certified organic," Nicky said. "She came by and introduced herself once she got her first crop in. She was really into the whole organic thing."

"Did you buy anything?"

"I said I'd think about it. The apples looked okay, and she had some interesting older varietals. She told me she'd saved some of the old trees in her orchard. The problem was, back then at least, that there weren't enough of those varieties to sell. She hoped that we could use them, but again, she didn't have enough that we could put them on the menu on any long-term basis. To be fair, I suppose we could have held an organic night and advertised it. Maybe this season. I'll be happy to talk to her again."

"I think I can stand the competition," Meg said wryly.

"I know!" Nicky snapped her fingers. "You wanted to poison Ginny, to eliminate the competition, and killed Monica by accident. Or killed her first in order to throw everyone off the scent, and then you'd go back after Ginny later. You'll wait until the furor dies down and then, bam! Ginny dies."

Meg grimaced. "I'm flattered you think I'm that devious. I think. Tell me, how did I do it? I didn't know either of them until recently."

Nicky waved a dismissive hand. "Details. You're smart—I'm sure you could have found an undetectable method. I'll let the police sort it out now that I've got the answer." She checked the clock on the mantel. "Oops, gotta get back to the stove. You staying for lunch?"

"Maybe—Seth got an emergency call about somebody's plumbing, and I have no idea when he'll be back. We're kind of out of food, and that's why I was at the market, but I panicked and fled after explaining what little I know for the fifth or tenth time, so I picked up only half the things I needed."

"Poor baby," Nicky said, laughing. "I'll fix you something, and then you can go your merry way. Oh, how's your new manager working out? I don't think I've met him yet."

"So far, so good, but I haven't seen much of him, either. That's not a problem, since there's nothing urgent to do in the orchard, but things should pick up in a couple of weeks.

I'll try and introduce him to a few more people in town—
he needs to know you guys, and our local vendors."

Happily stuffed with a variety of Nicky's winter dishes,
Meg made her way home by noon, to find Seth had returned. "Hey, there," he greeted her. "Where'd you disap-
pear to?"

"I went to the market to stock up, but everybody and
his sister wanted to talk about Monica, so I went over to
Gran's and Nicky fed me lunch. Don't worry—I brought
you a doggy bag."

"You are a mind reader." Seth grabbed it from her, leaving her to wrestle with the skimpy grocery bags. Once that
food was stowed away, she sat down to watch Seth eat.

"How'd your plumbing job go?"

"I could have done it in my sleep. Burst pipe to the
outdoor hose spigot—the owner had forgotten to shut it
off for the winter, and then he couldn't remember where
the shut-off was inside. I'm surprised it held as long as it
did. Didn't take long to fix. But as you were saying about
the market, he wanted to talk about the fair and Monica's
death. Are we surrounded by ghouls?"

"No, I think they're unsettled, maybe afraid, so they
want to know what's going on. Which Marcus isn't going
to tell them, not that he's under any obligation to. If we're
lucky he'll keep Art in the loop, and Art will fill us in. Oh,
I asked Nicky and Brian if they had seen anything odd in
Doug's behavior, and they hadn't noticed anything out of
the ordinary. He was quiet and polite and appeared happy,
and Monica did all the talking. So we don't know anything
more. You haven't heard from Art today?"

"No, or not yet—yes, I checked the phones for messages. I have to admit I keep wondering about whatever it was Monica ingested that could have killed her, and how the heck a lab can identify it. It's one of those circular problems: you have to know what you're looking for in order to use the right test to find what you're looking for. Unless it's something simple like arsenic or cyanide, or an overdose of street drugs."

"All of which have already been ruled out by the obvious tests. Make haste slowly."

"Indeed. Nicky can sure cook," Seth added, now that he'd emptied his plate.

"She can. Oh, and the police collected food samples, but the restaurant has been cleared. And business is booming, which kind of tells you that nobody in town suspects them. Wow—we've eliminated one suspect, or pair of suspects. Does that help anything?"

"Not really, since we never suspected Nicky or Brian to begin with."

"Maybe it was a passing tourist who jabbed Monica with a lethal pinprick of a rare Indian cobra venom?"

"Wrong symptoms, not to mention timing. You don't really believe that, do you?"

"Of course I don't. But I'd rather believe in the random tourist theory than suspect anyone in Granford."

"I know what you mean. There's always the possibility of suicide."

"I suppose. Monica put on a bold face in dealing with the town, but she had Douglas to worry about—by the way, do you think anybody medical is going to look at him?—and who knows how they were fixed financially. Maybe she just couldn't deal with it all anymore. Maybe the Winter-

Fare was her last farewell. We'll have to see what the cause was, and if she had access to whatever it was."

"In other words, we've done all we can do," Seth said. "Do we have any of our own work to tend to?"

"I'm still working on my business taxes. I should inventory some of my apple crates to see how many need replacing. I have to get the tractor tuned up so it will keep running for another year, unless I find a financial windfall and can afford a new one. But those are expensive, and I think the well pump is more important than the tractor. No water, no crop. You?"

Seth sighed. "As a good businessman, I should be contacting all my prior and potential customers to see if they are planning any building improvements, repairs, alterations, and so on in the coming year. Maybe I'll go play on my computer and design a fancy brochure with lots of pretty pictures."

"Old-house pictures are always nice. No big projects in sight?"

"Well, I told you before that since the library moved out of the town center, that building is up for grabs. The town assembly is making noises about selling town hall and taking over another building—not necessarily the old library, which I'll agree is probably too small—but they've been talking about that for years. Besides, I would have to disqualify myself. Maybe I'll sniff around the neighboring towns and see what they're planning. If anything."

"I hear the Emily Dickinson house needs a bit of work," Meg offered.

"I think I'd feel compelled to do that pro bono—as long as they let me put a sign up so my name would be linked to the repairs."

"We could clean out the attic," Meg suggested.

"Oh, that sounds like a lot of fun," Seth replied.

"Build a fire and sit and do a jigsaw puzzle?"

"Better. Let's get the basic chores out of the way and think again. Feed goats and clean up their pen. Change cat litter. Give Max a good run."

"Don't forget laundry!"

"What an exciting life we lead," Seth said, smiling.

Meg carried Seth's dishes over to the sink and, looking out the window, saw Art Preston's car pull into the driveway. "Looks like it might get more exciting pretty quickly."

14

Meg hurried to the door to let Art in before he could knock. He looked tired. "Come on in, Art," Meg said quickly. "Have you eaten? Want some coffee?"

"Coffee's fine. Hey, Seth," Art said as he walked into the kitchen.

"Art." Seth nodded. "Why do I think you're not bringing good news?"

Art dropped into a chair, and Meg set about boiling water and grinding beans. "More like no news. It's not that Marcus isn't sharing—it's that he doesn't know anything more than he did yesterday. And of course that makes him angry, and he's likely to take it out on me, probably because he figures that I'm covering for you two."

"I'm sorry, Art. You don't deserve the wrath of an angry

Marcus. What happened with Douglas Whitman?" Meg asked.

"Not much, from what I hear. It didn't take Marcus long to realize that Douglas wasn't quite in touch with reality, and to his credit he let me call elder services so Douglas could be evaluated. He didn't want to be accused of brow-beating a helpless man. I guess he's got some scruples."

"Good for him. So Douglas was taken somewhere to be looked at?"

"So it seems, at least temporarily. I'm glad there are some good people involved. In the meantime the forensic folks have been having a wonderful time scraping every-thing in the house. I hope you didn't get too close to any-thing, Meg."

"Well, I did wash the dishes. I looked for some rubber gloves but couldn't find any."

"Any symptoms of anything?" Art asked.

"No, unless you count frustration. I feel fine." The wa-ter boiled, and Meg poured it over the coffee grounds. "I went to the market today and everybody was still talking about the murder. I tried not to say too much, but just be-ing polite to people was tricky. I ended up leaving fast."

"I know what you mean," Art said as Meg poured him a cup of coffee. "I can't go anywhere without getting ques-tions."

"I also stopped by Gran's while I was out. Nicky told me the police had come and gone, but they were allowed to stay open—and nobody in town has been too afraid to eat there. It's been well over twenty-four hours since . . . Any new cases?"

"All the kids are fine—like we guessed, mostly they were overexcited and stuffed their faces too fast. I'm sure

Marcus and his crew have talked to all the food vendors by now."

"So what does that tell us?" Meg asked. "Monica went to the fair and ate who knows what; she goes home and shortly after that she gets sick, then sicker. That suggests that whatever Monica took might have come from the fair, rather than her own home?"

"Maybe." Art rubbed his hands over his face, then took a large swallow of coffee. "It's been, what—three days since I got back from vacation? A nice, peaceful vacation, with nobody pestering me with questions I can't begin to answer. Feels like I never left Granford. And why am I not surprised to find you two in the middle of all this? Seth, you've been pretty quiet. What're you thinking?"

"I'll take the easy answer first: I was involved because I represent the town," Seth told him. "Meg is involved because she grows apples, and she was one of a whole bunch of people who sold edible products at the fair. Nothing suspicious there. Two unrelated reasons for us to be part of this."

"I know, I know," Art said, holding up his hands. "Just a lousy coincidence. I'm grasping at straws. I'd really like to help Marcus out, but I don't have anything to offer him. Where's Sherlock Holmes when you need him?" He mustered up a weak smile.

"If he was still alive after all this time, he'd be in London, I'd guess," Meg said. "No help there. What happens next?"

"The state police continue to interview anyone who swallowed anything at the WinterFare—I don't know how far they've gotten with that list. The lab keeps applying their fabulous high-tech toys to identify the poison or toxin—but they are neither as fast nor as fancy as those TV shows would have you believe. Marcus keeps chewing on the furniture. And life goes on in peaceful Granford. Seth, if anybody proposes another public event, give me a heads-up and I'll plan another vacation. Maybe to Alaska. Without a phone."

"I can't see anyone doing that soon, Art," Seth told him. "Which is a shame, because this one worked well, until the end of it."

Art hauled himself out of his seat. "I guess I'll be heading back to my office, where I will find yet more questions I can't answer. You'll let me know if you hear anything?"

"Of course we will, Art," Meg assured him.

"I'll walk you to your car," Seth said. "Max? Walk?" The Golden Retriever bounded to his feet and followed the two men out the door.

Meg found herself wondering why the killer had chosen to poison Monica in a peculiarly unpleasant way. He could have used something that let her die quietly in her sleep, but instead he had used something that caused repugnant symptoms, and led to a very undignified death. That almost sounded personal, and definitely cruel. And why did she keep saying "he" even in her head? A woman could administer poison easily. But Meg kept circling around to the same issue: nobody in Granford knew Monica, or not well enough to wish her dead. She assumed that Detective Marcus was looking at earlier parts of her life, with Doug, and he was best equipped to do that. Maybe back in her teaching days Monica had somehow harmed a child, and the parents had borne a grudge all these years and tracked her down here, thinking no one would connect them with a long-ago incident? The fair had offered the ideal opportunity to mingle with the crowd, and to somehow slip something to Monica. But wouldn't Monica have recognized them?

Could it be payback for something Douglas had done in the past? If there had been any warnings, or anything suspicious, in his current state he might not have noticed. Would Monica have seen them, and known about whatever inspired them? Maybe in another life Douglas had been a Mob accountant, had made off with documents the Mob didn't want to go public, and they had killed Monica to send him a message?

This is ridiculous, Meg thought. She was spinning her wheels, trying to understand something when she didn't have anywhere near enough information to make even an informed guess and no way of getting any more information—and it wasn't even her business. Or maybe only indirectly, as an apple seller and the wife (*wife!*) of a town assemblyman. Which put her only one notch above most of the population of Granford. *Leave the problem to the experts—Marcus and Art—and get back to your own business!*

She could work on her profit-loss statement for the year just ended. That would be a responsible adult thing to do, even if it bored her. Or maybe she should meet with Larry again. They should talk about specific ideas for the spring, which was approaching rapidly. And Seth could chat with him about the tiny house idea—and if Larry hated it, Seth could stop thinking about it and go back to taking care of *his* business. Before she could overthink her decision, she pulled out her cell phone and called Larry.

He answered on the third ring. "'Lo?"

"Hey, Larry, it's Meg." Which he could see on his own phone, duh. "I thought we should sit down and start working on details of what we're doing over the next few months. What's a good time for you?"

"Uh, the afternoon's okay."

"Why don't you come over late afternoon, and you can have supper here? You ought to get to know Seth since you'll be crossing paths a lot, and he has something he wants to talk with you about. Does that work?"

"Yeah, fine. Thanks. I'll come by around four, okay?"

"Sounds good to me. See you then." After they'd hung up, she wondered if Larry had heard the news about Monica's death over the weekend. She had little idea where he was living at the moment, and he said he didn't really watch television. But it was unlikely that he had crossed paths with Monica, so he shouldn't be too upset about the news.

Seth and Max came bounding in the back door, panting. "That was quite a walk," Meg commented.

"We both needed the exercise. It felt good out there, and we might as well use the time when we've got it."

"I wish I felt that way about the orchard accounts. I just invited Larry over for supper—we'll meet first to go over orchard plans for the next few months. I didn't mention the tiny house, just that you wanted to talk to him about something. But you don't have to if you don't want to."

"I'll be happy to run it by him. And we should talk about any changes we need to make in the barn, and what equipment to order."

"Hey, isn't that my business?" Meg said, mock-serious.

"Lady, if you want to talk about tractors to local mechanics, be my guest."

"I'm so glad to know you're not going to be sexist about women and machines. I recognize one when I see it, and

I know which end the gas goes into, but that's the end of my expertise. I let Bree take care of it, and she was good at it. But I would be delighted if you would do the talking when it comes to tractors, oh big strong man." Meg batted her non-mascaraed eyelashes in an exaggerated way. "I suppose we should find out how much Larry knows while we're at it."

"Good idea. I can't say I know whether they cover farm machinery at the university. What're you going to feed Larry?"

"Whatever is lurking in the freezer, I guess. I suppose I could bake a cake. That's much more interesting than compiling financial statements."

"I've got to replace some of the supplies I've used up lately, and I want to look at tools, so I'm headed out for the box stores. I should be back by the time Larry gets here."

After Seth had left, Meg's search of the freezer yielded the bare requirements for spaghetti sauce, but she suspected that Larry wouldn't complain. She pulled out a package of sausage to let it thaw, and found canned tomatoes and a couple of onions, and set to chopping. An hour later a large pot was simmering on the back of the stove, and she had to face the dreaded financial summaries: no more excuses. It was hard to believe that she had formerly been a competent financial analyst for a major Boston bank, given her reluctance now. Maybe that was because she was afraid of what she might find. She knew there was money in the bank, and the crop had been fairly good. She and Bree had identified some new outlets for her apples with local farmers' markets, and there was always a steady demand at Gran's, although she tried to keep the prices low for them since their business was still fairly new. But the looming question remained: would she break even for the past year? Would there be a respectable profit that would let her invest in a new wellhead and irrigation system or a new tractor—or, by some miracle, both? *Only one way to find out, Meg.*

After two hours with her computer, with invoices and estimates and charges and bank statements spread all over the dining room table (which seemed to have become their permanent home), Meg was feeling much better. At least her gut estimate of the state of the business had not been far off, and while she wasn't going to get rich from the orchard, she could at least cover the expenses for both the business and for herself. An income! It had been a while since she'd seen that.

She and Seth hadn't really talked a lot about how they would pool expenses. They each had a business, and kept the accounting separate for those. The house had been paid for—for a couple of centuries!—but there were still ongoing expenses like utilities and taxes and maintenance. They had to eat, and pay for health insurance. They each had middle-aged cars that required upkeep and gas and would have to be replaced eventually. And Meg couldn't remember the last time she had bought clothes—her mother had given her a wedding outfit. So she and Seth were getting by, but a lavish lifestyle was out of their reach. Their brief honeymoon would have to do as a vacation for a while.

But Meg refused to play the Little Wifey and depend on Seth for financial support. They were going to be equal partners in this marriage thing. At least, that was the plan.

Meg had tidied up the dining room table and made a neat stack of her documents, and was stirring the sauce when Larry came up to the back door. Meg let him in. "Have I given you a key yet? You should have one. We might ask you to feed the animals now and then, or something like that."

"Okay, sure—that'd be good." Larry lapsed into silence again. What would it take to make him relax and open up, at least a little? Meg wondered.

"Why don't we go sit in the dining room?" she suggested. "This is only my third season with the orchard, and I'd like to hear your ideas about what we could do to improve yield. I've got the numbers together."

"Sure. Lead the way."

Larry followed Meg into the dining room, where they sat down and spent a productive hour reviewing the status quo, even though Larry hadn't seen the orchard when it was bearing, and then he had moved on to suggestions for a number of changes. Meg listened, and as he talked, her respect for his expertise grew. It was clear that he'd given the matter some serious thought, and he suggested a few things Meg hadn't even heard about. When he slowed down, Meg said, "Can you map out something like a five-year plan? This is a lot for me to take in all at once, and I don't yet know how much we could tackle this year, but if I could see how it lays out over several years I'd appreciate it. Oh, and figure out if our current picking crew will be adequate or if we need to look for more."

"You've been working with the same guys for a while now, right?"

"Yes, and they've been great. What matters to me is that they take pride in their work. They know we're all in this together. So I'd like to keep them together, if it makes sense."

"Sure, no problem. I don't think you'd need to change

much, not more than one or two people, up or down. You've been selling to a pretty limited group—the restaurant, a couple of small markets around here. You think about expanding? Cider? Jellies?"

Meg laughed. "So far I've been lucky to stay afloat doing only what needs to be done. I'm not into cooking, certainly not in large amounts, and I think I'd need an officially approved kitchen. I could see a cider operation somewhere down the line, but I don't know what's required in the way of machinery or regulations. Let's see how things work out this year, and we can talk again after the crop is in."

Seth came in, brushing a scattering of snow off his jacket. "Hey, Larry. Glad you could make it."

"Hey, Mr. Chapin. Meg said there was something you wanted to talk about?"

"Call me Seth, please. Let's wait and do it over dinner. I guarantee you it won't spoil your appetite."

"Sounds good to me," Larry said, giving Meg one of his rare smiles.

15

After they were seated around the kitchen table with steaming bowls of pasta and sauce, grated Parmesan on the side, Meg asked Larry, "Maybe we talked about it before, but I'm not sure where you're living now. I think I mentioned a couple of options. You have any new plans?"

Larry chewed a large forkful of pasta vigorously before answering. "I'm crashing with friends for now. It's hard to find an apartment this time of year, much easier for the summer, once the students leave. And if you get your foot in the door, you might get to keep the place past the summer. No big deal."

Seth spoke up. "Larry, I think Meg mentioned the idea of using the foundation for the old chicken coop to build a tiny house the first time you were here. I've been looking around online, and I kind of like the thought of building one—at the very least it would be good advertising for my business, although only the foundation and some of the framing would be old, so no renovation angle—unless I re-create a nineteenth-century chicken coop just for show, which probably isn't worth the effort. Anyway, I measured what's there, and I think it would come out to be about five hundred square feet. Not large, but enough for one person, or for short-term use."

"You want me to live there?" Larry asked, staring at his spaghetti.

"No obligation, Larry," Seth said. "I just wondered if you'd be interested. You can certainly say no if you want— it's not a kind of space for everyone. Or you could wait and see how it turns out before you make up your mind. How're your construction skills?"

"I can handle a hammer and a drill. I've done my share of repairs and stuff, but nothing fancy, and never from scratch. Why're you so interested in this, uh, Seth?"

"Mainly because he's looking for a distraction before his own business picks up in the spring," Meg said quickly. "You heard about Monica Whitman's death?"

"The lady who died after the fair on Saturday? Yeah, people in Amherst were talking about it. Something fishy about it?"

"Kind of," Seth told him. "It looks like she was murdered. Poisoned."

Larry stared blankly at Seth, then Meg. Finally he said, "That's too bad. Who did it?"

"Nobody knows yet. She hadn't lived around here too long, so nobody had a chance to get to know her. As the saying goes, the police are baffled."

Larry nodded. "And you want something to keep you busy so you don't have to worry about it?"

Meg leaned over and put her hand on Seth's. "You know, we never told him about, you know, the other deaths."

Larry looked from one to the other of them again, confused. "You serial killers or something?"

Seth and Meg exchanged a smile at that comment. "No, but we've been involved in helping the police with some local crimes," Seth told him. "The town police chief, Art Preston, is an old friend of mine, and he was in our wedding. But it's the state police who handle homicides. We just fill in the gaps about the more personal aspects of Granford and its citizens."

"Huh," Larry said, apparently digesting that information. "But you said nobody really knew this Monica person? So you can't help, can you?"

"True. Mostly we serve as a sounding board for Art to bounce ideas off. So far nobody's come up with a suspect."

"You said she was poisoned?" Larry asked.

"That's what the medical examiner says," Meg told him. "But nobody knows which poison yet. A few other people who were at the fair got sick, but they've all pretty much recovered, so we don't think that was the same thing."

"Wow. You never know what's going to happen, do you? So, Seth, you got a concept for this tiny house thing? All one big room? Or divided up?" Apparently Larry had lost interest in the murder, Meg thought. But he was showing some enthusiasm for Seth's idea.

"I can show you some floor plans after supper if you want. You can go either way, structurally, but most people want a little privacy for bathrooms and such."

"Yeah, that makes sense."

Meg watched as the guys lapsed into guy-speak, about tools and materials and layouts. Larry was more animated than she'd seen him before. He hadn't committed to actually living in the space, but since that space existed only in Seth's head, and maybe on a few sheets of paper, that wasn't a problem. She realized that she hadn't said if she would charge Larry for living there, but she didn't mind giving him five hundred square feet—with his own kitchen and bath—rent free. And maybe Seth could write off the construction costs as a business expense if he used it as a showcase for his skills. She was pretty sure the space wouldn't go to waste, whatever they did with it. Maybe she could get a loom and start weaving goat-hair scarves . . . With a jerk, she realized she was nodding off.

"There's cake, if anybody's interested," she said, standing up. "Coffee with it?"

"Cake sounds good," Larry said. Seth nodded agreement.

"Coming up." Moving around the kitchen helped keep her awake as she distributed apple cake and coffee. But her energy started flagging after another half hour, and Seth noticed.

"Maybe we should call it a night. You want to come back by daylight, Larry, and we can take some measurements?"

"Sure, that sounds good. Thank you for inviting me, Meg. I've got some ideas about increasing yield per tree that we didn't get around to discussing, but I can show you tomorrow. Ten okay, Seth?"

"Sure. See you then."

Side by side, Meg and Seth washed up and were in bed by ten thirty.

The next morning, pets fed and Max walked, Meg and Seth were enjoying a second cup of coffee in the kitchen when Christopher knocked at the back door and let himself in. "Would you happen to have any more of that?" he asked, nodding toward the coffee cups.

"Always," Meg said, smiling. "It's good to see you. Did you come looking for coffee, or did you want to talk to one or the other of us?"

"A bit of both, perhaps. I'm on my way to work, but I wanted to see how you and young Larry are getting along."

Meg handed him a mug of coffee. "We're still getting to know each other, but he seems to know his stuff as far as the orchard goes. I don't see any problems, at least not yet. Do you have any reason to be worried?"

"No, no, nothing like that. He's a good boy—man, I guess I should say. He's well into his twenties. What he might lack in scientific expertise he more than makes up for in hands-on experience. Both are necessary in agricultural pursuits." He accepted the mug of coffee that Meg handed him.

"I agree, from what I've seen, but you're the expert. Speaking of experts, I may be in the market for a new irrigation system if the numbers work out. What should I be looking at, and how much should I have to spend for it?"

They spent a few minutes discussing the pros and cons of various commercial systems intended for small farms, and Meg was beginning to think it might, just might, be in the range of possible. "When would I need to decide? I mean, to get it set up for this growing season?"

"You'd have to wait until the ground thaws, but I'd start talking to vendors now," Christopher said. "With the unusual weather patterns of the past few years, people are increasingly concerned about managing their water. You're lucky that you have that well. Have you had the water tested?"

"Uh, no? I didn't know I needed to. Actually I've only used it the once, I guess—it hasn't been necessary. What am I testing for?"

"I won't trouble you with the menu of chemicals, both natural and man-made, that you might find. And you need to assess your water pressure as well, in choosing the right system for you. You can ask Larry to follow up on that."

"I had the water tested at the family house a few years ago," Seth told Christopher. "I can't swear that we share the same aquifer here, but that test came up pretty clean. There's never been anything but farming in this neighborhood."

"I'm glad to know that, Seth. In any case, Meg, I'll send you a list of people you should talk to. And take Larry along—if he doesn't have this information, he should, and he can learn something."

"Thank you. You and Lydia didn't go to the WinterFare this weekend, did you?"

"Lydia was not in the mood for socializing, so we spent a quiet day together."

"But you heard about what happened?"

"The death of Monica Whitman? Of course. News travels fast around here."

"That it does," Seth said.

"Do the authorities have any, uh, leads?" Christopher asked. "If that's the correct term in this country."

"Not yet. Or not that they've shared," Seth told him.

"How very sad," Christopher said, almost to himself. "It seems that the poor woman declined quite rapidly."

"That's true," Seth said. She got sick on Saturday night and passed away Sunday. I've heard that organ failure was the cause, due to an as yet undetermined poison."

"That was rather abrupt, if she consumed something toxic at the fair. It suggests it might have been ingested earlier."

Seth shrugged. "We don't know. The forensic people are still looking for the cause. Do you know about her husband?"

"I've heard nothing. What should I know?"

"I met him on Sunday," Meg said, "and I wondered if he's suffering from some form of dementia. He was definitely acting strange, and thought his wife was out on an errand and would be back any minute. And the house was a mess—rotting food all over the place."

"Might that have been the source of her illness?" Christopher asked.

"We don't know, but you can be sure the state police are looking at that. If there's anything left of it—I made the mistake of washing the dishes. Nobody said it was a crime scene before I started, but when the state police arrived it was too late to do anything about it. Except for the trash."

"So you, my dear, are once again under the magnifying glass. You do seem to have an attraction for problems of this nature."

"Tell me about it," Meg said with a rueful smile. "You'd think we would have been safe from it, on a honeymoon in a different state, but nooo . . . Christopher, I do have one question, and you're about the only senior scientist I know. From what little I've heard and read, this sounded like typical stomach flu, which would be an illness, or gastroenteritis, which could have any number of causes, or even norovirus. That would account for the worst of the symptoms—the nausea, vomiting, and diarrhea. But the rapid organ failure doesn't fit. Does it?"

"It does seem rather abrupt, although there are exceptions to almost every rule. We don't know anything about her medical history, do we?"

"Not the last time I talked to anyone. I'm not even sure what town the Whitmans came from, although I'm sure the police will figure that out. You're not thinking drug allergy or something like that, are you?"

"I think not, Meg. If I may set foot on your turf, so to speak, once again we find ourselves confronted with the basic elements of a crime: means, motive, and opportunity. We also find ourselves with only the shakiest of suggestions for any of those. Perhaps the opportunity is the strongest. Mrs. Whitman attended the WinterFare and was deeply involved with planning and execution. She would no doubt have felt it her duty to taste everything that was presented. Therefore there were multiple opportunities for someone to have slipped something into an item she was going to eat, then or later. That person had only to either sell it to her directly, or follow her about and slip it into or onto what she was intending to consume."

"Okay," Meg said cautiously. "Assuming, of course, that the poisonous substance would not be obvious if applied externally. I'm less convinced that someone could have injected a food product with so many people watching."

"A valid point. Next, let us move on to means. How was she killed? With a quick-acting poison—assuming your fears about the bacteria circus at her house are unfounded—that attacked the digestive system and, slightly later, the liver and kidneys, and that acted rapidly once it was established. Will you accept that hypothesis?"

"We have to, don't we?" Seth asked. "I mean, she wasn't electrocuted, she wasn't shot or stabbed or strangled. She wasn't drowned. She didn't have a heart attack or a stroke. There were no physical marks on her body, or so Art led me to believe. So we have to go with poison. But which one?"

"That is where we have an unfortunate lacuna in our hypothesis. I would have to do some research on what agents would produce those symptoms with such rapidity. But to continue, last we have motive."

"And there we're at a dead end," Seth said. "Nobody had a motive."

Christopher held up one finger. "That we are aware of. She may have led an entirely different life before she arrived in Granford. What of the husband, who is always the first suspect to consider?"

"As I said, he appears to have Alzheimer's or something similar."

"To your untrained eye, my dear. He may be a consummate actor. And even those poor souls in the grip of Alzheimer's do have moments of clarity. If he had the poison at hand, he could have made use of it during one of those moments, then forgot entirely shortly afterward. In which case he may never remember what he's done."

"So now you're back to suggesting that I destroyed possible evidence."

"In the eyes of the law, you may have. Not with any

malice, I assume, but the damage was done. Has this analysis been fruitful?"

"Not exactly." Meg sighed. "Thank you for trying, though."

"I'm always glad to assist," Christopher said as he stood up. "I must get to the university, but thank you for the interesting diversion. I hope the killer is identified quickly. Let me know if anything significant is uncovered."

"You too, Christopher," Meg said, hugging him.

She and Seth watched as Christopher started his engine and headed out the driveway.

16

After seeing Christopher in the morning, Meg was surprised to recognize his car pulling into the driveway at the end of the day. She dried her hands at the sink then went to open the door for him.

"Twice in one day!" she greeted him. "To what do we owe this honor?"

He didn't answer until Meg had closed the door behind him. "There was something nagging at me, after our meeting earlier today. Remind me, how many people sold apples at the WinterFare?"

"Around five, I think. Me, Ginny Morris, and a few others who had some, in addition to other fruits and vegetables. Do you want to sit down, have some coffee?"

"I'll sit, but don't worry about the coffee. And there were others who sold or served apple-based products such as jellies, am I correct?"

He took a seat on one side of the kitchen table, and Meg sat down across from him. "Yes, although I couldn't tell you how many. I was pretty much tied to my own table. But this isn't new information, is it? What does it have to do with anything?"

"Bear with me, my dear. The only person who became seriously ill after the event was Monica, correct?" Meg nodded, so Christopher continued, "We'll dismiss the few children who did, and some other adults. The children, who all recovered quickly, were no doubt overexcited and ate too much and too quickly. The adults might have been suggestible and shared the symptoms, but none of those suffered any lasting effects."

"Yes. What point are you trying to make?"

"The initial symptoms appeared to be those of an ordinary illness, as we discussed. Even in Monica's case, she appeared to throw it off, for a short time. And then she sickened rapidly and died."

"Christopher, you're driving me crazy," Meg said. "I assume you have a point, but you're skating all around it. What's the problem?"

He sighed. "I happened to be reading a recent journal article, and it led me to a footnote about one element discussed in the article. Are you at all familiar with colchicine?"

"I've heard the word, but I don't think I've ever encountered it personally. Why?"

"For many years, colchicine has been used to attempt to enhance plant growth, in a variety of manifestations— larger fruits, increased yield, disease resistance—although success has been mixed."

"And has this been used on apples?" Meg was beginning to get an inkling of where he was heading, although she couldn't figure out why.

"It has. Some tetraploid varieties of apples have been created, but they never achieved wide commercial distribution."

"I've never heard of that, but I'm still pretty new to all of this. How is it delivered to the plant?"

"The colchicine is applied to the terminal bud of a branch, and all the cells in the branch when it develops will have additional chromosomes. Some of the early articles about this process are quite amusing, but those researchers carrying out the experiments were sincere in their efforts to find a way to enhance food supplies."

Meg was beginning to get impatient with Christopher's scholarly yet apparently aimless lecture. She wanted to get dinner started. "But basically, it never caught on?"

"That's correct."

"So why are you telling me this?"

"Colchicine is extremely poisonous if consumed. And Monica's symptoms follow the usual course of colchicine poisoning."

A dozen questions popped up in Meg's head, and she waited until she could sort them out before responding. "Why would anyone have colchicine? Where do you even find it?"

"Oddly enough, it was approved a few years ago by the Food and Drug Administration for use in treatment of a limited number of human illnesses. In other words, it's commercially available. There are also some holistic practitioners who may use—or perhaps I might say misuse—it for non-approved purposes. It is available in tablet form. And let me add, it is also found in the plant generally called

wild garlic, as well as in autumn crocus or meadow saf-
fron. Grazing animals have been known to suffer fatal
consequences from eating it. I should note that it is extremely bitter in flavor, so it would be difficult for a person
to consume it accidentally in any quantity. Although most
medicinal doses are rather small. It can be tricky to prescribe."

"Okay, so it's nasty stuff and I'll do my best not to eat
any, if I happen to find it. But what does this have to do
with Monica's death?"

"I may be overstepping my bounds, but I would like to
ask Art Preston to request that Monica's blood be tested
for the presence of this substance."

"Oh," Meg said. She thought about that for a moment.
"But how on earth would Monica have gotten hold of any?
From what little we know about her, it seems unlikely that
she could have known about it herself, much less found
any."

"That I cannot tell you. It is not something that a common household mold would produce as an undesirable
by-product, so I doubt that you'd be implicated in any way
for your kind efforts to clean up Monica's kitchen. I cannot
say whether Douglas could have obtained any, or how he
might have administered it. Or if he would remember having done either, if indeed as you observed, his condition
is so uncertain. I have no knowledge of any preexisting
medical history for Monica, so I won't speculate about
how, and how quickly, the effects would have occurred."

More and more it sounded to Meg that Christopher was
trying *not* to say something. "Christopher, I'm still not
sure I understand. You're a respected scientist—you could
have gone directly to Art, or even to Detective Marcus,

and laid out what you just told me. Why are you talking to me at all?"

Christopher turned away from her, staring out of the window. "There is a reason that perhaps strikes closer to home for you. It involves Larry."

He paused, leaving Meg even more confused. "What's Larry got to do with Monica's death? He didn't know her. He didn't attend the WinterFare."

"I told you when I recommended him that Larry had been my student at the university, taking postgraduate courses. I even helped him to procure funding for that. He was then, and may be still, a bit rough around the edges, but he's more than competent. While he was at Cornell he wrote an undergraduate thesis on the use of colchicine to enhance growth of certain plants, and at the university he continued those studies. He had a small research plot set up on university land. It was a modest undertaking, but he designed his project well and carried it out scrupulously."

"You were his advisor for that?" Meg asked.

"I was. And, if you will, his mentor. I believed in his fundamental abilities—and I still do. But you, and I presume law enforcement officials, need to know that he has direct, personal knowledge of the uses of colchicine, *if* in fact that is the substance that was given to Monica."

"Ah." Meg thought again. "But why would Larry have poisoned anyone? Much less someone he didn't even know?"

"Now you see my dilemma, my dear. I believe Larry is a good scientist with no animus toward anyone, much less Monica. But he does know about colchicine. If I were to go to the authorities, they would make a single linear deduction: Larry knows this rather arcane drug colchicine, and presumably how to obtain it, if he doesn't already possess a supply. Larry lives in the same town as Monica. And the police will take a pencil and connect those two dots. End of story."

"Assuming that it was colchicine that killed Monica. Which we don't know, and won't until we get someone to test for it," Meg pointed out.

"Precisely. Which is the reason I am attempting to tread lightly here. Will you agree with me that we need to ascertain that fact before we proceed?"

"In theory, yes. But even if you go to Art directly—and you could because he's a friend—someone up the line is going to want to know why you are looking at this particular poison. The fact that Monica suffered from awful gastric symptoms in her last hours is not enough to ask a lab to test the blood of a possible murder victim."

"I agree. I wish I could say I felt better for sharing my problem with you, but I fear I've only dragged you into a greater mess. But since you are nominally Larry's employer, that would be inevitable in any case."

"Is there some simple way we can test Monica's blood? No, what am I saying? You and I, and even Art, can't hope to get a sample, much less find a lab to test it for us. And even if we did, no doubt some lawyer would argue that we tampered with evidence and jeopardized an active murder investigation and probably even more stuff along those lines."

"Exactly. So you can see why I was reluctant to voice my concerns," Christopher said, looking relieved.

"But you're right to voice them, if only to see that they're dismissed," Meg protested. "Do you have any suggestions about what to do now?"

Christopher shook his head. "I wouldn't mention anything to Larry just yet. He would take it as a criticism or even an accusation and probably walk out on you, which would benefit neither himself nor the investigation."

"I can understand that. So why don't we talk to Art, off the record, and see what he recommends?" *Poor Art,* Meg thought—*we don't make life easy for him, do we?*

"I would be grateful if you could do that, Meg. As you point out, I could approach him myself, but you have a closer relationship, and you've worked together in difficult situations in the past."

"Let me give him a call now. Do you want to be here when I talk to him, or should I lay the groundwork first?"

"I will stay if you like, if only to explain the scientific side of the issue."

Meg stood up. "Then I'll try to catch him now."

Meg retrieved her cell phone from her bag and walked into the dining room to call Art. When he answered, she asked, "You still at the office, or are you home?"

"And hello to you, too, Meg. I was just getting ready to head home. Is this urgent?"

"You mean, is someone bleeding to death? No. But Christopher Ramsdell is here, and he's raised an issue about Monica's death that we'd like to run by you. It shouldn't take long."

Art sighed. "All right. I'll swing by on the way home. But if I'm late for dinner, you can explain it to my wife. I'll be there in, oh, fifteen."

"Thanks, Art."

After they'd hung up, Meg went back to the kitchen, where Christopher was still sitting at the table, lost in thought. "He'll be here in a few minutes. You do know that there's not a lot he can do? He's not officially involved in this investigation."

"Yes, I'm aware of that. I merely want to get my concerns on the record, but I don't want to see Larry dragged into this unless there's good reason."

"Fair enough. And you know Art will help if he can. Now do you want coffee?" Meg was beginning to wonder how long her supply of beans would last at the rate she was using them.

"Might I ask for a cup of tea?"

"Of course. I've just made a pot."

Seth wandered in from his office at the back of the property and was startled to see Christopher in the kitchen. "What's going on?"

"Christopher has raised an interesting point about a possible cause for Monica's death, and we thought we needed another opinion, so I called Art and asked him to come over so we could discuss it. Do you mind waiting until he arrives so we don't have to repeat the whole explanation? He'll be here in a few minutes."

"I can't leave you alone for an hour without you getting into trouble, can I? Hello, Christopher."

"Seth." Christopher nodded to him. "I'm afraid I'm the guilty party here—I thought she needed to hear my concerns. Or perhaps I simply wanted a sympathetic ear while I tried to articulate them intelligently."

Seth looked bewildered. "Then I guess I'll wait until Art gets here, and you can fill us both in. Is there tea in that pot?"

"There is. Help yourself," Meg told him.

Art arrived quickly, and Meg greeted him at the back door. "Thanks for coming, Art. Seth's here, too, and he hasn't heard any of this." Meg realized she had no idea where Larry might be, but it was still too early to bring him in. "Tea? Or I could make coffee."

Art surveyed the group in the kitchen. "Christopher, Seth. So you've got another problem to dump in my lap? What I'd really like is a glass of twelve-year-old Scotch, but I'm an officer of the law, so I'll take tea."

Meg filled a cup for him as he pulled up another chair to the table. When everyone had a cup in front of them, Meg joined the others. "Christopher, this is mainly your story. Please tell Art what you told me."

And they listened while Christopher explained again.

17

Art listened carefully, and Meg and Seth didn't interrupt Christopher's explanation. Seth was hearing it for the first time, and Meg was glad of a chance to hear it again. She wanted to see if the theory seemed logical the second time around. Her quick judgment was that it stayed within the range of possible, although there were a lot of details that should be filled in.

When Christopher finished, Art rubbed his hands over his face. "It's been a long time since high school biology class. Let me see if I've got this right. The colchicine you're talking about is"—here he started ticking off points on his fingers—"used for agricultural purposes, including enhanced apple-growing, is readily available legally, and produces symptoms such as those that Monica showed before she died." Christopher nodded his agreement, so Art went on. "This substance has more than one application, including some medicinal ones, but we don't have medical histories for the people who got sick."

"Monica was the only one affected, if you discount the greedy kids," Meg pointed out. "It's not like you have to check everyone who was at the fair."

Art nodded. "All right. Now you lot are hoping that I can somehow finagle the state police into testing Monica's blood for this pretty obscure substance that most people have never heard of?"

"I will concede that it's somewhat improbable," Christopher admitted. "But the symptoms do fit."

"They also fit a lot of other things," Art said, beginning to sound testy. "Sorry, it's been a long day. But let me finish. You also don't want me to explain to whichever authorities *why* I have reason to think that this stuff is what poisoned Monica because it might implicate someone you both know and apparently like, and you don't want to get him into trouble?"

It did sound pretty ridiculous, Meg had to admit. "Art, we're not trying to conceal anything. If Christopher were to talk to the authorities, which he is willing to do, no doubt someone will ask why he knows about this stuff and if it's used at the university, and he would tell the truth, and ultimately that would point to Larry."

"I would," Christopher agreed. "I don't want to raise any other issues unless it's necessary."

"Other issues being this Larry guy. Meg, I know how long you've known him, which isn't exactly long, so I can't give a lot of weight to your defense of him. Christopher, you've worked with him for a couple of years, right? You're willing to stand up for him?"

"I am. He's a hard worker and a good scientist. And I

can't believe that he would jeopardize all that he's worked
for by trying to kill someone."

Seth spoke at last. "Which of course brings us around to
motive. Christopher, you're saying he has no motive—that
you know of—to harm Monica or anybody else. Art, I know
motive isn't necessarily a legal criterion for this investigation, but everybody thinks about it. Why would Larry want
to harm Monica? Why would anyone? Don't police usually
look to family and friends first for a suspect? Well, you and
Meg are telling me that Monica's husband is in no shape to
plan and carry out murdering his wife, and they haven't
lived around here long enough to make any close friends—
much less enemies. Are we supposed to go back through
their entire history looking for a suspect?"

"If this is in fact murder, then the answer is yes. Of
course Marcus and his pals would look at Douglas first—
and would check his medical records, to see if any doctor
has confirmed his current condition and he's not just faking
it. And if he's really that out of it, then they'd have to expand
their search. But we're still stumped for a motive for
anybody."

"I suppose 'just because they could' or 'they wanted to
see what happened' wouldn't work?" Meg said.

Art sat back in his chair to look at her. "You don't think
much of our local population, do you?"

"Sorry. I have no reason to believe any of them are mur-
derers, or even up for pulling a prank that went wrong. But
if Monica was killed by a stranger, how do you—or
Marcus—investigate?"

"I won't say it's easy. Family and locals are always the
first people to look at." Art slapped both hands on the
table. "Listen, folks, I want to get home before my dinner

gets cold. Let me think about this overnight, and decide if and how to approach Marcus with it. Maybe I could tell him he should take a harder look at agricultural chemicals, since there's no shortage of those in Granford, but this one of yours is pretty obscure, so that might not help. Maybe there's some secret manual that matches symptoms to drugs, but we've already agreed that Monica's symptoms were pretty ordinary, except that they came on real fast and then killed her. Maybe her doctor—if we can find him or her—will tell us Monica had a previous condition that was aggravated by something she ate, and we're barking up the wrong tree. But I think it can wait until tomorrow. Will that satisfy you?"

Christopher stood up. "That's all I ask, Art, and I appreciate your taking the time to listen to us. I would be more than happy if this death turned out to be no more than an unfortunate accident—perhaps Monica grabbed the wrong medication—and we can put this all behind us. Meg, Seth, I'll take my leave now as well, but we should keep in touch if there are any new developments."

"You got it, Christopher. Meg, Seth—try not to call me again tonight, unless something really big happens."

"We'll do our best, Art," Meg told him.

After Art and Christopher had left, Meg and Seth faced each other in the kitchen. "Well," Meg began.

"Exactly," Seth answered.

"Christopher just dropped by, you know. I didn't invite him."

"I know. We both know Christopher, and we know he is scrupulously honest. And precise. In this case he's torn between two goals: finding out whether this colchicine is the poison—if there even was a poison—and protecting

Larry, who he seems to feel rather paternal about. And that troubles him."

"Of course it does."

"Now that we don't have an audience, what's your gut feeling about Larry?"

"I certainly don't see him as a killer, especially of someone he doesn't even know. And I can't see how he could have had access to anything Monica ate or touched."

"Maybe she's his long-lost mother or something."

"According to Christopher, he had a mother and father."

"Maybe she gave him up for adoption when he was an infant," Seth countered.

"And in between managing his parents' orchard and getting a college degree, he tracked her down and plotted his revenge?"

"I'm not serious, you know."

"I know. Still, just because he has no apparent reason doesn't mean there isn't one. But I understand why Christopher doesn't want to set Marcus on him. I need a glass of wine."

"I'll join you. Are we eating dinner or just grazing?"

"Let's see what the fridge is hiding."

Over a patchy meal, Meg asked, "Okay, you're a guy, and you're not his employer. What's *your* take on Larry?"

"Mostly I feel sorry for him. He definitely has skills, but he's not good with people. It's understandable based on what Christopher's told us about his background, but I'm not sure there's much to be done to fix him, so to speak. Is he more comfortable with you, as a woman?"

"I haven't seen him comfortable with anyone yet. He says he's staying with friends, so I hope he actually has some and isn't just living out of his car. But it's early days yet, and I haven't spent a lot of time with him. He seemed enthusiastic about your tiny house idea—more than I've seen before."

"He did," Seth agreed. "Maybe we can spend some quality time together over that. Dessert?"

"I think there's cake somewhere in there."

Later, after they were settled in bed, each with a book, fighting to keep their eyes open, Meg said, "If no one finds the killer, what happens?"

"Maybe we should back up and ask if there really was a killer. Maybe she died of a heart attack brought on by something else, and it was a natural death."

"Do you really think that's true?" Meg asked.

"I'd like to. But the medical examiner seems to think otherwise."

"Seth Chapin, you just ducked my question. Go back to the start: was Monica Whitman murdered?"

"Meg, I really don't know. It may still prove to have been an accidental overdose of something. Or suicide."

"Fair enough. What happens to Douglas Whitman now?"

"If there are no relatives to be found? That might depend on what kind of money he's got. Well, first somebody would have to appoint an executor for Monica's estate, and see if there's a will. If she was aware of his condition—and it would be hard not to be—and if she'd updated her will recently, maybe she made provisions for his long-term care."

"They don't have poorhouses anymore, do they?" Meg asked, settling herself closer to Seth.

"Not lately. And if Douglas has a work history, he should get Social Security and Medicare. He may have a pension from his prior employer. And there's the house."

"We don't know if it's mortgaged. Poor Monica—she

was trying so hard. She didn't deserve to die, no matter how it happened."

Meg's last comment was greeted by Seth's snore, so Meg turned off her light.

She'd thought it would be easy to sleep, but it wasn't. Part of that was the lack of physical exertion, since she hadn't been doing her usual orchard chores. She probed her wandering mind to figure out what was bothering her. She'd finished most of the number crunching she needed to do for taxes and for planning for the coming year, and they'd turned out better than she'd expected. She knew now she could afford a few investments in new equipment. Or at least upgrades. Like an up-to-date irrigation system. Nothing in the house needed fixing urgently.

Which left Monica's death and Larry to worry about. It was a peculiar situation all around. Nobody had known Monica well, and she hadn't had time to find her place in the community. It was oddly frustrating, because over the past couple of years Meg had become accustomed to knowing something about the background and connections of her Granford neighbors. With Monica she had no connections, which could prove helpful in determining why she had died. Coming upon her husband, Douglas, was disturbing, because the poor man clearly wasn't able to function on his own, but there was nobody obvious to turn to for help for him. Which led Meg to realize she did want to help him, but she had no experience in anything resembling eldercare.

Meg was pretty sure Monica had been murdered. Ninety percent, anyway. But she had no way of knowing why. There was no clear reason for anyone to want Monica dead. The woman might have been overexcitable, but that was no reason to kill her. It seemed unlikely that Douglas could have done it, although he might have wanted silence from her, just for a bit, and he'd found a way to silence her permanently, whether or not he meant to.

And to suspect Larry was pretty close to laughable. Meg didn't pretend even to herself that she was a perceptive judge of character, but she couldn't see Larry as a killer—and she'd made the acquaintance of more than one over the past couple of years. Shy, awkward, clumsy Larry might be, but homicidal? She was not ready to believe that, not without convincing proof.

Then, who? She fell asleep with that question bouncing slowly around her head, like an ancient game of Pong, which she used to see when she was a child . . .

It was the middle of the night when Meg woke from a sound sleep and sat bolt upright, with questions ringing in her head: What if Monica wasn't the target? What if her death was a mistake? What if somebody else was the intended victim and was still in danger?

18

Meg slept fitfully the rest of the night. When she finally admitted she wasn't going to get any more sleep, the sky outside was already graying with morning. She lay in bed, staring at the ceiling and wondering if she'd hit on something important or had merely lost her mind in the middle of the night.

There was no proof that Monica had been murdered. Sure, the chronology of her final illness was a little suspicious, but it wasn't impossible to attribute it to natural causes.

On the other hand, Meg—and Seth and Art—couldn't come up with a single credible candidate who had any murderous hostility toward Monica.

Back to Hand One: Could Douglas have done it, having had his fill of her endless prattle, and was he now faking his illness? As far as Meg knew, there were no physical tests to confirm Alzheimer's or dementia, so how could anyone prove it, yes or no? And she had read that people suffering from either condition could have moments when they were "themselves" again, if only briefly. Could he have done something in such a moment?

Why was Seth so strongly affected by Monica's death? Sure, he was a selectman, and he had always felt a degree of responsibility for the affairs of the town, which was admirable. But for some reason Monica's death had hit him hard. Maybe that was her fault. Since she'd arrived, and after they'd become a couple, the local death rate, or at least the crime rate, had risen dramatically. And it followed her—witness what had happened at her parents' home. Had Seth simply reached a tipping point with all this crime? Was he blaming her? Was she cursed?

Oh, stop it, Meg! she told herself firmly. This was not her responsibility. She had listened to Christopher and given him her opinion, and it was up to him and Art and Detective Marcus to decide what the next step would be. She was involved only at arm's length because she was Larry's employer, but all things willing the investigation would never reach him. Right now she had plans to make for the orchard, and a well pump to find. Oh, and a new husband to coddle.

She snorted at that image, and Seth said, "You're awake."

"Well, yes. I was running through my to-do list and I reached the item 'coddle husband' and I laughed."

"Do you know how to coddle?"

"Are you questioning my wide range of abilities? Of course I do. Would you like breakfast in bed? A back rub? You know, we really need to find something to do—leisure is apparently wasted on us."

"That's exactly what I thought," Seth replied. "You can help me find that well pump you need."

"In that case, I'll make you breakfast in the kitchen."

"Deal."

While Seth showered, Meg went downstairs and assembled the ingredients for pancakes. She might as well indulge in cooking while she had the time. At least she had plenty of maple syrup on hand. Seth ambled down after a few minutes. "Will there be bacon?"

"Your wish is my command," Meg said, and extricated the package of bacon from the fridge.

"Coffee?" he asked next.

"Wow, you really are needy! If you want breakfast before lunch, you can pour yourself a cup. I'm busy."

"Well, the coddling was nice while it lasted. Do I have time to walk Max?" At the sound of his name, Max looked up and wagged his tail enthusiastically.

"Go for it," Meg told him.

Seth pulled on a jacket and opened the door, and Max bounded past him. No leash for him. He and Seth set off toward the back of the property, while Meg whisked eggs for the batter. The goats had wandered over to their fence and watched as Seth and Max passed them, and Meg made a mental note to make sure she had enough goat feed on hand. She could pick some up when she went out to look at well pumps—wherever that was. She'd better take Seth along—he knew a heck of a lot more about plumbing than she did. Maybe it was sexist of her to need a big strong man to do the talking for her under circumstances like these, but it would probably be more effective in the long run. One more reason a husband was handy to have around.

The landline rang, and Meg put down the bowl of batter to answer it. "Hey, Art, what's up?"

"I got to thinking about what we talked about yesterday, and, well, I kind of decided to take things into my own hands rather than pass it up the line for now. I've got a buddy at the state lab, so I called in a favor and asked him to check Monica's blood for colchicine."

"Oh. Well, thank you—that's above and beyond the call of duty. How long will it take until he—or she?—has results?"

"Probably by the end of the day, since he's working on those blood tests today anyway."

"That's fast. Did he say whether the state police had asked for anything special?"

"I didn't want to pry, but I think he said something about checking a standard drug panel. All we'll get is a yes or no, and maybe how large the dose might have been."

"Again, thank you. You shouldn't get yourself in trouble, or waste all your favors, on this long-shot theory of ours. I'll wait to hear from you, okay?"

"I'll call when I know anything. Pass this on to Seth, will you?"

"Of course."

When she'd hung up the phone, Meg tried to figure out how she felt about that. If it had been impossible to get Monica's blood tested, that would have been the end of it—they had no clout, no way to make the state police pay attention to them. Meg wasn't sure what would happen if the test came back positive for colchicine, but they'd cross that road when they came to it. Right now she needed to make a batch of pancakes. First things first.

Seth and Max came back about ten minutes later,

looking windblown and pleased with themselves. "Where's my breakfast, woman?" Seth demanded.

"Take a seat and I will serve you, sir."

Meg waited until they'd each finished their first stack before mentioning, "Art called while you were gone."

Seth set down his fork and looked at her. "And?"

"He took what we said seriously enough to get in touch with a friend of his at the lab and ask him to run the tests for colchicine, off the books."

"Ah. And how is he going to explain this to Marcus?"

"Maybe he won't have to. But if the test is positive, that opens up a whole new can of worms. Wow—nobody is going to be happy with us. Want to leave town again?"

"That's not exactly a solution. Was there something else you wanted to do today, apart from waiting for a phone call?"

"I told you, I need to take a serious look at well pumps. Can you help?"

"So you did, and that's why you've been softening me up with pancakes. Sure, no problem. Just give me the specs."

"I don't have the specs because I don't know what I need. We know the acreage and the number of trees, and we know we have a natural spring, but that's the end of my expertise. Besides, this is just an exploratory mission. I don't plan to buy one today."

"Got it. You're just using me."

"Exactly. For your vast plumbing knowledge and your undeniable charm."

"How can I say no?"

"You can't. Was there something you needed to get done today?"

"I've got a shopping list for stuff I'm out of, so I'll need to check the barn to see if I've missed anything. But my supply stores overlap your supply stores, so that all works out. There might be an ad hoc selectman's meeting, but I'd rather wait until we know more about Monica's death before we schedule that."

"I can be ready in fifteen minutes. Just tell me when you want to go."

Meg had never expected that talking about flow velocity and pipe diameters could be fun, but she found herself entertained by their quest for the perfect pump. Seth clearly knew everybody in western Massachusetts, although she should have realized that he'd followed in his father's footsteps as a local businessman. And he was an elected town official. And he was an all-around nice guy and even paid his bills on time. So of course he'd be an asset in getting what she needed for her orchard. She even enjoyed following him around supersized stores that sold tools, half of which she couldn't even recognize. Seth assembled a cart of basic construction supplies, which they loaded into his van. They stopped by the feed store near town and bought a couple of large bags of goat feed before heading home.

"I'm going to put this stuff in the barn," Seth said as they pulled up at the back of the driveway.

"Need help?" Meg asked as she climbed down from her seat.

"Can you handle the bags of feed?"

"Surely you jest. I am a farmer—of course I can handle fifty-pound bags."

"Go for it, then."

Once the van was empty, Seth said, "You want to walk up to the wellhead?"

"What, you think we haven't had enough exercise today?"

"No, that's not it. I just wondered if you'd like to see where your fabulous new pump will be going, now that you've seen a few."

"Sure, why not?"

They walked companionably up the hill to where the spring emerged from the ground, halfway up the orchard. It was capped for now. There were two buildings that had served it over time, one older and crumbling, the newer one sagging. "Are you going to build me a new well house?" Meg asked Seth.

"Of course. Who else? Any requests?"

"Like, do I want pink gingerbread? I'll trust your taste—it's just a functional building, but it should be sturdy. When can we start?"

"The pump can't really go in before the ground thaws. Let's see how the weather goes." Seth fell silent, turning to study the lay of the land. The house he had occupied when Meg had first arrived in Granford was visible over the crest of the hill.

"I have to decide something about the house," he said.

"No rush. I can understand why you want to keep it," Meg told him.

"But it takes maintenance, and some heat in the winter. Besides, a house should be lived in—that's what keeps it alive. But once I've sold it, I lose control of it. I'd like to see a young family living there, raising kids, but once it's out of my hands, I have no say."

"What does your mother think? After all, she lives next door."

"She says it's my decision—it's in my name, and she's happy with her own house, or at least as long as a heavy metal band doesn't move in next door and practice at three a.m. And if that happens, she figures I can pass a town ordinance to take care of it."

"Would you rather we sold my house?"

"No," he said without hesitation. "It's more practical for our needs, and besides, your business is there. And my office. Don't worry—I'll get my head wrapped around it soon enough. I've given myself until summer to decide—that's when a lot of families relocate, once the school year is over."

"Okay," Meg said simply. "You ready to walk down again? And I bet Max is going to be mad that we took a walk without him."

"No doubt."

They reached the bottom of the hill in time to hear a ringing phone, but it had stopped by the time they had unlocked the door and made it inside. Meg took a steadying breath before checking the caller record: it had been Art. Did he have an answer so soon? She noticed that he'd left a voice mail, and punched in the code. It was short and to the point: "The test was positive. We need to talk later."

Meg set the phone receiver down carefully. Had she really believed—hoped—that the elaborate story they had pieced together the day before was just a fantasy? Well, now it looked like they'd been right, and things suddenly got a lot more complicated.

She walked back into the kitchen, where Seth was looking through the cabinets at their ingredients, but when he saw her face he stopped. "Art?"

Meg nodded. "It was colchicine."

"Damn," Seth muttered.

"Exactly," Meg replied.

19

"What do we do now?" Meg asked.

"I take it Art's message didn't say what he planned to do?" Seth replied.

"Nope. So you're suggesting that we talk to him first?"

"I think so. Find out what he thinks *he* should do, which affects what *we* should do."

"Right," Meg said, though she wasn't convinced. "What about Christopher?"

"Let Art deal with him."

"And Larry?" Meg asked softly.

"I . . . don't know. You have his cell number, right?"

"Yes. That's the only way I know to contact him. He doesn't exactly have a fixed address."

Seth sighed. "There's a part of me that thinks we should talk to him, one on one, before this goes any further. Then there's this other part of me that thinks it's absolutely the wrong thing to do. What if he just disappears after he's met with us? Marcus would probably find a way to accuse us of interfering with a criminal investigation."

"It's possible, even if it isn't an official criminal investigation yet," Meg agreed cautiously. "But I don't think he would."

"Meg, you're splitting hairs. It's only inches from being a criminal investigation. You're saying that you want to go with your gut, rather than follow official procedure?"

Meg was beginning to get mad. "Doesn't that sound a bit familiar? It's not like we haven't done that before. Look, I respect the law and I know you represent the town so you have additional obligations, but you and I both know Marcus, and we know we're not his favorite people. If we tell him anything about what we've learned it will probably just annoy him because he'll see it as trampling all over his official turf, and to tell the truth, it is. And that will make things worse for Larry."

"I can't disagree with you, Meg. But let me ask you this: how much are you willing to give up for Larry?"

"I don't know what you mean."

"I'm saying that you risk jeopardizing your relationships with Art and the state police, and maybe Christopher, for the sake of a young man you don't know very well. Sure, you need someone to step into Bree's shoes and manage your orchard for you. But there are other people out there who can do that job, and Christopher could find you one."

"Christopher believes in Larry," Meg said, hating the sullen tone in her voice. "And I trust Christopher. He's known Larry for years."

"Then you owe it to Christopher to talk to him before you talk to Larry."

"Yes, I agree with you on that. But what about Art?"

"That's trickier, I'll admit. He's already skating on thin ice, since he's asked for information from the lab that technically he shouldn't have. Whether that's because he's our friend or because he thinks there's more to this death than meets the eye is not clear. He heard us out, but I don't think he's made up his mind about where Larry may fit. And he's got to maintain a good working relationship with the detective or he'll never have access to anything again."

Meg thought about her three a.m. fantasies. Oh well—might as well drag everything out into the open now so Seth could shoot them down. "I don't know that this is the best time to mention this, but there's something else, Seth."

He looked pained. "What?"

"It occurred to me last night, or rather, very early this morning, that maybe Monica wasn't the intended victim."

"What?"

"That she wasn't the one who was meant to die. She just happened to get a dose of this stuff somehow and it killed her, but maybe it wasn't supposed to."

Seth stared at her for a few beats before responding. "Let me get this straight. Fact: we now know—unofficially—that Monica was poisoned, presumably with colchicine. Theory number one: somebody had a reason to sicken or kill Monica and found a way to do it, using a somewhat obscure poison. Now you've added theory number two: Monica somehow ingested this poison, whether she knew it or not, and died quickly, but she wasn't supposed to get that dose. Did she eat someone else's cookie? And who was supposed to die, and at whose hand? And finally, tell me again what you and I are supposed to be doing about any of this. I'm sorry, but I think your theory kind of falls apart pretty fast."

"I know it sounds crazy—hey, it was three o'clock in the morning when this occurred to me. But remember this: *we're* the ones Christopher came to when he made the connection between Monica's symptoms and the chemical that he knew Larry had been working with. He didn't talk to Art or the state police first, he talked to *us*. So I'm guessing that means that he has his doubts that Larry could have been involved. When we brought Art in, he took it seriously enough that he went to the next level and confirmed the poison. He told us, but as of a few minutes ago he hadn't told anyone else. There are too many 'ifs' and 'buts' in all of this."

"Hold it," Seth interrupted. "You've now gone all the way back to the beginning, and you have no motive and no suspect, and the poison reached the wrong person by unknown means?"

"Well, sort of. Maybe. So what are our goals, apart from figuring out why Monica is dead?" Meg asked. "One, protect Art. Two, protect Larry. At least until we get more facts."

Seth sighed. "Whoever ran the test in the lab may report it to the state police, with or without implicating Art. He—or she—may regard it as a legal obligation."

"True. So let's assume the state police will know, sooner or later. But what if *nobody* was supposed to die? Maybe the whole thing was a stupid accident."

"Then tell me, why was Monica the only person affected? Not Douglas, not anyone else at the WinterFare. And where did this colchicine come from?"

"Seth, I don't know! But what do we do now?"

"Are you asking me for my opinion, or do you want me to tell you what to do?"

For a brief moment Meg indulged in the fantasy of letting Seth make all the difficult decisions, taking them out of her hands. She squashed that quickly. "That's not the way we operate. Is it?"

"No, I hope not. We're partners. We discuss things. I don't give you orders."

"I'm glad to hear that."

Meg didn't know what to do. She couldn't just walk away, although she could use some time alone to try to fit the pieces together. But they had to work this out together, because that's what she wanted from this marriage, and she hoped Seth did, too.

She took a deep breath. "Look, we're tired, we're hungry, and we're frustrated. Those are not good conditions under which to be making decisions. Plus we've got a muddy mix of legal and ethical and moral issues all tangled up in this. One solution would be to do nothing and let anybody else handle it, or if they choose, ignore it."

"But that's not the way we do things, right?" Seth said, almost smiling.

"Obviously not. Monica died Sunday. We and a very few other people know she died from a poison that is available legally but that most ordinary people have never heard of. She could have taken it herself—maybe she thought she'd failed somehow with the WinterFare, or she couldn't face nursing her husband through a debilitating illness that could last decades, or they were out of money. Maybe she had cancer or some other illness herself and couldn't handle all these pressures at once. Unless or until we can find her doctor, and maybe Douglas's, we can't say. But some random stranger poisoning her is less likely than any of those, isn't it?"

"Maybe," Seth agreed. "But, Meg, this is not our responsibility. Let the authorities handle it. Let the state police decide if they want to make public the way Monica died. If asked, Larry should admit he knows about colchicine, but it's unlikely that anyone will take him seriously as a suspect. And you and I stay out of it and go about our business. That's the simplest solution."

"I know. So why do I feel bad about doing nothing?"

"Because you care about people, and about this town."

"I'm beginning to understand why people become hermits."

"You wouldn't last a month."

A few minutes later Art rapped on the back door, interrupting a nicely distracting intimate moment in the kitchen. Seth went to let him in.

"You got my message?" Art said without preamble.

"We did. I wish we hadn't been right," Meg told him.

"You need to know that my lab buddy felt that he had to put that into the report to the state police, although in it he said that test was his own idea, not mine."

"We thought that might happen," Seth said. "So the state police know it was a poison, and they know which one. What's their next step?"

"They don't exactly share with me, but my guess would be that they'd go back to Monica's house and do a more thorough search, looking for colchicine."

"How's Douglas holding up?" Meg asked.

"Social services let him go home after they'd evaluated him. Apparently he's more coherent than he was when we first saw him, but if it's Alzheimer's or dementia or some combination, his clear moments may come and go."

"Can he stay alone?"

"For now. They'll send someone regularly to check him out, but that's not a long-term solution. Nobody's got a better idea, anyway." Art hesitated. "Look, you guys, it really would be best if you just keep your distance from here on out. Let Marcus and his gang work through the steps, just the way we did. They can talk to people at the university about the stuff, and they may come across Christopher that way. What he says is up to him, but it doesn't have to involve you two."

"So you're ordering us off the case?" Meg asked, smiling to soften the question.

"I'm asking. I know I can't possibly control either one of you. How about I add 'please'?"

Meg glanced at Seth. "We promise we'll behave ourselves, Art."

Art cocked one eyebrow, clearly not believing her. "Uh-huh. You wouldn't happen to know where Larry is, would you?"

"No," Meg told him. "I have his cell number, but I haven't seen him lately."

"Let me know when he shows up or checks in, okay?"

"We will. Thanks for coming by," Seth said.

"Night, you two," Art tossed back over his shoulder as he left.

"So that's that. Should we call Larry? Wait for tomorrow? Throw him to the wolves?"

"Meg, let's just eat dinner like normal people and talk about anything except murder, okay?"

"Mr. Chapin, I think that's an excellent idea."

As they were getting ready for bed a couple of hours later, Meg said, "You know, I think I'll call Ginny Morris tomorrow. We chatted for about two minutes at the fair, and I said I'd love to know more about how she manages an organic orchard. Since we've already figured out that this is the slowest part of the year for us, maybe I could invite her for lunch and then we could go look at her trees? Do you know anything about the place?"

"I didn't know the people who owned it, but I'm pretty sure it stood empty for a few years, which can't have helped the trees or the house. They must have gotten a good price on it. Anyway, you'd know better than I would what it would take to bring the orchard back to full production."

"A couple of seasons, probably, but that's only a guess," Meg told him. "I know I really lucked out here, since Christopher and the university had maintained my orchard all along. Do you know Mr. Ginny? Darn, why do I keep forgetting his name?"

"Al, I think Ginny said. I've met him a time or two, mostly in passing. If there were any permit issues regarding the organic status of the orchard, they didn't come through me. And as far as I know, they haven't done anything in the way of improvements to the house—maybe cash is tight. I know they've got a couple of kids in school here now, but I couldn't tell you ages or genders."

"Well, then, I will meet with Ginny and endeavor to fill in the gaps in your knowledge, tomorrow or later this week."

"An excellent idea, Mrs. Chapin. Bed?"

"Most definitely bed."

20

Four days after Monica's death, Meg found herself sitting at the table with her third cup of breakfast coffee with nothing to do. For all of her life she'd been busy—first school, then school plus after-school activities, then college, then a job, followed by another job. And now farming. Orcharding? She'd been prepared for the hard work, or so she told herself, but not for the downtime, like right now in winter. Maybe she should try dairy farming—the cows needed milking year-round, didn't they? But she dismissed that quickly: cows were messy, and she wasn't a big fan of manure. Cleaning up after two goats was plenty for her.

She should be sightseeing. Catching up on her reading. Reupholstering her tattered furniture. Just sitting didn't work for her. And Seth had gone off to do man things somewhere else. *Bad Meg—sexist!* Doing plumbing things? Official Granford things? Anyway, he wasn't around to play with, so it was up to her to entertain herself, or use her time wisely. While trying to avoid thinking about Monica Whitman's untimely death.

She was both relieved and dismayed when she looked out the door to see Larry Bennett. She wanted to see him, wanted to talk to him, but she wasn't sure what she should say—or shouldn't say. But he'd seen her sitting there, so she had to let him in.

"Hi, stranger!" Meg greeted him. "You haven't been around much this week."

He shrugged off his coat. "You didn't say you needed me. Did I miss something?"

"No. I think everything's covered. You want to sit down, have some coffee? Or do you have other plans?"

"I can sit, sure. Feels kind of funny, you know. I mean, I'm working for you, and you're paying me for it, but right now there's not much to do."

"I know. I was just complaining to myself about the same thing." Meg hesitated before saying, "Listen, Larry, you should talk to Art Preston—he's the local police chief. He's been trying to reach you."

"Why?" Larry asked.

"Christopher told him that he suspected that Monica Whitman had died from colchicine poisoning, based on her symptoms. The lab confirmed it, and the lab told the state police. You worked with colchicine at UMass. But rather than throwing you under the bus and telling the state police, Art wants to talk to you. Will you? If you don't, it looks suspicious."

"Huh," Larry answered unhelpfully. "Okay."

Okay? Meg said to herself. *Okay, yes, I'll talk to Art, or okay, I hear you?* Still, she'd done her duty. "Good. Things will get busy soon, won't they? When do we start pruning?"

"In a few weeks, depending on the weather. You want to get it done before bud-break."

"That's about what I figured." Meg stood up and put on more water to boil, then filled the coffeemaker. While she worked, she said, "You haven't been in touch with the pickers yet, have you? I know, it's kind of early to be thinking about the harvest, but I'd hate to find out they'd agreed to work for someone else."

"I don't have their contact information. And they don't know me. How do we handle that?"

At least he'd said "we." "How about this—I write to them, or maybe see if I can call Reynard, who's the foreman, and introduce you and explain what's happened— heaven forbid they should think I fired Bree—and then once they know who you are, you can take it from there?"

"Yeah, that could work. But you gotta know, I'm not good at telling other people what to do."

"Well, I had a heck of a time myself, at first. I mean, there I was, supposedly bossing around a lot of guys who were older than I am and who knew a heck of a lot more about what they were supposed to do than I did. But it all worked out. And I trust them, and they know with me they'll get paid a fair rate. I'm sure you can manage. If you respect them, they'll respect you." The water boiled, so Meg poured it over the grounds, then waited until she could fill a mug for Larry.

When they were both settled at the table again, Meg said, "Seth and I were looking at well pumps yesterday."

Larry added two spoons of sugar. "Yeah? What did you find out?"

"Well, I got a lot of brochures and a lot of recommendations, and I'm very glad I'm married to a plumber who understands these things. But I did want to get your input. Say we have an extreme drought, which is not unheard of around here—how much watering will I need to plan for?"

"What do you know about your spring?"

"Not a lot. I know it held up well during the last dry stretch we had, when Bree and I were hand-watering. But how much water the trees got was kind of set by how much the two of us could handle, which might not be the same as what the trees needed. How do I plan?"

Larry proved to be surprisingly well informed about water stress and timing of watering, so Meg listened respectfully. He ended by saying, "I guess you've got to figure your budget into the equation, right? And then you need to give your newest trees special treatment, because you want them to get established, but they're the farthest from the source, which means running more pipes."

Meg was already shaking her head. "How about I let you and Seth put your heads together and work it out? I simply don't know enough. I can tell you what I think we can afford to spend, but you're going to have to tell me the best way to spend the money."

"Yeah. I can talk to him, set up a time if you want."

"Good. Then I can check that off my list."

Meg paused. Here was Larry, the prime suspect in Monica's death in at least one of the theories. But sitting here in her kitchen with Larry in front of her, try as she might she couldn't picture him as a killer. Maybe of apple maggots, but not a middle-aged woman. Maybe there was a middle ground.

"You know, I don't think we've talked about longer-range plans for the orchard. When Christopher was managing things, he had no reason to plan for the future, except maybe on paper for his students. What's your overall assessment? What should we be thinking about for the next two to five years?"

Larry leaned back in his chair and thought before answering. "You've got some trees that are past their prime and they should be replaced, but I don't have to tell you it'll be a couple-few years before they produce a crop. I think you were smart to expand where and when you did, but they won't pay off right away. Good mix of heirlooms and dependable varieties, by the way. Bree's choices?"

"Yes. I wanted the heirlooms more for sentimental reasons than for whatever income they'll bring in, but there is a market for them in this area. Would going organic be worth considering?"

Larry shook his head. "I'm not a big fan. Too much regulation. You say you've stuck to biological control options rather than spraying anything that moved, and I think that's good, but I don't think trying to shift now would pay off. And you'd be competing with the Morrises."

"How're they doing?"

"Hard to tell. Struggling right now, but the orchard was neglected for a while, and it takes time to turn that around. You know them?"

"I met Ginny briefly at the WinterFare, but I was thinking of getting together with her. It would be nice if we didn't have to compete head-to-head. There's room for both of us, isn't there?"

"Yeah, I think so."

All right, Meg, you've created the opening—now go for it. "If I'm not going to worry about purist organic standards, are there any other strategies we should think about? Fertilizers? New chemical treatments? Any changes in apple-growing coming along?"

She all but held her breath, waiting to see how Larry would respond.

He didn't seem troubled. "I worked with some stuff like that when I was at UMass, with Christopher. You know, ways to increase crop yield, or pest or disease resistance. Interesting to study, but I don't think the results are in. Doesn't mean people aren't trying, but most of the treatments aren't ready for general use. Probably wouldn't be worth the effort in your orchard anyway—if the applications didn't work, you'd have wasted your money."

"Is this stuff expensive? Experimental only?"

"Nah, some of the products have been around for a long time, but it's how they're being used that's changed. Like colchicine—people fifty years ago thought it could work miracles, grow giant vegetables. Didn't work out. I ran some experiments with it. Can't say I raised any giant tomatoes"—he grinned at Meg—"but I came to the conclusion that under certain specific conditions it could make a difference. Needs more research, though. I don't have the time for that."

"Is Christopher working on it?"

"There might be some students who are. You probably know that Christopher's gotten more into administration, with the new science building and all. I'll bet he misses being out in the field, though. He's around here a lot, isn't he?"

"Yes. He's a friend and he knows the orchard inside out, as you know. But he's also got a more personal reason." She wondered if Christopher's relationship with Lydia Chapin was public knowledge yet.

"You mean Mrs. Chapin?" Larry asked, smiling. "Not you—the other one?"

"Exactly. And we're all happy about that. Did he tell you?"

"I've seen them together now and then. It's kind of obvious."

He was right—they kind of glowed, in a mature sedate way, when they were together.

Had she poked enough? Larry seemed perfectly comfortable talking about colchicine. She decided to drop the matter for the moment and changed the subject.

"Have you given any more thought to the tiny house idea?"

Larry shrugged. "It's kind of cool, but Seth doesn't have to do it on my account. I'll figure out something soon enough."

"Look, Larry—Seth likes being helpful, but if he says he wants to do this, he means it, and it's not just a favor for you. I think I like the idea, now that I've gotten used to it. I bet Rachel's kids would love it when they come over."

"Rachel?" Larry asked.

"Seth's sister. She's got two school-age kids and a new baby. She lives in Amherst, not far from Emily Dickinson's house."

"Okay. Yeah, I bet kids would like something their size. And maybe for sleepovers later. Well, I'm happy to help out with the work if Seth needs it."

"I'll let him know. Or you can, if you see him first. Was there anything else you wanted to talk about?" *Like, have you killed anyone lately? No, Meg, that's simply not possible, end of story.*

"That's about it—just trying to do my job. If Seth wants me to talk with him about well pumps, he can give me a call. But I'd try to get the system in as soon as the ground's soft enough."

"That makes sense. I'll tell him what you said."

"Thanks for the coffee, Meg. Call me if you need anything else."

She let him out the back door and watched as he stopped to greet the goats, who'd come over to the fence in case anything interesting was happening. He scratched Dorcas's head, then Isabel's. *Goats, are you good judges of character?* How could a guy who patted her goats be a killer?

Seth came in from his office about an hour later. "Was that Larry's car earlier?"

"Yup," Meg told him. "He was just checking in. I told him you two should talk about the well pumps, because either one of you knows more than I do. He seemed knowledgeable, anyway. Oh, and he'd noticed that Christopher and Lydia were an item, or whatever the kids call it these days. Have they gone public?"

"I'm not sure what that means, but they're certainly going out as a couple, in public. I don't think either one has posted their status on social media, but then, I don't look at it very often. Or ever."

"One more thing . . ."

"Meg, I'm beginning to dread your sentences that start that way. What?"

"Since Larry was here, I told him that it was colchicine that killed Monica. He didn't flinch. He said he'd worked with it at UMass. No hesitation."

"And your woman's intuition told you he was innocent?"

"You're being condescending, you know. No, I would say that based on my close observations of his body language and micro-expressions, he did not exhibit any anxiety or other suspicious responses to the mention of colchicine. That might not stand up in court, but I'm satisfied."

"I stand corrected. I guess I don't have any reason to talk to him about it. You were smart to work it into your conversation."

"I'm a smart woman. Oh, and he seems to like the tiny house idea, even if I had to drag that admission out of him. If you decide to go ahead with it, you can call him and spend some buddy time with him and pump him for information on your own. When are you going to make up your mind about it?"

"Soon, I promise." He strolled over to the sink and looked out the window. "You know, you'll be able to see it, or at least a corner of it, from here."

"I can live with that. Look, I was thinking of calling Ginny about lunch and an orchard tour. You need me for anything else today?"

"Nothing specific. I'm just catching up on my invoices. Some people are a little slow to pay during the holiday season."

"And don't forget taxes. Are we filing separately or together? We both have sole-proprietor businesses, so it may be a complicated return."

"That, my dear wife, is your area of expertise. I will bow to your superior wisdom."

Maybe his mother had been doing them all along. "Gee, thanks. I'll move it up my list. But you've got to work out your own Schedule C."

"Yes, ma'am!"

21

Seth vanished back to his office lair, leaving Meg at loose ends once again. She cleaned up the few breakfast dishes and was contemplating starting a long-range to-do list for occasions such as this, not that she was expecting many more, when yet another car pulled into her driveway, and this time it belonged to the state police. Unfortunately the appearance of Detective Marcus seldom meant good news, although she took some small comfort that he had come alone. Should she tell Seth to join them? No, she decided: if this was about Larry, she was his employer, and she didn't need to muddy the waters by including someone else in the discussion. If Marcus wanted to talk with Seth, he could ask himself.

She opened the back door—again—and waited for the detective to emerge from his vehicle and approach. "A word with you, Meg?" he said when he drew closer.

"Of course. Come on in. Coffee?" He'd called her Meg, so this was only semiofficial at best—or worst. Maybe he was trying to lull her into a false sense of security. No, not likely—he was usually a direct person.

"That'd be good. Cold out there." William Marcus stepped into the kitchen and slid off his coat.

With Detective Marcus, that passed for social chitchat. "Please, sit down. I'll just be a minute." For the third time in the day Meg made coffee. She did her best to keep her mind blank: she didn't want to jump to any conclusions, and she had to avoid acting defensive if there turned out to be no need. And if Detective Marcus asked her a direct question about Larry or poisons, she'd answer honestly. Probably.

Three minutes later they were seated around the kitchen table with mugs filled with hot coffee. "So, what can I do for you today?" Maybe it was about a fundraiser for the state police? Or the state lab needed money for a new Amazing Thing? But Meg doubted it.

Marcus cleared his throat. "Our department has a few questions about Larry Bennett. We understand he works for you?"

Meg couldn't say she was surprised. "Yes, he does, but he's only just started. He's replacing Bree Stewart, who left for an internship in Australia. What do you want to know?"

"How well do you know him?"

"Not very. But he came highly recommended by Christopher Ramsdell, who was a professor of his at UMass. Christopher knows this orchard well and knows what I need here."

"Do you have an address for Mr. Bennett?"

"No, actually I don't. He's told me he's looking for a new place to live now that he has a steady job with me, but so far he's been camping out with anyone who has a spare bed. I have his cell phone number, if that's any help."

"We already have that, thank you. He's not answering it at this time. Did he fill out any type of formal job application?"

"No, or at least, not yet. I realize I need to do the paperwork on him as an employee of my own business, but I haven't gotten around to it. He's barely started working for me." *Take it easy, Meg. Don't overexplain. Don't volunteer information. Let him come to you.* "Why are you interested in him? Is there something I need to know about him?"

Detective Marcus ignored her question. "How well did you know Monica Whitman?"

So that's the way the wind is blowing. She wasn't surprised. "I met her just once, when she dropped by to introduce herself and to talk about the WinterFare. That must have been the middle of last month sometime. And then we chatted for a couple of minutes at the fair itself. That's all."

"Have you ever seen Larry Bennett and Monica Whitman together?"

"No. Do—did they know each other?"

"That's something we're trying to ascertain. You were at the Whitman house the other day. Why?"

"Art Preston asked me to accompany him to talk to Monica's husband, Doug. At that time we all thought it was a natural death, and we wanted to make sure Douglas was all right. Art thought a woman's touch might make things easier. I told you that before."

"You had never been to the Whitman house prior to that?"

"No, I hadn't."

"Yet you took it upon yourself to wash the dishes and clean up the place," the detective said implacably.

"Yes, because I thought it was an unhealthy situation. Douglas was clearly in distress and seemed to believe that his wife was still alive and would be home soon. He appeared not to notice that the kitchen was filled with rotting food. So, yes, I did clean up. As I said, no one thought it might be a suspicious death, and I didn't want him to get sick."

"Did you take anything away from the house with you?"

"No, of course not. I might have taken the garbage away, but your officers arrived before I could, so I left things where they were. Detective, what is this about?"

Detective Marcus focused a stony stare at her, giving nothing away. *Aw, come on, give me a hint,* Meg pleaded silently. Finally he cleared his throat. "As you already know, Monica Whitman did not die from natural causes. She ingested a poisonous substance."

And why does he believe I know that? Meg wondered. But she could play along. "Which was?"

He paused—for dramatic effect, Meg wondered?—then said, "Colchicine. Are you familiar with it?"

"I've heard of it. I understand it has some agricultural applications."

"That's correct. Have you used it in your orchard?"

"Not personally. If Bree used it, she didn't consult with me because I couldn't give her any sort of advice. I trusted her judgment in anything to do with the orchard. Why are you asking?"

"Christopher Ramsdell has informed us that Larry Bennett carried out studies involving the use of colchicine while he was taking classes at the university. He is aware of its applications and properties."

"Why does that matter?"

"Don't you find it a curious coincidence that Monica Whitman dies from colchicine poisoning at the same time Larry Bennett starts working in the same town?"

"A coincidence, yes. I can't guess what it means. Is there something you want me to do?"

"If you should see or speak to Larry Bennett, please ask him to contact us at this number." Detective Marcus handed her a business card.

"I will be happy to do that. Anything else?"

"Not at this time." Marcus stood up.

"Oh, wait," Meg said. "Can you tell me anything about how Douglas Whitman is? He seemed kind of lost when I last saw him."

"He seems to be in better control of himself. The professional assessment was that he could stay in his home for now, with some periodic supervision, but there is no long-term solution in place yet. Thank you for your time, Meg."

Meg meekly followed the detective to the door, shutting it behind him and watching as he pulled out of the driveway. She felt like she had been playing a part in an obscure play, saying the right lines, but there were hidden subtexts littering the scene. Did Marcus know she knew more about Larry than she had let on? But she hadn't lied. She'd answered his questions honestly. And did he only want to talk with Larry, or was he contemplating an arrest? Did he know more about Larry than Larry had shared with her, or even with Christopher?

She shook her head to clear it. Better tell Seth, in case

Marcus decided to drop by again. She pulled on her jacket and went out to Seth's office in the back. Seth greeted her after she had trudged up the stairs to his workspace. "Marcus?"

"Yup. I thought about asking you to join us, but then I decided that I should play big girl and handle it. After all, I'm the one who hired Larry."

"I figured you could handle Marcus, so I stayed out of it. Anything unexpected?"

"Not really. He knows about the colchicine poisoning, duh. He knows Larry has worked with the stuff, and that Christopher advised him on it. He knows we know about the colchicine, although he didn't say anything outright, but he knows we're close to Christopher. He hasn't talked to Larry yet because he hasn't been able to find him. I told him in all honesty that I had no idea where he was, although I kind of forgot to mention that I'd seen him earlier today. Marcus already has his cell number, but Larry's not picking up. But I'm not going to make too much of that. Yet. And that, sir, is all I know."

"What now?"

"Got me. It's too late in the day to call Ginny—I'll wait until tomorrow to call her. Oh, has anyone said anything about a funeral for Monica? Is Douglas up to handling that?"

"I doubt that the state police are in any hurry to release her body," Seth told her, "and I also doubt that Douglas is pushing for it. I wonder where he'd like to see her buried?"

"I hope somebody is looking after the poor man."

"I'll see if I can push the town to help out, but I'm not sure what we can do. Which reminds me—you and I need to revise our wills, what with the changes in our status."

"Uh, I've never made a will. I didn't own much of anything until I moved here—well, sometime after that, because my mother transferred the property to my name a year or so ago. And I had no one to leave anything to. I guess that was ducking the issue—if a tree had fallen on me and killed me, it would have been up to my parents to sort things out. Unless Massachusetts laws say something different. Wow, I'm feeling more and more stupid. What about you? If I thought about it, I would expect you'd like to help out your mother, or maybe your sister. I don't exactly need your property or your vast bank account. God, I feel like we're playing at being grown-ups. Do you have any suggestions? Do you even have a lawyer?"

"I could ask the town lawyer to help us out—I know him, and he's a good guy. It doesn't have to be complicated. Just something along the lines of 'I leave all my worldly goods to my beloved wife'—I think Nicholas Biddle did that."

"*The* Nicholas Biddle? Didn't he finance the American Revolution?"

"He certainly had a hand in it."

"I'm not sure why you happen to know that. He must have been a trusting soul. But then, maybe he had an exemplary and competent wife. So, should I put 'draw up wills' on our to-do list?"

"Before or after 'solve this latest murder'?" Seth grinned at her.

"Uh, at the risk of repeating what you keep telling me, that's not our job. But I still don't think Larry did anything to Monica."

"Let Marcus figure out who did."

"I plan to." Meg sighed. "So I'll set up something with

Ginny in the morning. You have any plans I need to know about?"

"Not that I've heard. Maybe we should invite Mom over for dinner."

"With or without Christopher?"

"Her choice."

22

The next morning it took Meg only a couple of minutes online to find Ginny's phone number in Granford. She punched in the number, and Ginny answered. "Morris Orchards, Ginny speaking," she said brusquely.

"Ginny, this is Meg Corey, uh, Chapin." She really should make up her mind what name she was using. "Remember, we met at the WinterFare?"

"Oh, yeah, sure. You've got that orchard on the south side of town. What can I do for you?"

"I thought maybe we could get together and have lunch, and compare notes on running an orchard? Or, heck, just get to know each other, since we're in the same business. I'm guessing your schedule right now isn't too full, if mine is any indication."

"Uh, yeah, sure, that sounds good. The kids are in

school and won't be back until three. Where you want to go?"

"Can I take you to Gran's? You mentioned you hoped to sell the owners some apples, but I don't know if you know the full history of the place. Anyway, they're good people there, and you should get to know them better."

"I haven't had a lot of time for lunches and socializing. I'm sorry about that, because you and I should have met sooner."

"Look, I know how that goes. I was overwhelmed when I first moved here, and I didn't know anything about growing apples. If I'd had a choice . . . Well, why don't we get together and talk?"

"Okay. Noonish at Gran's?"

"Sounds good to me. See you there."

Meg grabbed a quick shower, dressed warmly, and then, failing to find Seth in the house, left a note for him: "Lunch with Ginny at Gran's. Back later." She stuck it in the middle of the kitchen table and set the salt shaker on it, grabbed her bag and keys, and set out for the center of town.

She arrived a bit before twelve. It looked like a slow day: there were only a couple of cars in the parking lot and, once inside, she noted that only three tables had any people seated at them, and two of those tables held only one person each. She decided to check in with Nicky if she was in the kitchen. She stopped in the doorway and stood watching as Nicky and her sous chef worked efficiently side by side in a well-choreographed routine. Nobody noticed her, so Meg finally said, "Something smells wonderful."

Nicky look up and smiled. "Oh, hi, Meg. Was I expecting you today?"

"Nope. I invited Ginny Morris to lunch. You talked to her about apples a while back, didn't you?"

Nicky stared up at the ceiling for a moment. "Uh, short woman, curly hair—grows organic, right?"

"That's the woman. How on earth do you remember these things?"

"That's a visual memory—recipes are harder, which is why I have scribbled notes all over the kitchen. I didn't buy anything from her, did I?"

"She said not. Any particular reason?"

"I could guilt-trip you, because I buy most of mine from you, but I don't think she had enough of any one variety to make one of our desserts and keep it on the menu. We couldn't call it organic if some of the fruit wasn't."

"Got it. Is organic a good selling point around here?"

"To some people. You thinking of joining the other side?"

"I'm still learning the 'environmentally responsible' side—I'll think about it."

"She was at the WinterFare, wasn't she?"

"Yes, at the end opposite me—closer to you, I guess. I didn't get a chance to really talk to her then and I felt guilty, so I wanted us to get together and chat. Seth says it's an old orchard but it had been neglected for a while."

"Before my time in Granford, Meg. Why don't you go wait for her in front, and I'll bring you menus when she arrives and say hi?"

"In other words, you want me out of your kitchen. No problem. See you in a bit."

Meg returned to the main room and stood in front of the large windows that overlooked the town green. By any standards it was a quiet time of year. She counted only a handful of cars passing, and this was the main road through town. Finally she saw a battered pickup truck with some kind of apple logo on the door pull into the parking lot, so she went out to the wide porch to wait for Ginny.

Ginny climbed out of the truck and hurried up the path. "Sorry I'm late—something always comes up at the last minute."

Meg laughed. "No need to apologize—it happens to me all the time. And I have to say if I'm not crazy busy I don't know what to do with myself, so my timing is off. Have you eaten here?"

"No," Ginny said, without explanation. "Lovely old building, isn't it?"

"It is. I'm glad to see it put to good use. I was afraid someone would tear it down, or put in a blah insurance office. It really anchors this end of the green. Come on, let's go in and sit down."

Nicky must have been watching, because she came out of the kitchen as soon as Meg and Ginny were settled. "Hey, ladies! I love winter cooking. There may not be a lot of fresh ingredients available, but you can do such interesting things with the old hardy ones! Ginny, I'm sorry we haven't spoken lately. I wish we could have bought your apples, but we needed more volume. But come back to us again when your crop is in."

"Thanks, Nicky. I heard the same story from other restaurants and markets, so I don't take it personally. My husband and I are working to bring our trees back to what they once were, but it takes time. As I'm sure Meg here knows. What should we order?"

"I've got an amazing winter vegetable soup, from an

antique recipe, and some house-made country bread. Sound good?"

"Great," Ginny said, and Meg nodded agreement.

When Nicky had gone back with their order, Meg said, "You've actually lived here longer than I have. You bought your orchard? I mean, you're not just renting it?"

"Yes, and this past fall was our third season. You want the whole boring story?"

"Sure—I don't have any other plans for the day."

"Well, you asked for it. My husband and I were living the mid-level corporate life, working full-time, with two kids in school. We had two cars and a nice house, and we took a two-week vacation to a different place every year. Sounds perfect, right? So one morning I woke up and thought I would scream if I had to do the same damn thing every day forever. But then I had to decide what I *did* want to do. That took a while, and when I figured out I wanted to make something or grow something, it took a while longer to convince my husband. He thought everything was just fine the way it was."

"How did you land on apples as the answer?" Meg asked.

"Well, I didn't like cows," Ginny said.

Meg laughed out loud. "I hear you! Too messy. Did you have any background in agriculture?"

"Nope. I was a public defense lawyer, and Al—my husband—was a mid-level manager at a midsize pharmaceutical firm outside of Providence. So once we had our dream picked out, we started alternating taking courses at night to learn what we needed to know. After a few semesters of that, we went looking for a place with an orchard,

and that's when we found Granford. Kind of like we followed the Connecticut River north."

"I don't think I've seen your place, or maybe I have but
didn't notice. Although I usually notice apple trees. Even
in my sleep, I think. From what I've heard, the place was
pretty run-down, wasn't it?"

"That's a polite way to say it. But it was what we could
afford. Once we sold our house, we set aside a chunk of
the proceeds as a cushion, because we knew it would take
time for us to get up and running. More than we expected,
I'm afraid. If everything goes right, we might see a profit
with this year's crop. What about you? How'd you end up
here?"

"Backed into it, kind of. My mother inherited the place
from two aunts or great-aunts or whatever who never married and outlived the rest of their family. She brought me
out here to meet them when I was a kid, and I hated the
whole thing—two dotty old ladies cooped up in a shabby
farmhouse that hadn't changed for more than a century.
Not a good first impression! So when I got downsized out
of a job in Boston, Mother thought it would be a great idea
if I came out here and fixed up the house to sell it—she'd
never even been back since she'd inherited it. Wow, that
was two years ago last month! Things got a little more
complicated along the way." *That was a massive under-
statement*, Meg thought. Maybe Ginny had slept through
the time when Meg had single-handedly upended a town
meeting and torpedoed a planned development project—
and that was in the first couple of months. "I learned a lot
about the business, and in December I married the guy
next door."

"Yeah, Seth Chapin. I've met him a couple of times,

usually on town business. Seems like a good guy. Of course I'd have to say that to your face, wouldn't I?"

"Yes, but we didn't get along in the beginning. He was a plumber when we met, but he's kind of moved laterally into restoring old buildings and he's much happier with that. I've managed to keep the orchard growing, and last year we collaborated and planted three acres of new trees—Seth's land, my trees. Is your husband involved in the hands-on stuff?"

"He does the heavy lifting, I guess you'd say. You've got what, fifteen acres?"

"Plus the new three, but they won't produce for a while," Meg confirmed.

"We've got ten, and we had a lot of work to do. Some trees were beyond salvage, and others needed a lot of pruning and feeding. I also wanted to make the soil around the trees healthier, and I've been adding beneficial plants between them. I think we've turned the corner."

Nicky arrived with a tray laden with heavy stoneware bowls of soup, and plates with hearty bread, both white and whole grain. When she set down the bowls, Meg laughed. "This looks amazing. Of course so did that last soup of yours that I tried—the bright red one. What's in this?"

Nicky leaned in conspiratorially. "What you'd expect after a long Massachusetts winter. But I threw in a lot of herbs that I grew last year, for flavor."

After a taste, Meg said, "Whatever you did, it works!"

Nicky straightened up. "Can I get you anything else? Coffee? Tea? Water?"

"Coffee for me," Meg said. Ginny just nodded.

Nicky went off to get their drinks, and Meg turned to Ginny. "You're not going to insist on organic coffee?"

"No, too much hassle. Look, I believe in the whole concept of organic farming, and I'm sticking to the rules, but I'm not some wild-eyed evangelist. It's a market niche and a healthy one, and I can get behind that. But in the rest of my life I do eat other food. Certainly my kids do, at least outside of our house, but I don't tell them sugar and processed flour are evil or anything like that."

"Sounds like a reasonable approach. We're probably not that far apart in our growing practices, but I haven't felt up to going through whatever it would take to get certified. It's been hard enough without it."

"You like it now, after two years?" Ginny asked. She spooned up a mouthful of the soup, swallowed it, and said, "Wow! This is terrific. Think Nicky will give me the recipe?"

"Just ask. She's good people, and so's her husband, Brian. As for your question, yes, I think I do. I thought I liked what I was doing in Boston, but looking back on it now, it seems so stuffy—I was crunching a lot of numbers in a back room. I work a lot harder now—I'm sure you know what that's like—but I feel stronger and more productive. A bushel of apples is a lot more interesting than a financial report, at the end of the day."

"No argument from me!"

They chatted amiably through Nicky's excellent lunch, until finally Meg said, "Would it be rude of me to ask to see your orchard? You said your kids wouldn't be home for a while."

"Sure, I'd love to show you. Like I said, it won't take long—it's smaller than yours. And you know that the trees look pretty bare at this time of year."

"Yes, of course I do. I'd just like to see the lay of the

land, how you handle the apples, stuff like that. I've got an old barn that came with my place, and Seth built some refrigerated storage units for the apples inside it, but I figure it's good to consider other options."

"So we're skipping dessert?" Ginny asked slyly.

"Maybe we can ask Nicky for something to go," Meg said, grinning.

They settled the check, which Meg insisted on paying for, since she'd been the one to invite Ginny, and accepted two pieces of cake from Nicky. Then Ginny led the way out to her truck. "You want to follow me?"

"Sure," Meg told her. "I know the general area, but I might not find your place. Lead the way!"

Ginny's home was about as far from Meg's as possible within the boundaries of Granford. When they came close, and Ginny slowed, Meg realized she had in fact driven by the place plenty of times, but she couldn't see the apple trees or the house from the road. The shrubbery surrounding the property was high and untrimmed, and there was a long driveway leading to a one-story house that looked like it dated from about 1900. Ginny parked at the side and waited for Meg to park and get out of her car. "You up for walking?"

"Sure. I don't get a lot of chances to walk without working, and I'm looking forward to seeing what you've got here."

23

 "Well, this is it," Ginny said. Meg found it hard to read her expression. Was she defensive? Proud? Worried?

"You said ten acres?" Meg asked.

"For the orchard, not including the house and buildings. It's about ten, but they're kind of spread out. If you look over that way"—Ginny pointed past the house—"you can see the ground gets marshy. We also left a lot of the native trees in place. You want me to walk you through it?"

"Sure. I could use the exercise."

They strolled among the irregular rows. The trees varied in size, shape, and age, and Ginny treated each one like an old friend. "I know some of these will have to go, to make way for more productive ones, but they've hung on for so long, with so little care, that I feel guilty taking them down."

"I know what you mean. When you bought the place, did it come with any history?"

"No. Yours?"

"As I keep saying, I was lucky. The university managed it for at least a decade, and of course they collected whatever information they could—or more likely, asked students to do the research. They went back through property records and old maps, and even genealogies. Did I mention there's a series of diaries, written by a woman who lived on my property in the later nineteenth century? The Historical Society in town has them now, but I've read through them. The author writes about the whole family—grandparents, parents, and their two girls—going out to shake the trees and harvest the apples. And then the husband would take some into town and sell them, and I guess they'd keep or somehow preserve the rest. I know the woman was manic about baking pies almost daily, more than her own family could possibly have eaten, so I'm guessing there were some hired hands to help with the harvest. You could find something like that at the Society, too."

"I wish I had the time!" Ginny said. "I thought about home-schooling my kids, but there was no way we could do that and run the orchard at the same time. You don't have any kids, right?"

Meg laughed. "We've been married about three minutes, so no. Seth was married before, but they didn't have any, either. Still, as far as I know, the schools around here are pretty good—there are plenty of academic types living in town."

"Well, that's reassuring. You want me to explain what I plant between the trees? That's something you could do, and it doesn't take much work."

"Sure. What should I know?" As they meandered along, Ginny pointed out clumps of dried vegetation, which didn't mean much to Meg. "What's your plan here?" she asked.

"I've chosen plants that provide needed nutrients for the trees and enrich the soil—and keep the weeds down, by the way. I prefer it to adding chemicals, even when they are acceptable to the organic purists."

"Makes sense. And they don't take much maintenance, right?" When Ginny shook her head, Meg added, "Maybe you could give me a list, or point me to something I could read about these?"

"I'd be happy to."

When they'd completed the circuit of the orchard, Meg asked, "Have you considered adding other money-makers? Cider-making, or jellies?"

"Well, as you probably know, both would take an up-front investment in equipment, or bringing the kitchen up to code if we were going to sell a cooked product, and we'd probably have to hire somebody to manage whatever it was. So the short answer is no: no money and no time. Kind of a Catch-22, isn't it? We could make more money if only we had money to spend to make it possible."

"That is a problem. I think about making cider now and then, but I know nothing about the process, and like you, I'd have to bring in someone who did, and set up the whole operation. Makes me tired just thinking about it."

"Exactly. Seen enough?"

"I guess so. Your place here, it seems almost like a secret garden. You kept all the trees around the perimeter. Would it help if you opened it up more, maybe put up a sign to let people know you were here?"

"Maybe. But in a way, I like the trees. You look out the

windows and it could be a past century. I want the kids to have a sense of that. I know they're going to grow up with malls and electronic stuff coming at them all the time, but I'd like them to see there are simpler ways to live. Come on in and I'll show you the house."

As they walked toward the house, Meg studied it: one story, with unpainted but nicely weathered board siding and a low-pitched roof. A shallow porch ran along the front. Set back on one side was a small sale area, with a table and tiers of shelves for baskets—empty now, no surprise. Meg followed Ginny into the front room, where a fireplace occupied most of the wall to the right, with a kitchen on the other side of it. Meg assumed there were bedrooms to the rear. It was small, but it felt comfortable and well lived in.

"I've driven by yours," Ginny said, watching as Meg took in the room. "Nice Colonial. Original?"

"Yes, it is, built around 1760, which was before Granford was even founded. Luckily nobody's messed around with it much, except that around 1850 one of the owners decided that having a single central chimney with fireplaces on each side took up too much space, and replaced it on the first and second floors, which allowed him to put in a central stair. But the brick base is still in place in the basement. It's massive."

"That's cool. I mean, that it's still there. And that you can follow the history of the people who made it. Is it hard to heat?"

Meg laughed. "Let's say I've bought a lot of sweaters over the past two years. But both Seth and I don't want to pop in aluminum windows, which would spoil the look, and we haven't had time to make our own replacements."

"Must be nice having a plumber plus woodworker on hand," Ginny said almost wistfully.

Maybe her husband wasn't handy around the house—a lot of men weren't anymore. "He grew up doing it, and his mother still lives in the Colonial he grew up in. Me, I grew up in the suburbs, so I never knew anything about any of this. But I'm learning."

"Hey, where are my manners? You want some tea or something? The kids won't be back for another half hour."

"Sure." Meg followed Ginny into the kitchen, which ran the depth of the small building.

"Sit down—it won't take long." Ginny filled a kettle and set it on the stove, then pulled a glass jar out of a cupboard. "Hope you don't mind herbal—it's my own blend."

"That's fine. You have an herb garden?"

"I do. That's kind of my little kingdom, and it's easy to maintain. I let the kids help weed." When the water boiled, Ginny spooned her tea into a pot and brought it to the table, along with a pair of mugs.

"Give it a minute or two to steep. So, do you miss the corporate world?"

"Every now and then, when I'm hot and sticky and too exhausted to even take a shower. Funny, isn't it? The first thing I think of is being clean. But I like learning new skills, and I like using my body. I'm probably more fit than I've been in years, even though I used to do a lot of walking in Boston. It's not the same, though."

"No, it's not," Ginny said, laughing. She poured tea into the mugs. "Taste it before you add sugar."

"You don't use sugar?"

"Yes, in moderation, and also honey. But the sugar masks the flavor, so you should see what it's like on its own."

Meg sipped cautiously. The blend proved to be fruity and spicy at the same time—it was pleasant, with a slightly tart aftertaste. "Nice."

"I read up on old recipes, when the orchard isn't eating up all my time. I like to experiment. It really is nice to have the break from dawn-to-dusk work in winter, you know? All that hauling stuff around and lifting really does a number on my joints. And muscles, too."

"Believe me, I know what you mean. You don't hire any pickers?"

"No, it's just us, but like I said, the crop hasn't been all that large for the last couple of years. Maybe this year, fingers crossed!"

"My manager and I had to hand-water the orchard during a long dry spell. We have a well, so there was water, but we had to distribute the water by hauling the tank around the orchard with a truck. Water is heavy!"

"You've got that right."

"The only thing that saved me was the old claw-foot bathtub that must date from before 1900. I could fill that up with hot water and just wallow in it until I got the kinks out."

"I envy you—we don't have one like that, just a modern one that's too shallow to really submerge yourself in. Just as well, I guess—I don't think our boiler could manage to fill a bigger one anyway. That's another thing we need to replace. But I have found one thing that helps when I ache all over."

"What's that? I just use ibuprofen."

"I used to use that, but it really didn't help, so my doctor told me to try this other thing. Let me show you." Ginny got up and went through the living room, presumably to the bathroom, and returned shortly with a small cardboard box, which she handed to Meg. "It's really good for joint pains—it's been used for treating arthritis. And it's a natural product. Have you tried it?"

Meg took the box and glanced briefly at it—then looked back. The package was clearly labeled "Colchicine."

Meg wondered what her face showed. Was this just a coincidence? Or was there more to it? "No, I haven't. Where do you get it?" she said carefully, trying to keep her voice normal.

"You can ask at the pharmacy. But once I found out it worked, I started ordering it over the Internet—it's cheaper that way. Hey, why don't you take that box? I've got more."

"Sure. Thanks." Meg found she didn't know what to say next, but she was saved at the sound of young voices coming down the long driveway: the children were home. "That sounds like your kids. I should be going. Thanks for the tour, Ginny. I'd be happy to show you around my place if you like."

"I would. I'll give you a call and we can set up something. Hey, kids, welcome home! This is Meg Chapin—she has an orchard, too, on the other side of town. Meg, this is my daughter, Alice, and my son, Joey."

"Hello, Mrs. Chapin," the children answered dutifully. *Funny how they assumed that because I'm a grown-up, I must be married,* Meg thought.

"Nice to meet you. Sorry I have to run, but you can come over with your mother if you like some afternoon. I have a pair of goats."

"Thank you," the older child, Alice, said. "Mom, are there any cookies?"

"In the kitchen. We'll talk later, Meg."

Meg carefully put the box of colchicine in her bag and zipped it, and went out to her car. She felt like she was in a daze, so instead of starting the car immediately, she tried to sort out what she'd learned and what she wanted to know now. One, she liked Ginny. They had a lot in common, on more than one level. They could become friends. Two, Ginny took colchicine for muscle or joint aches. It had been recommended or prescribed for her by a doctor. She apparently kept it in her bathroom, not hidden away or under lock and key. It was commercially available without a prescription to ordinary consumers. How had she missed finding that fact? Three, she really needed to know if Ginny had met Monica, and if Ginny had suggested the same remedy to her. Ginny had been part of the WinterFare. Monica had made a point of meeting all the vendors, so she had probably paid a call to Ginny at some point, just as she had with Meg. So the odds were good that Monica had sought out Ginny. Could Ginny have handed Monica a box of the stuff? Too bad the arrival of the children had prevented her from asking just a few more questions.

But surely Monica wouldn't have taken more than prescribed. The medical lab had said there was colchicine in Monica's system—but how much? A therapeutic dose? Or a fatal one?

Now what was she supposed to do? For all she knew, there was a package of these same tablets in half the households in Granford. It was legal and available, so why shouldn't people have it? But had Monica taken it herself, in a safe dose or a deadly one? Or had somebody slipped it to her? She needed to talk to Seth. And Art. Not Marcus. That was her immediate to-do list, short and simple.

She turned on the car and headed for home.

Seth was in the kitchen when she arrived. When he looked at her, he asked immediately, "What's wrong?"

"I went over to Ginny's to take a look at her orchard. While I was there, she gave me something she said helped with her aches and pains, better than ibuprofen." Meg fished in her bag and pulled out the box, then offered it to Seth. "This."

He took it and his expression changed. He turned it over in his hands, read the back label, opened the box, and pulled out a blister pack of capsules. They weren't very large, Meg saw. "These are legal?" he asked.

"Apparently so. They might keep them behind the counter at the pharmacy, because we know they can be toxic, but you don't seem to need a prescription."

"Ginny volunteered these?"

"She gave me the package. Her doctor recommended it when she said ibuprofen didn't work, and she thought I should try it. We both know what kind of physical work an orchard demands. It's hard to imagine that she wouldn't have suggested it to Monica, if they met, which seems likely. I didn't get a chance to ask because the school bus dropped her children off right then."

"Huh. How'd you two get along?"

"I liked her. We have a lot in common."

"So you don't think she's trying to kill you to reduce the competition in Granford?"

Meg checked his expression to see if he was kidding. "By handing me poison pills? You don't really mean that?"

"No, of course I don't. So now we know there's at least one innocent use for this stuff, and plenty of people could have it. I wonder if there's a lab that could tell if this is the same formula as what they found in Monica?"

"I'd like to know what concentration was found in

Monica," Meg replied. "I have read that it's bitter, and it looks to me like it would take a whole bunch of those capsules to do any real harm, and odds are you'd taste that something was off. And we need to know if Ginny gave her a box, the way she did me, or if it came from somewhere else. What do we do now?"

"I'd say talk to Art again. If he's still willing to pick up the phone when he sees who's calling."

"I vote for that, too. Is Lydia coming for dinner tomorrow, and is she bringing Christopher? You said you were going to ask."

"Yes and yes."

24

"You want to flip to see who calls Art this time?" Seth asked.

Meg sighed. "This was my conversation with Ginny, so I should do it. Why do I keep finding myself in the middle of things? I went over just to see Ginny's orchard, and to get to know a neighbor, and look what happens. Okay, I'll do it now before I lose my courage."

"Great. You still okay if Mom brings Christopher for dinner?"

"Of course I am. We need to talk to him anyway. When was the last time we had a simple meal talking about happy stuff? I can't even remember." Meg retrieved her cell phone and walked into the dining room to call while Seth made his call from the kitchen. She checked her watch: Art should still be at the office. That was all right, because this was official business, sort of, and she trusted him not to blab it around. She hit his speed-dial number, wondering yet again how it happened that she had the Granford chief of police on speed dial.

"Meg," he answered cautiously. "What is it this time?"

"I just discovered something that troubled me, and I thought you might want to know. Can you talk, or do we have to do it face-to-face?"

"Let me shut my door."

Meg heard voices in the background, and then silence as the door shut. Then Art picked up again. "Okay, hit me with it."

"I was over at Ginny Morris's house this afternoon, looking at her orchard."

"Do you consider that a crime now? Industrial espionage?"

"No, of course not. But we had a cup of herbal tea afterward, and got to talking about the physical demands of running an orchard. She said she'd tried the standard over-the-counter pain relievers and they hadn't really worked for her, but then her doctor recommended something different. You can probably guess what."

Art sighed. "Our current favorite poison?"

"Yes. Sold legally, in stores and available by mail order and online. I never knew. I've been looking at it online myself, but mainly its agricultural applications. It never occurred to me that it would be so available and so ordinary. And potentially deadly."

"I didn't know, either, Meg. So you're saying just about anybody could have gotten hold of it?"

"That's what it looks like. In fact, Ginny gave me a package of the stuff."

Art was silent for a few moments. "Does the package

say anything about a fatal dose? Or that it can be fatal at all?"

"Hold on—let me get it." Meg retrieved the box from where she had set it on the mantelpiece, so she could read the label. "Shoot, only that exceeding the maximum recommended dose can be dangerous. How is that even legal?"

"I'm not the person to ask. Anyway, from all I know about the Morrises, they're pretty straight-arrow folk, so I don't think they'd knowingly use something illegal or dangerous."

"That's what I thought. And of course that got me wondering . . . You know Monica came by the house here, a couple of weeks before the WinterFare, mostly to introduce herself? Well, she probably did the same thing with Ginny. What if Ginny handed her a package of these things and said, 'try this,' like she did with me?"

"Did you ask Ginny?"

"No, because the kids came home from school then, so I didn't have a chance. But think about it: if Ginny's actually taking the stuff herself, I can't imagine she's using it to poison people. I mean, her kids could get hold of it. It's not like it's hidden, or even under lock and key. She just walked to her bathroom, which I could see from where I was sitting, and came back with a box."

Art was silent a moment. "Let's say she did give Monica a box, and Monica forgot about it, or didn't feel the need for any pain relievers for a couple of weeks. The fair must have been a lot of work, and maybe that was the first time she remembered she had it, or needed it."

"That's what I'd like to think, Art. So now I've got two questions. One, can your lab buddy tell if this is the same formula as what he found in Monica's body, and two, how high was the dose Monica took? I mean, given the size of the capsules, did Monica take one or half a dozen? What was the lethal dose?"

Art chuckled. "This is why I love talking to you and Seth, Meg. You ask such interesting questions, and I have to work hard to find answers. I don't know what I'd do at my job if I didn't have you two. I cannot answer either of your questions, but I can put the question to my friend. It's late Friday afternoon, and I doubt he's going to hang around the lab checking this out, if he's there at all. He might be able to answer your second question, about how much Monica had taken and if that dose was fatal. If he says no, he wouldn't have to worry about the other question. Of course Marcus would have something new to worry about, but that's his problem. And I will bend over backward and jump through hoops to keep all of our names out of this discussion, if ever it becomes official."

"Thank you, Art," Meg said meekly. "I'll try not to bother you again, at least for a day or two."

"Yeah, right," he muttered. "I'll call if I get any further information. If I don't, please allow me to enjoy a peaceful weekend with my wife. Deal?"

"Deal."

When Meg walked back into the kitchen, Seth asked, "How'd it go?"

"About what you'd expect. What the heck did Art do with himself before I moved here?"

"Oh, lots of exciting stuff about missing dogs and tomatoes thrown at the high school. You have definitely altered the quality of his life. Did he have any practical ideas?"

"He said he'd ask his friend about the dosage Monica

took—we never asked if it was enough to kill her. Other than that he more or less said we should leave him alone. What news on your end?"

"We're a go for Mom and Christopher. Should we set a moratorium on any discussion of murder, in whatever form?"

"You mean, try to be normal? It's probably not worth it. Do you think they'll end up together, or just keep going along the way they are now?"

"You mean, will they want to get married? Or move into one or the other's home? I have no information on either front."

"Would it be rude to ask? Or should I leave well enough alone?"

"I pick Door Number Two. They're adults, and they've earned the right to do what they want."

"Got it. Now, what about food?"

"Oh, that."

"Yes, that," Meg retorted. "Either we should get a large freezer so we can stock up for occasions like this, or I need to find a cookbook that combines random foods and conceals them in a tasty gravy."

"I don't think Christopher and Mom will complain no matter what we put in front of them," Seth told her.

"Too true. And I for one always appreciate any meal that someone else has cooked." Meg went to the freezer to rummage around. Too bad she couldn't use apples for everything, because that was all she had in ample supply. Apple soup, apple filets, apple burgers? She sighed, which she realized she was doing far too often these days.

She managed to cobble together something that seemed edible and smelled far better than it had any right to, and welcomed Christopher and Lydia shortly after six. They had decided to walk across the fields and through the orchard, despite the early darkness and rapidly cooling air.

Lydia hugged Meg when she walked in. "What a lovely night it is. So many stars, even this early. I swear I could smell a hint of spring in the air."

"I'm glad you could come, both of you. Hello, Christopher. There's no snow left, is there?" Meg asked.

"Not really, and it's easy to see the patches of it, even in the dark. Something smells awfully good."

"I'm glad to hear it. I have no idea what it is, but if I have to give it a name, it's got to include 'Surprise.'"

"Can I do anything to help?" Lydia asked.

"I guess you can set the table with me." Meg wondered if Lydia had already guessed that she and Seth had an ulterior motive in asking them over. "Come on into the kitchen. We'll let the men do man things."

"For shame, Meg—you know we can do anything they can do, only better and faster."

Meg grinned at her. "Yes, I think I've noticed that."

In the kitchen, Seth stepped in to find drinks for Christopher and himself, then discreetly disappeared, leaving Lydia and Meg alone. "So, what's up?" Lydia asked. "Murder or whatever's happening between Christopher and me?"

"I knew you'd see through me. It's Monica's death. What you two do is your own business, unless you want to share?" Meg quirked an eyebrow.

"Nothing noteworthy as of this moment. But Christopher's lease is up in a couple of months, which may precipitate some changes."

"In case you're wondering, Seth and I approve."

"I figured as much. So, Monica. What's the issue?"

"How much do you know?" Meg began cautiously.

"About what? How she died? She was poisoned, right? Look, Christopher explained what you talked about earlier this week, about the poison. He said you'd passed the information on to the lab, by way of Art Preston, and the lab reported it to the state police. So what's the problem now?"

"A couple of things actually, although they're related to that. Why don't I dish up, so we can all hear this?"

"I'll get the table set."

Five minutes later they were assembled around the dining room table, with candles glowing in the middle, and a bottle of wine to share. "And what is the price we must pay for this delightful meal?" Christopher asked.

"I'm sorry," Meg said. "We enjoy seeing you under any circumstances, but we've come up with some more questions since we talked to you on Tuesday. Please, go ahead and start eating—as long as talking about poisons doesn't spoil your appetite."

"Not to worry, my dear," Christopher said. "What seems to be the problem?"

"Apparently you already know that the state police know that Monica had colchicine in her system?"

"Yes, they talked to me briefly about that."

"Did they ask about Larry?"

"They did. I told you I would be honest with them."

"Of course. I wouldn't expect you to lie. Do they suspect him of having anything to do with all this?"

"That's something they would be unlikely to share with me, under any circumstances."

"Do you have any reason to believe that Larry would want to do harm to Monica—or anyone else, for that matter?"

"As I've already told you, he is a good young man. I

cannot see how he could possibly benefit from murdering anyone. Do you have doubts?"

"No, I don't. I trust your judgment, and based on what dealings I've had with Larry, I agree with your opinion of him," Meg told him.

"So where does the difficulty arise?"

"It's the presence of colchicine that runs through this whole mess."

"There's more?"

"I'm afraid so. I'll explain in a minute. The other issue is, where is Larry? I told the police that I didn't know, and they said that he wasn't answering his cell phone, which is the only way of contacting him that I have. I'm not sure they believed me. But technically it was correct. I did not know where Larry was staying. I did not mention I had seen him quite recently, so I knew he was still in town."

"And why would you be concealing his whereabouts?"

"I don't know. Detective Marcus is not my biggest fan, and I suppose he's just being thorough. I guess I'm afraid that if the state police bring him in for questioning, it might spook him. I need him here. Does that make me selfish? Christopher, do you know where he's living now?"

Christopher and Lydia exchanged a glance, but it was Lydia who answered. "In fact, we do."

"Mom! You've been harboring a potential suspect in a murder investigation?" Seth protested.

"Well, nobody has identified him as a suspect, exactly. The fact is, he's been staying at your house, Seth."

"What?"

"It was vacant, and he needed a place to stay. All quite innocent, until this other business came up."

"And you didn't tell the police? Even Art? Or me?"

"No, Seth, we did not. I know Art is a friend, but he's also an honest man and he would probably feel compelled to inform the state police. While they did talk to Christopher, they did not ask him where Larry might be, and Christopher did not volunteer that information."

"Why on earth are you protecting him?" Seth demanded.

Christopher responded, "Because he is a vulnerable young man who has few allies around here, and who is socially inept. I was concerned that the police would take advantage of that."

"Does he actually have any colchicine?" Meg asked suddenly.

Christopher sighed. "I'm afraid he does. Or did. He retained a small quantity following his university experiments, and he meant to speak to you about doing some additional research with some of your trees—not without your permission, of course. He left it in your barn, along with some of his other possessions."

Meg shut her eyes. "So you're telling me that you two have been harboring a potential suspect on Seth's property without telling him, and said suspect has concealed a potentially dangerous chemical on my property, without my knowledge?"

Meg turned to Seth, who after a few seconds started laughing. "If I had to guess, I'd say these two were trying to protect *us*," he said. "This way we could answer in all honesty that we don't know where Larry is and we don't have any of that particular poison. You know you're not a very good liar, Meg."

"Precisely," Christopher said, beaming.

Meg was surprised to find she was angry. "I appreciate your thought, but I'm an adult, and I'd prefer to make my own decisions about what I say or don't say. I'll let Seth speak for himself," she ended stiffly.

Seth had stopped laughing. "I'm afraid I agree with Meg. I'm not saying we would run to the police and tell them everything, but I'd rather make that choice myself. I hope that doesn't offend you. I know you meant well."

"No offense taken, my boy," Christopher said, his tone contrite. "We're only trying to help the people we care about."

Meg sighed—again. "I understand." She stopped to consider, then decided she'd better get the whole story out in the open. "I said earlier that there was more to the story, and I think you need to hear it."

"And what would that be, my dear?" Christopher asked.

Meg stood up. "I think we need dessert for this."

25

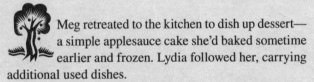Meg retreated to the kitchen to dish up dessert—a simple applesauce cake she'd baked sometime earlier and frozen. Lydia followed her, carrying additional used dishes.

"I'm sorry we didn't let you know," Lydia began.

"Don't apologize, Lydia. I know you were trying to help. This is such a mess!"

"Murder isn't supposed to be neat and tidy."

"I know, but right now I'd give a lot for an axe covered with the victim's blood, stuck under the killer's bed, and covered with his fingerprints. All we have now is a whole bunch of maybes."

"There was no blood, if you recall. Can you hand it all over to the police?" Lydia asked.

Meg set about slicing the cake, although in her current mood she felt like stabbing the blasted thing instead. "That would be the sensible thing to do, wouldn't it?" she said bitterly. "Dump it all in Art's lap, and he can take it to the state police and leave us out of it."

"Then why don't you?" Lydia said gently.

Meg pulled plates out of a cupboard, set them on the counter, and turned to face Lydia. "Because I know how the police work. Not that I'm saying they're incompetent or they take shortcuts. I do respect them. But I've been on the wrong end of one of their investigations, remember? They go for the easiest solution first. And that's understandable. What's the silly saying? 'When you hear hoof beats, you don't look for zebras'? Why should the police look at anything other than the most linear, direct solution?"

"Which is what in this case?"

"I'm thinking Larry is the obvious first choice. He has a demonstrated knowledge of colchicine. Plus he's an outsider, not from Granford, with a sketchy background. That's two strikes."

"But why would Larry kill anyone in Granford?" Lydia asked.

"That's a minor sticking point. I'm just afraid that if the police get hold of Larry, they'll stop looking any further. But my opinion is suspect because I'm his employer, which makes me guilty by association, and I want to keep him out of jail because I need him to work for me, which gives me a motive to cover for him. And I'll admit it—my gut feeling about his innocence is not exactly evidence. I have no right to judge—that's for the courts."

Lydia was looking increasingly distressed. "Meg, what can I tell you?"

"Sorry, Lydia—I don't mean to put you in a tough spot.

I hate it that somehow I've dragged you and Christopher into this."

"Christopher was already in the middle of it, as Larry's advisor. And like you, I can act as I choose. It was my idea to conceal Larry's presence, although Christopher backed me up on it."

"So how do we fix this?" Meg asked, hating that she sounded whiny.

"Without digging yourself in deeper?" Lydia countered.

"If possible. We've already sucked Art into it. I hate to keep doing that, because he has to work with the state police in his job, and we're just making life more difficult for him."

"That *is* his job—he knows Granford. Detective Marcus should welcome his input when he's faced with a crime in Granford."

"True. All right, how about this? I feel bad because we're putting Art in a position where he has to lie to the detective, or at least conceal information."

"You mean, by not telling the detective where he's getting his information—that is, you two? You think Detective Marcus is stupid? He must know. But he can't admit that he's getting tips from a couple of amateurs, so he has to at least pretend to get the details from Art."

Meg stared at Lydia. "You know, you're making an awful lot of sense. I hadn't looked at it that way. You want to explain that to Art?"

"He's not dumb, either. Meg, you said there was something else that you need to tell us. Is that part of this whole mess?"

"It is. Let's take the dessert in and I'll explain."

Meg and Lydia ferried dessert to the table, and Meg

sent Seth back to the kitchen to make coffee. "Do we need to wait for Seth?" Lydia asked anxiously.

"No, he's heard all this before. He makes a good sounding board. The reason I think you need to hear what I'm going to tell you is because I think it points away from Larry. Christopher, what do you know about non-agricultural applications for colchicine?"

"I'm not sure I am aware there are any. I know that what Larry and others have purchased come with warnings about the hazards of using it because of its potential toxicity. You're saying there are beneficial uses?"

"I am. Some doctors prescribe it for pain relief, as well as other rather specific ailments. Like gout. I've read that it is virtually the only medication that treats gout effectively. That's why it remains available to the public."

"You mean, in pill form?" Lydia asked.

"Yes, and liquid. Suffice it to say, it's out there. And Ginny Morris gave me a package of it, told me it would be good for my aches and pains, if the standard OTC pain relievers didn't work. She orders it in bulk, online."

Lydia understood quickly. "So you made the assumption that if Ginny was handing it out like that, she may have done the same thing with Monica. With no evil intent."

"Exactly. But almost anyone else could have obtained it, too. The tricky part is getting Monica to consume it."

Seth slipped into the room quietly and distributed coffee, then sat down.

"Have you informed the authorities?" Christopher asked.

"I told Art," Meg said. "It's up to him what he does with this information."

"Did you tell us his friend works at the lab where the testing is done?" Christopher pressed.

"Yes, they're the ones who found the colchicine in her body. And then told the state police, which the lab felt they had to do."

"Ah. Would it then be possible to determine chemically whether Ginny's pills match what was found in Monica's body?"

"In theory, I guess," Meg told Christopher. "But I'm not sure Art can call in any more favors, and I don't know if the state police would think to check."

"What if there's only one basic formula? Or the differences are so subtle that only some super-secret lab can figure it out?" Lydia shot back.

"I have no idea, Lydia. What if we come at it from the other side?" Meg said. "Find out how many other people in town have colchicine?"

"You think the police aren't doing that already? They should have found the pills that Monica had—if she had any. That's still an assumption," Seth pointed out. "At least they should have checked for prescriptions, wherever she kept them."

"True," Meg admitted. "They wouldn't tell *us* whatever they found. They'd probably tell Art. But would they interview everyone in town and search their homes? That sounds like a lot of work. But back this up a sec. Here we are sitting on a piece of information they may or may not have—Ginny's stash of pills. Of which I now have a sample, which, if the police find out, could get me into trouble. And we don't know if the police found any at Monica's place. She might have taken them all and destroyed the package. She might have hidden it so well that the police couldn't find it, at least not on a first pass."

"You're thinking that Monica might have killed herself?" Lydia said carefully. "With the pills that Ginny gave her?"

"Maybe. If in fact Ginny did give her pills, and then Monica went home and read the label and the warning about high dosages, and took an easy way out."

"Leaving poor Douglas to cope? That seems so cruel," Lydia said.

"I know," Meg said. "But how do we know what really goes on in people's minds? None of us knew Monica well. We don't know how long Douglas has been sick, or what his prognosis is going forward. Maybe she just couldn't deal with it. I mean, here she was, in an unfamiliar town, with no family or support network anywhere nearby. She was trying desperately hard to fit in and make friends, to make herself useful, but that's not easy on top of everything else she was facing. I'm not condoning it if that's what happened, but I can understand it."

Lydia smiled sadly. "I think you're right. But what can we do?"

"That's what I can't figure out. All I know is that I don't want anyone to suffer under suspicion—I've tried it, and I didn't like it."

"If I may interrupt," Christopher said, "you—*we*—need to know what, if anything, the police have found at Ginny's and Douglas's homes, and I'll assume the state police won't share that information. Which means you have to drag poor Art into it again. They owe it to him to keep him up to speed since this death occurred in his town. Or if not, he can get that information for you from his friend."

"I think you're right."

"And I agree," Seth said. "But can we wait until morning? Give the poor guy a break?"

"Of course. There's little to be gained by telling him now."

"Actually, I'm more worried about his wife. We're not high on her friends list right now."

"So what have we decided?" Meg asked. "Art knows about the pills. Now we want him to find out how many it would have taken to kill Monica? And which variety of the chemical it might have been? And also find out whether Art has given the information to the state police."

"I think that sums it up," Seth said firmly. "Now, can we enjoy dessert?"

The talk around the table turned away from murder and mayhem to more pleasant items, and the rest of the evening passed quickly. It was close to ten when Christopher pushed back his chair and stretched. "Much as I enjoy such delightful company, I should escort this lovely lady home."

"You want a ride?" Seth volunteered.

Christopher glanced at Lydia, then shook his head. "I think we'd rather walk. It's not far, as you well know."

Seth looked briefly at Meg. "Give our regards to Larry, then. I think it's better that he knows that we know, if you know what I mean. Any more lies and evasions and we'll never sort this out. But you can keep him under wraps for now."

"I concur," Christopher said, then drained his coffee. He got up to collect his coat and Lydia's, then helped Lydia put hers on. "Thank you for an . . . interesting evening. We'll be sure to share any new information we might come across, and I hope you'll do the same."

"We will. We're on the same side, you know."

Meg and Seth stood in the doorway and watched as Christopher's flashlight bobbed up the hill, then disappeared over the crest. Then Meg went to retrieve the dessert dishes and washed them while Seth took Max out for one last ramble. He was back in five minutes, just as Meg was washing down the countertops. "So you and Mom took care of everything?"

"No. Mainly we decided that you and I need to talk to Art again."

Seth groaned. "He won't be happy."

"I know, but this is a murder. Hard to believe that Monica's death was less than a week ago."

"It is. Remind me why we need to see Art?"

"So we can find out if the state police have told him if they've searched Ginny's and Monica's homes, and what they've found."

"Because they won't tell us," Seth said flatly.

"Exactly. They may not even have told Art, although they should. Lydia thinks Marcus must know that Art is a conduit to and from us."

"That doesn't sound very flattering to Art."

"I don't mean to put him down. He's certainly capable of thinking for himself, and he knows this town well. It's just that sometimes you and I seem to think outside the box. Now and then that produces some good ideas."

"Tomorrow is time enough to bother him?"

"I'm pretty sure it is. You have some ideas for the rest of the evening?"

"What's left of it. Turn out the lights, and let's go upstairs."

26

Over coffee the next morning Meg asked, "Whose turn is it to call Art?"

"Seriously?" Seth asked.

"Why, you don't think we should talk to him, after sleeping on it?"

"No," he said reluctantly, "we need to talk to him. But his patience is wearing thin."

"Blame the killer, not me. We give him any new information we get, and he can decide what to do with it. I'm not claiming we do things faster or better than any of the police involved, but we might be better at putting unrelated pieces together to get a full picture, and we know Granford. You don't think we're just meddling, do you?"

"I guess not. My turn, I suppose. But when his wife whacks him over the head with a shovel, I'll point to you as the cause."

He finished his coffee, picked up his phone, and went out the back door, followed by Max once again. Meg refilled her cup and eyed Lolly, dozing on top of the refrigerator. "You get off easy, you know that? Your whole life is made up of eating, sleeping, and keeping warm, with an occasional mouse chase. I want your life, at least for a while." Lolly ignored her.

Seth came back ten minutes later. "He's on his way."

Fifteen minutes later Art's car pulled into the driveway. As he came in the back door he said, "Much more of this and I'll block your calls."

"I apologize, Art," Meg was quick to say. "But you know we don't bother you frivolously."

"Yeah, yeah, I know. Is there more coffee?"

"Always." Meg filled a cup and passed it to him, then she sat down again at the table.

"Okay, what's so important?"

"We keep coming back to the colchicine," Seth told him.

"Yeah. So?"

"There seems to be an awful lot of it around in Granford," Seth added.

"What's a lot?"

"Larry's a minor expert, sort of. Ginny's handing it out like candy. Before you get hot and bothered, we all know that it's legally obtained over the counter, for a variety of illnesses and complaints."

"Yes, I know that. What have you got that's new?"

"You told us that the lab confirmed that there was colchicine in Monica's body and that's what killed her. But how big was the dose she took? Did your pal tell you? Or did Marcus?"

Art shook his head, but then he said, "You two sure do

know the right questions to ask. The lab says there was enough of that stuff in her blood to kill a horse."

"What?" Meg said, incredulous. "I thought it acted pretty fast."

"Well, that kind of depends on who's taking it. It can act in hours, or it can drag on. We went over this, remember? The vomiting and so on comes on early, but then the victim might feel better for a while—until his or her kidneys shut down. Unpredictable stuff."

"Wow," Meg said. "So we know Monica was all right through the afternoon of the fair—goodness, was that really only a week ago? She got sick, with those first symptoms, that night and went to the hospital, and then she died the following day. Is that fast for that drug?"

"Yeah, relatively," Art said. "But she had a pretty big dose in her."

"When would she have taken it?" Seth asked.

"Probably no later than a few hours before she got really sick," Art told him. "I'm told it could be as little as two hours, although usually it's longer. The fair shut down at three, right? It would be getting dark soon, and we wanted to give people time to break down their booths and such, and pack up, so most people were still there until about four. I don't recall if she hung around for that, but I would have expected her to stay on for a bit to enjoy what she had accomplished, so say she was home by five. It's possible she took the stuff before she left the fair or after she got home. She called an ambulance around eleven that night."

"*She* called? Not her husband?" Seth asked.

"Yup. Her husband seemed kind of out of it. He doesn't drive anymore, but the EMTs let him ride along to the hospital with his wife."

Meg tried to work out the timeline. "So, she could have eaten or drunk something at the fair, toward the end. Or she could have purchased something for later and taken it home with her. Douglas didn't ever show any symptoms, right?"

"Nope, he was fine. What're you getting at?"

"I'm trying to figure out when that happened. If Ginny happened to give her some of her pills, she might have taken them after she got home—she must have been exhausted by then, and Ginny would have told her they were good for aches and pains. Then she started feeling bad, and it kept getting worse, and finally she called for the ambulance. Does that fit so far?"

"Yeah. But there's one thing you need to know: there was more than one package of colchicine tablets in her house."

Meg was stunned, and it was several seconds before she could speak. "Okay, let me get this straight. There were two *different* packages of colchicine in her house?"

"Yup," Art said, then waited.

"Was one from Ginny? Wait—did Marcus and his minions talk to Ginny?"

"Of course they did."

"But you didn't even know the whole story until yesterday!" Meg protested.

"I talked to Marcus. He followed up and got back to me. Ginny says she orders the stuff in bulk. All nice and legal. She says she gave Monica a full package, back when she stopped by a week or two before she died. Monica thanked her and took them home with her. One of the packages at her house is the same brand as Ginny's. That box has Ginny's fingerprints on it. The logical assumption is that the other package was Monica's, but she didn't mention to Ginny that she was already taking colchicine. Or so Ginny says."

"Okay." Meg was beginning to wonder if they were playing a game like Twenty Questions, and she had to choose the right questions to ask. When would Art get fed up and cut her off? "How many tablets were missing from the box Ginny gave her?"

"Maybe six or eight? It wasn't full, but it wasn't empty, either. And before you ask, we can't say when she might have taken those. Could have been over several days, or could have been all at once."

"And the second box?" Seth asked.

"Different brand, same dosage. Also partially used. Her fingerprints were on the other box."

"Were the boxes found in different parts of the house?" Meg asked.

"One in the bathroom, one in a cabinet in the kitchen. The kitchen box was the one Ginny gave her."

"Hidden or in plain sight?"

"Not hidden, but not just lying around, either. Next question? Come on, you two—this is almost fun, but Monica is dead and we want answers."

Meg thought hard. "Say she had consumed all the missing tablets at once. Would that have been enough to kill her?"

"Nope," Art said triumphantly. "As she had way more in her bloodstream than that many pills would account for."

"That doesn't make sense . . ." Meg said to no one in particular. "Was there an empty package in the trash somewhere?"

"No. Not unless you came across one with your clean-up and brought it home with you."

"If I'd found an empty package when I was there—which I didn't—I would have tossed it in the trash," Meg replied tartly. "I wouldn't have known what it was. Was the trash still there in the house?"

"Yes. Douglas is not exactly into housecleaning, as you may have noticed. The trash was still in the kitchen. The state police took it with them."

"And they didn't find any trace of another box?"

"Nope. Now you want three boxes?"

"Well, you did say that the amount missing from the boxes the state police *did* find was still less than what was found in Monica."

"You want to take a shot at stating the obvious conclusions?" Art challenged.

"Absent another box, we can rule out suicide, right?" Seth said. "She hadn't taken enough of the stuff in the house."

"I think we can," Art said, "although that's not conclusive. Still, she could have taken every pill she could lay her hands on and hidden the evidence. Burned it, buried it, whatever."

"Then why some of the boxes but not all? Oh—maybe she didn't want it to look like suicide," Meg offered. "Do we know anything about her will, or any insurance policies? Maybe there was a clause that nullified the insurance if she died by her own hand, and she was worried about what her husband would live on if he didn't get any insurance."

"The state police are looking into that, as well as the Whitmans' finances. Doug's no help." Art looked at each of them in turn. "Come on, guys, there are more possibilities."

"You've had time to think about this, haven't you?" Seth protested. "You just threw this at us. Okay, say it wasn't suicide. No sign that Ginny slipped her something? I mean, was the original packaging tampered with?"

"Not that I know of, but the state guys might not have told me. I assume they're looking into that. Still, those packages are hard to mess with deliberately. It probably would have been obvious if somebody had switched pills. You suggesting that Ginny might have given Monica a bigger dose than she could handle? If so, why?"

"It does seem unlikely," Meg said cautiously. "Okay, I know Ginny had means and opportunity, but she had no reason to kill someone she barely knew. What threat could Monica have been to her?"

"Maybe Monica dropped by and caught Ginny spraying pesticides on everything," Art suggested. "Could Monica have been blackmailing her?"

"Wrong time of year for spraying," Meg said absently. "From what little I know about Ginny, I think she is a true believer in organic farming. She's worked hard to bring the orchard back, and she's proud of what she's done."

"But her farm was struggling, and she had a family to feed," Art pointed out. "Maybe she strayed."

Seth seemed to be getting impatient. "Fine, keep Ginny on the possibles list. Who else have we got?"

Meg said slowly, "Let's say there was nothing out of the ordinary about the pills Monica had at home—she already knew about them and was taking them anyway, for the same reason Ginny was—basic aches and pains. She accepted Ginny's pills just to be polite. Could someone at the fair have slipped some others to her?"

Art shook his head. "Seriously, a third source for the

pills? You're thinking of a homicidal joker? Unlikely. Nobody else got sick. It would have been hard to give Monica something she'd be sure to consume. And the timing's wrong. Odds are if she ate or drank something at the fair earlier in the day, she would have gotten sicker faster."

"So who's left?" Seth asked. "We're running out of suspects. What are the state police thinking?"

Art shook his head. "You and I have talked about them wanting to arrest someone, anyone, for this, and even if that wasn't true at the beginning, it's true now. It's been a week since Monica died. They're not happy campers. They've even asked me if I might have some insights, but I can't offer them anything new, so now they're mad at me, too."

"Are they going to put this on the shelf, or are they going to haul someone in, just so they look like they're doing something?" Seth demanded.

"I can't speak for them," Art said, "but if I had to guess, I'd say Ginny is the obvious target. They'll look harder at her."

Meg got up and started pacing around the room. "But that's ridiculous! Ginny had no reason to harm Monica! She gave her the pills because she wanted to help. She'd taken them herself, and she must have believed they were safe."

"I agree, Meg," Art said. "But the truth is, *somebody* killed Monica. And it's our job to figure out who. By 'our' I mean the state and local police—not you two."

"I know, I know," Meg said. "And I don't have any better ideas. It's hard to meddle when you have no idea what you're looking for."

"Don't beat yourself up, Meg," Art told her. "It's a small town, which means there aren't a whole lot of suspects."

"Tell me about it. So what happens now, Art?"

Art shrugged. "I really can't say, and I'm not just blowing smoke. I'd guess they'll question Ginny again, but I doubt they'll find anything, or not enough to hold her. And then the well runs dry, as far as suspects go." Art stood up. "Guys, it's Saturday, and my wife has a to-do list as long as my arm. I have nothing more to share with you. And I hope you'll tell me if you find anything new." He headed for the door and pulled on his coat, but before he left he turned to Seth. "Oh, by the way—you wouldn't happen to know where Larry is now, would you?"

"I think I can safely say he hasn't left town," Seth said with a straight face.

Art nodded once. "That's what I figured. Next time you call, you'd better have something solid for me."

"Thanks for coming, Art," Meg said.

After he'd left and they shut the door, Meg said, "I hate this."

"Which part?" Seth asked.

"All of it. Monica shouldn't have died. I don't want anyone in town to have killed her. Why are we in the middle of the whole mess—again?"

"Karma," Seth said.

"I don't believe in karma. Or maybe I mean I refuse to accept that I have lousy karma, despite the evidence. This is ridiculous, and it's made worse because I don't have any real work to keep me busy and distract me, so I can't stop thinking about it. Maybe we should get together with Larry again, and you two can talk some more about the tiny house idea? I'll be happy to help with the construction. I can use a hammer and a drill, but I don't like power saws."

"You want to talk with Larry about something that isn't

the murder? Or you think he might have something to contribute?"

"I don't care which. You think it's a bad idea?"

"No, not really. Should we smuggle him in after dark, wrapped in a burlap sack or something?"

"I don't think that's really necessary. Just call your mom and tell her to send him over, say around seven?"

"Whatever you say. At the risk of invoking your wrath, may I point out that we have even less food than we had last night?"

"Hey, I'm getting into this improvising thing. How about frozen ham with maraschino cherries and peanuts?"

"I'll go look for my antacids."

"Chicken!"

Meg had improvised a pasta dish with ham but minus the cherries and peanuts when Larry rapped tentatively at the back door. Meg let him in quickly. "Hi, Larry. Good to see you again."

"You mean, good that I'm not in jail? Or that I haven't left the county?"

Meg faced him squarely. "Larry, I have never believed that you did anything wrong. Did you ever even meet Monica?"

"No. Never even saw the woman. But I guess you didn't find the colchicine I left in the barn?"

Meg stared at him, then burst out laughing. "No, I did not. Thank heavens the state police didn't decide to search the barn, or they might have arrested me. Is it gone now?"

Larry nodded. "And nobody's going to find it."

"Good," Meg said firmly. "I didn't have anything

against Monica, so I have no motive, but I can't find anyone who *did* have a motive. You know, this poisoning business is almost a comedy of errors, except that the poor woman is dead. A week ago I'd never heard of colchicine, and now it keeps popping up all over town. Ginny Morris even gave some to *me*. Is that ridiculous or what? Sit down, will you? You want something to drink? Wine, beer, coffee?"

"Coffee's good. I'm not really much of a drinker."

"Is there anything I should know about colchicine that I don't already? Have you ever heard of any accidental overdoses? Did you have to take special precautions when you were using it?" Meg asked as she put the kettle on to boil.

"I was always careful when I used it," Larry said. "For farm research applications, we used to buy it in powder form and mix it to the right concentration. We didn't keep it anywhere near food that we were going to eat. I read somewhere that for medical purposes, sometimes it's measured out by grains, not even spoonfuls."

"What about tablets or capsules?" Meg added coffee grounds to her pot, then poured water over them.

"I'm pretty sure they're mixed with other stuff, although I haven't seen them myself. I've heard they were used to treat some specific conditions, but I don't know what." He flashed a brief smile. "If you want to see something funny, you should read the questions that marijuana growers post online about how to use it to boost their crop. It's pretty clear they've been sampling their own product when they log on."

"I'll add that to my list of irrelevant information. Did you ever meet Ginny Morris and her husband?"

"Yeah, sure. I think I told you, Christopher sent me over

there to check out her farm, see what she was doing, back when I was still at the university. I think she'd just arrived then."

Meg felt a small chill. "She gave me the tour of her place earlier this week, after I saw you last. She had a lot of work to do to bring back that orchard. Going organic must have made it even more difficult for her."

"Yeah, but she's one of those people who's really into it, although maybe she didn't know how much work it would be. Did she tell you she'd had some important job in the city before she decided to move here? Both her and her husband. I'm not sure he's as into farming as she is."

"Because he has to do all the hard physical work?" Meg asked.

"No, I think they split that pretty evenly. Hey, if you can do it, so can Ginny Morris. You're about the same size, right? But I don't think he was cut out to be a country boy. You met him?"

"No. He wasn't home when I stopped by at their house." *Maybe it's time I talk to him.* "Hey, you want to track down Seth in his office and tell him dinner's ready? And you can talk about tiny houses."

"No problem." Larry loped out the back door into the dark, leaving Meg with the troubling thought that maybe everyone had overlooked Al Morris.

27

The three of them managed to spend a pleasant dinner without talking about crimes. Meg watched Larry covertly, and what she saw reinforced her original opinion: he wasn't hiding anything. She had no reason to suspect him of anything, despite his history with colchicine, and neither did anybody else. End of story. He and Seth seemed to be having fun tossing around ideas for building out the former chicken coop.

"I won't ask exactly where you've been staying," Seth said cautiously, "but assuming it's a house and not a cave in the woods, has that changed your thinking about what kind of space you'd like to live in?"

"Don't think so. I don't want to be responsible for a whole house. Like I think I told you. It's too much space for me, and I don't want a bunch of roommates. The tiny house thing sounds cool, and it's all that I'd need. But I don't want you to go ahead and build one just for me. If you want one for other people, or other uses, fine. I'd be happy to help out. At least until we get into the orchard season." He shot a quick glance at Meg.

"I know, I know," she said. "You tell me when we need to do something, and I'll be there. And you and Seth need to work out the details for the well pump installation."

"Got it." He looked down at his empty plate. "Hey, if I haven't said it already, I appreciate you trusting me. I mean, you don't know me from Adam, and I really could be a serial killer."

Seth let Meg answer him. "I trust Christopher's opinion, and he trusts you. That covers your professional skills *and* your character. I don't think you've killed anybody, deliberately or accidentally."

"So why've you been hiding me?" Larry asked, looking back and forth between Meg and Seth. "Or your family, at least?"

"Because we know the police can make mistakes," Seth said, avoiding the last question. "Not out of malice, but because they want to solve cases, particularly in a small town like this one, where it should be easy. Once you've been around us for a while, you'll understand why we feel the way we do."

"Yeah, I think Christopher might have said something like that. Thanks for the vote of confidence anyway. I appreciate it. Not too many people have ever believed in me."

Fighting tears—she must be more tired than she thought—Meg glanced at the clock. "Wow, it's almost ten. If you guys have any business to talk about for the house— houselet?—maybe you can go over it tomorrow?"

"No problem," Larry said. "I'll head back now, but to-morrow's good. Seth, that work for you?"

"Sure. I'm kind of wiped out, too. Seems that crime-solving is hard work. I'll give you a call in the morning. You will answer your phone, right?"

"Yeah, if I see it's you or Meg on caller ID."

Meg yawned. "You know, I think 'solving' is kind of overstating things. Maybe 'investigating' is more like it."

"Art would say 'snooping,'" Seth added. "And I don't want to guess what Marcus would say. Interfering? Meddling? Annoying him?"

"All of the above," Meg said, smiling. "Thanks for coming by, Larry. Safe home."

"I'll go partway with you," Seth volunteered. "Max needs walking again."

The two men left, along with Max, leaving Meg with the dirty dishes. She sighed and turned on the tap.

Meg had been asleep by the time Seth returned. In the morning she said, "You were gone for a long time. Did you and Larry hash out all the details for the house? Shoot, can we call it something else? Tiny house just sounds silly, even if that's what it is."

"Chicken coop?" Seth suggested.

"Sure, why not? That's what it was. Wouldn't you enjoy telling people, 'Sure, come visit—you can stay in the chicken coop'?"

"Might put off people who we want to keep out."

"There is that. So, what's on the calendar for today? Larry hasn't given me any chores yet. Maybe I should learn to make my own apple baskets. If someone else will cut the slats for them, that is. I can bend and nail them."

"I thought you were using plastic bins these days?" Seth countered.

"Yes, I am, for the harvest, anyway. They're sturdier and easier to haul around, and will probably last longer than the old wooden crates. But they kind of lack charm. I guess if I had new wooden baskets, they'd be for a more boutique market."

"Whatever you want. Breakfast?"

"If you're volunteering."

Seth had produced waffles with local maple syrup by the time Meg had showered and arrived in the kitchen. Lolly was sitting at one place at the table, washing her face with one paw, and Max was sitting beneath the table, hoping for scraps. It was a lovely domestic scene, and Meg was seized with a sudden surge of emotion. Her husband, her home. She could not have foreseen this when she had arrived two years earlier. If she'd followed through on her original plan—fix up the house and leave as fast as she could—where would she be now?

Seth set a plate of waffles in front of her and slid a pitcher of warm syrup toward her. He fixed one for himself then sat down next to her. "Sorry I bailed on the dishes last night."

"This goes a long way toward making up for it," Meg said with her mouth full. "Clean up after breakfast and we'll be even." She chewed pensively for a while. "So, Larry is absolutely definitely off the suspect list. Now what?"

"You don't plan to follow Art's suggestion and stay out of this?" Seth asked.

"He's right, I know. And I don't have any ideas for where to look next. I just hate to let it go and go on about my business. It feels wrong."

"Meg, you can't solve all the world's problems. Not even Granford's problems. I love you for caring, but you've got to step back."

"I know. I shall take up embroidery, or learn to play the piano. Oh, right, we don't have a piano."

"You want one?"

"No, not really. Although we have the space for one."

"Be nice if the kids could learn to play," Seth said carefully, concentrating on cutting a piece of waffle.

Meg went still. Kids. Something they hadn't talked about, not really, and now Seth had brought it up again, at least obliquely. He was great with kids—she'd watched him with his sister Rachel's family. And neither one of them was young, so that clock was ticking, at least for her. It wasn't that she didn't want kids, more that she didn't know *what* she wanted. She looked up from her own plate to find him watching her.

She managed a smile. "I hear you. But can I make a request? Can we put the idea on a shelf for a few months? We need time for just the two of us. I'm not saying no, but . . ." She stopped speaking, trying to gauge his expression. Disappointed? How much did this mean to him?

"Fair enough," he said, his tone neutral. "We can revisit this come summer. When you're ready." He turned back to his plate, ending the discussion, but leaving Meg feeling as though she'd hurt him somehow.

But now was not the time to push it. Quickly she changed the subject. "You know, I realized last night that I still don't know Ginny and her husband well. Would it be wrong of me to go over and offer some sympathy? I had the feeling that Ginny's been so wrapped up in her orchard that she really hasn't had time to make many friends around here. I think she could use one about now, if she really is a suspect. Do you think she knows she is?"

"Probably. You sure you don't just want to pick her brain about what she knows about colchicine?"

"Maybe twenty-five percent. Her kids came back before I could ask anything last time I was there. But since I've been in her shoes, and wrongly suspected, I know I would have appreciated that kind of support."

"She's already been here three years. You'd been here a month or two. Look how far you've come in two years."

"Are you trying to make a point? That she's been deliberately hiding out, avoiding the community?" Meg had to admit that Ginny could have made more effort, no matter how busy she was. The goodwill of the community would help her sell her apples.

Seth went on, "You've probably spent more time with Ginny than I have, even though you've known her for a shorter time. You don't need my blessing to go talk with the woman. It may be a good idea." He stood up, picking up her plate and his own. "I'll take care of the dishes now, and then Larry and I are getting together."

"Good." Meg got up and fled. What had just happened? Maybe she'd been stupid, not talking about something so important earlier in their relationship. Maybe she'd been avoiding the whole subject—but why? She'd had a happy childhood, albeit without siblings. She liked babies. She wasn't afraid of the physical side of childbirth—she was as strong and healthy as she had ever been. Had she been ducking the responsibility of having to raise a child or children? She'd spent two years learning to run an orchard, a skill set that was entirely foreign to her. Where was there time for raising a family?

Shut up, Meg, a voice inside her demanded. Seth had sent out the first feeler. She owed it to him to think it through and decide what she thought—no, *felt* about it. Having a baby was not necessarily a rational, reasoned decision. She had to *want* it, no matter how long the list of complications were. And the ball was in her court.

Upstairs, she pulled on clean jeans, a turtleneck, a knit sweater. She was uncomfortable with just dropping in on people, but that seemed to be a way of life in Granford. She knew Ginny should have some free time at the moment, although the kids would be home, since it was the weekend. Unless she'd left town for the duration of the investigation. Would the state police have allowed that? It didn't matter: she was going to go over and find out if Ginny was home.

Or was she trying to get away from the house—and Seth? No! She'd known this conversation was going to come sometime—she'd been in denial. Time to face it head-on.

She didn't see Seth downstairs and the dishes were done, so she figured he'd gone out to his office to wait for Larry and taken Max with him. She pulled on a coat and stuffed a hat and gloves into her pockets, then went out to her car.

The drive to the Morris farm didn't take long. Driving anywhere within the boundaries of Granford didn't take long, even though she lived at the southernmost edge. She had no trouble finding the place again, and pulled into the driveway. The battered pickup that Meg had seen at Gran's was there, but no other car. Still, she was there, so she might as well try the door. She turned off her engine and climbed up on the porch and knocked.

After a few moments she heard footsteps, and the door opened. She found she was facing Al, not Ginny. "Oh, hi. You're Al, right? I'm Meg Corey . . . Chapin. I've met Ginny a couple of times. Is she around?"

He didn't smile. "No. She took the kids to buy groceries. She should be back soon, if you want to wait." It wasn't exactly a warm and gracious welcome, but at least he'd asked.

"Sure, if you don't mind." She followed him in, shucking off her coat in the process, then tossing it on the back of a chair. "Ginny walked me around the farm the other day, and I'm sorry that we never got together sooner. But since we're in the same business, I know how busy she must be."

"Yeah, she is. We both are." The man still hadn't smiled.

"You've been here, what, three years now? Were you a farmer before you moved here?"

"Hell, no. I worked for a pharmaceutical company in Providence. Ginny was a lawyer. This place was *her* fantasy. Want some coffee? It's already made."

"Sure, thanks." She watched as he headed for the kitchen, returning a minute later with two heavy mugs.

He handed her one, then said, "Might as well sit down."

"Okay." Meg sat and considered her options. It was pretty clear that Al didn't want her here, and he was doing the bare minimum to maintain politeness. Although he could have ignored her knock on the door. What did he want?

He sat back in his shabby chair and stared at her for a couple of moments. "You here to talk about whether Ginny had something to do with that nosy woman's death?"

Well, there it was, on the table. "Actually, yes. But I don't think she was involved."

"You may be the only one in town who doesn't."

28

He had to be exaggerating, but Meg was getting fed up. "Al, do you want me to leave?"

Again the stare. "I guess not. Ginny would be pissed at me if I drove you off."

"You don't like people here? You don't like Granford? You don't like farming? What?"

"Yeah, most of that. Why are you here, snooping around?"

"Because I was suspected of murdering my ex-boyfriend when I first moved here, two years ago. He was found in my backyard, so I guess it was logical. But I didn't know a soul here, and people were all too happy to pin it on me because I was an outsider. Which is pretty much true of your family, even if you've been here longer than I have. I thought Ginny might like to have some support."

"And you don't think she killed Monica Whitman?"

"No, I don't. Do you?"

"No. But you got it right: I don't want to be here. I don't want to raise our kids here."

"So how did this all come about? Did you have family ties here?"

"Nope. You want the truth? I got fired. I might have screwed up some accounting, but nobody stopped to look very hard—they just canned me, after ten years with the company. We couldn't make it on Ginny's salary alone, not in a city. So my dear wife decided to make lemonade from our lemon crop and said getting fired was a great opportunity for us to try something else, make a real change in our lives. I'll admit I was pretty depressed by the whole thing, so I played along, and the next thing I knew she'd found this run-down orchard in East Nowhere and we were going to be farmers. Not just any old farmers, but organic farmers." The contempt in his voice was clear.

"And neither of you had any kind of agricultural background?"

"Hell, no. About all I knew was the roots were on the bottom and the leaves were on the top. But I didn't have the energy to argue with her. She was in love with this dump, and we sold our house and used what sorry proceeds we got out of it to buy it. We put a little away, but not enough. I'll admit this place was pretty cheap, but I've figured out why. We had to borrow money from her folks to pay the bills last year."

"Well, the orchard had been ignored for a long time— one of you should have realized it would take a little time to bring it back. Is she still in love with the place? Or with the whole idea?"

Al shrugged. "Beats me. At least we did better than break even with this past harvest, for the first time. But have I seen the light? No way. I don't much like the country. Or this house."

Meg's opinion of Al was sinking steadily. "Is that why neither of you has made an effort to make friends here? You figure you're just putting in time until Ginny wears herself out?"

"Maybe."

"You've told her how you feel?"

Al stood up and stalked into the kitchen, which still put him no more than ten feet away. "What the hell's the point? I can't offer her any other options. I don't even know if I can get a real job again, after what my old company did to me. We're stuck. What you see here is all we've got in the world. We can't go anywhere, even if we both wanted to."

My, this is going well, Meg thought to herself. "Look, Al, believe it or not, I understand. I got booted from my job, landed here in what you call East Nowhere because my mother thought it was a good idea, and then ended up with a body in the backyard. And then it got worse: I completely disrupted a town meeting and cost the town a major development project. I wasn't exactly anyone's best friend. If you want to have a mutual pity party, I'm your girl."

Al looked at her incredulously for a moment, then started laughing. "If you're trying to cheer me up, you're doing a lousy job. Why the hell are you still here?"

"I'm no Pollyanna, and it's not my job to make you feel better. But I know what it's like to be in Ginny's position, or something close to it. I wouldn't have made it through if I hadn't found some friends. I don't know Ginny well, but I like her. Problem is, the police who are investigating don't have a lot of suspects to choose from, and she's probably high on their list."

"Crap," Al said. "This just keeps getting better. What's next—a tornado? A plague of locusts?"

"Well, in the two years I've lived here we've had a blizzard, a drought, and an insect infestation that took out a lot of our trees. I think we're about due for an earthquake."

Al relaxed and came back to his chair. "Meg, I like you. Since we're being so open and honest and touchy-feely, tell me why the cops think Ginny could have killed Monica."

"This is off the record, Al. If those cops find out I've been sharing information, they might arrest me or ship me out of town. I'm not their favorite person. But here's the deal: Monica Whitman died from an overdose of colchicine." When Al started to speak, Meg held up one hand to stop him. "Your wife seems to have been handing out colchicine like candy, including to me. Now, I know it's legal, and I know she says she takes it all the time. The police know she gave some to Monica—they've got the box with Ginny's fingerprints on it. Then Monica died. I think you can see their logic."

"I don't believe this. All we've done is mind our own business, and now they think Ginny is a killer? That's ridiculous."

"Believe me, it happens." Meg took a deep breath. "You do know what colchicine is, right?"

"Yes. I was in pharmaceuticals, remember? My wife's been taking it for years, and I wouldn't have let her do that unless I'd checked it out."

"Did you ever tamper with the dosage? Swap out pills? Add something that shouldn't be there?"

Al stared at her. "Lady, you must be crazy. Say that to most people and they'd probably kill you and bury you in the backyard. We've got a handy swamp just beyond the driveway."

Yeah, not too bright, Meg. "My husband knows I'm here."

"I'd have to hide your car, too—that might be harder, what with Ginny expected home any minute now. Or maybe she's in on this and she'll help? We'll just tell the kids to watch television while we get rid of the evidence."

"At least I seem to have cheered you up, Al," Meg said, obscurely relieved.

"And I thank you. Look, Meg, I'm going to tell you something, and I guess I'll have to trust you that you don't tell Ginny. Yes, I did tamper with her pills."

"What? The stuff's poisonous!"

"I know that. But I didn't boost the dose, I cut it down. She's been using it for maybe two years now for pain relief, after she found that acetaminophen and ibuprofen didn't work."

"Is she addicted to it?" Meg asked.

"No, it's not addictive. I'm not proud to say this, but I was cutting back on what she was taking, without telling her, because I wanted her to feel like crap. I thought maybe she'd come to her senses and decide she just wasn't cut out for farmwork, and we could go back to our real lives some-where, and give our kids a normal childhood."

"How much did you cut back?"

"Half of what she was used to. I just swapped out the blister pack inside the box with a different one, and assured her it was just a packaging change when she opened a new one. If, as you say, the box that Monica got from her wasn't empty, any lab can test the dosage of those pills."

It made a weird kind of sense to Meg. Then she realized

the ramifications. "So you've just conveniently given yourself an alibi if the lab work confirms the dosage of the pills they took from Monica's house that came from Ginny."

"How so?"

"Monica died from a major overdose of the stuff. She didn't even finish the pills she had, or at least, there was no evidence of pills beyond the ones still in their packages. Unless she took a whole handful of your doctored pills, as well as a bunch of others, they couldn't have caused her overdose. Ergo, you and Ginny couldn't have killed her, unless Ginny had been stockpiling her pills for a long time and somehow force-fed them to Monica."

"Ah. Well, I'm happy to hear that, I guess. Are you going to tell Ginny?"

"I think you should tell her. Tell her how you feel about this whole package. You're not happy here. Is she?"

"She says she is, but she's stubborn. She wouldn't want to admit she made a mistake. She did it for me, you know— she thought we could get by with earning less money if we went back to the soil, or some such nonsense. I was depressed, and I let her talk me into it."

"And now?"

"I don't think it's working, financially—never mind the personal wear and tear on us. Maybe you can sit down with her and go over the books. Make some recommendations. Or tell her it's a lost cause."

"If it's her dream, I don't want to crush that. If she's willing, I'll look at the numbers—that was my area of expertise before I got myself into this. But I'm not going to lie to her. You're going to have to work this out together, sooner rather than later."

"I know," Al said. He cocked his head at her. "You sure

you belong in Granford? Because you seem a lot smarter than most of the yokels I've met around here."

"Gee, just when I was beginning to like you, Al, you go and say something stupid. You don't get out enough. You don't talk to people in Granford. You don't even know them. What right do you have to judge people here? You're no prize yourself. At least your wife has a plan, and she's worked hard to make it happen. You're just sitting here feeling smug and sorry for yourself. You owe it to her to at least try."

Al started applauding, slowly. "Nice speech."

Meg stood up. "I give up. It's too bad, because I like Ginny. I think we could be friends. But I'm not sure that's possible with you in the picture. Tell her I stopped by." She stalked out the door to her car. Al made no move to stop her. There was still no sign of Ginny.

Meg drove home, chewing over what Al had said. She didn't like him much. He'd been deliberately rude as well as sarcastic. In a way, she could sympathize. He'd had a decent job, and then he'd lost it, and that had started this whole avalanche. He'd implied that wasn't his fault, but Meg had no way of knowing. Maybe he was an embezzler or a drug addict or he'd groped female staff members. Now he was exiled to a pathetic orchard in the country against his will. And as a result he was sulking: he was letting his wife carry most of the burden, both physically and psychologically, because it was *her* dream, and definitely not his. How long had they been married? At least ten years, she guessed, based on the age of the kids she'd seen the other day. When had they stopped communicating? Why had Ginny made such an abrupt change? Hadn't Al said anything at the time? But maybe apathy was a symptom of his depression.

Did she believe what he'd told her about the dosage of the pills? Probably. He had the know-how to do it. He figured it couldn't hurt Ginny, although it might make her uncomfortable. He hadn't counted on her handing it out to other people, but even if he had known, he had probably assumed that the dose was low enough that it wouldn't hurt anyone else. And he'd probably know how much of a supply Ginny had, and how much had gone missing. Like the box she'd handed to Meg. The cops should have tested that by now. Or would they? They might just have said, okay, colchicine, check, without ever testing the pills themselves and checking dosages. She really didn't know how official labs worked and how thorough they were, or should be.

So now she knew that Al Morris had messed with Ginny's pills, and Ginny had given some to Monica, but the dosage had not been enough to cause Monica's death, or not by itself. Which left her right back where she had started, with one fewer potential suspect if she crossed off Al. Not worth calling Art about, much less Marcus: let them do their own legwork.

Seth was sitting at the kitchen table reading a magazine, a cup of coffee beside him. He looked up when she came in. "Good news or bad?"

"Both, I guess." She took off her coat and hung it up, then sat down across from Seth. Lolly appeared out of nowhere and jumped on her lap. "Quick summary: Ginny wasn't home. Al Morris admitted to doctoring the pills, but he said he *reduced* the dose because he wanted Ginny to feel bad so she'd give up her dream of running a farm, which he really doesn't like."

"You believe him?" Seth asked. "About the pills, I mean?"

"I do, more or less. He's depressed and sarcastic and contemptuous of the denizens of Granford—he called us yokels—but I don't think he'd lie about this. He had to know the police would be looking into all the pills and could figure it out easily enough if they tested them. He could have said nothing to me about any of it, but I think he told the truth. And I think their marriage sucks. They're not communicating, and they're pulling in different directions. I kind of read him the riot act about that. Very unlike me."

"What do you mean?"

"I told him he was screwing up. That he didn't have the right to complain if he'd never told Ginny what he really thought. And then he resorted to, what, reverse-poisoning her to get his way? Taking away a medication she chose rather than talking to her? That's low."

"That's a bad marriage," Seth said quietly.

"Yes, it is."

"I wish I could have seen you do it."

"Seth, if you ever think I'm shutting you out, or manipulating you, say something. Do something. I don't know where Ginny and Al went off the rails, and I'm not sure it can be fixed now. Let's not end up in that place."

"We won't. I promise."

29

"So, what now?" Meg asked.

"What do you mean?" Seth replied.

"We're out of suspects."

"Meg, that's not our responsibility."

"I know. But it doesn't seem right. Will there be any kind of memorial service for Monica in Granford?"

"I really don't know. The town assembly hasn't discussed it. Most people here didn't know her—she'd lived here only a short time. I'm afraid few people would attend."

"How sad. Has Art said anything else about her family? Would she be buried here? Cremated? Oh, and what's happening with Doug?"

"From what little I've heard, he seems to have recovered a bit since Monica's death."

"If it's Alzheimer's, it's going to get worse, isn't it? Can he function alone? Do you think he'll want to?"

"Why can't you ever ask me easy questions, Meg? As far as I know, yes, Alzheimer's is a progressive disease, although its course is unpredictable. But it goes only in one direction."

"Why do you think they moved here, if they knew Douglas was having problems that would only get worse?"

"Meg," Seth said patiently, "how can I answer that? I didn't know them. Nobody here really knew them, until Monica stepped up to suggest the WinterFare."

Meg refused to be derailed. "Maybe she thought that was her last chance to do something for herself, before her husband ate up more and more of her time. But as for coming here, maybe it was money—this place was cheaper than wherever they were before, and they may have been on a fixed income. Or maybe she wanted their friends from wherever they came from to remember Douglas the way he was, not the way he was headed. Is social services taking care of them?"

"I understand they are. They're evaluating Doug's condition, and they'll help sort out any in-home care, if that's appropriate. Or find a placement for him."

"And they'll figure out how he can pay for the care he doesn't even recognize he needs?"

"Meg," Seth said helplessly, "I don't know. We—by which I mean the town—can't be responsible for him. It's not our job."

"What if it was your mother?"

"Then I'd take care of her. You know that."

Meg summoned up a smile. "Yes, I do. And you'd take care of me. Heck, you'd take care of the whole town if you could, because that's who you are. I'm sorry—I don't know why this has got me so knotted up."

"Would it make you feel better if we went to see Doug?"

"Maybe. At least I'd feel that I was doing something."

"You haven't told Art about your conversation with Al, have you?"

"No, and I don't think I will. Let the lab do their stuff. Ginny and Al's personal problems are not police business, unless the two of them want to share. Can we go see Douglas now?"

"I guess. Maybe take him dinner?"

"Seth, as you keep reminding me, we don't have much food in the house. I can take him a cake from the freezer, which wouldn't involve him cooking or preparing anything. But maybe we should stop at the market on the way home before we starve?"

"It's a plan. You want to go now?"

"Yes. I can't seem to sit still, so I might as well put my energy to good use."

"I'll get our coats."

The ride to the Whitman house didn't take long. There was a car parked in the driveway at the rear of the house, but only the one. But at least the outside of the place looked tidy enough. Meg wondered if the inside had been tended to as well—she shuddered at the memory of the last time she'd seen it.

Seth parked in the driveway, and Meg got out and collected the carefully wrapped cake from the backseat. She led the way to the front door and rang the doorbell, wondering, as always, if they should have called first. She gave herself an excuse: she had a feeling that answering a phone and understanding who was calling and that they wanted to stop by might confuse Douglas. Seeing her face might make it easier for him to connect the dots. For almost a minute there was no sound from inside the house, but finally she heard shuffling, and then the click of locks. The door opened to reveal Douglas. Meg's first impression was that he looked better than he had on her first visit: his clothes were clean, his hair was combed, and he seemed to be alert.

"Hello? Can I help you?" he asked. Then his expression sharpened slightly. "Do I know you?" he asked, looking at Meg.

"Yes, you do. I'm Meg Corey. Chapin. I stopped by once before, after Monica . . ." Meg realized she didn't know how to finish that sentence.

"Monica isn't here anymore," Douglas said, as if by rote. "Would you like to come in?"

"If it's no trouble. I brought you a cake," Meg said, holding out her plate with the cake on it and feeling increasingly stupid.

"Oh, that's very nice of you. Please, come in. And who is this?" he asked, as if noticing Seth for the first time.

Seth stepped forward, closing the door behind him. "Mr. Whitman, I'm Seth Chapin, Meg's husband. She told me she'd met you, so I thought I'd come along and introduce myself. We live fairly close to you, on the other side of the highway."

"It's very nice to meet you, Mr., uh . . . Follow me to the kitchen—it's warmer there." Douglas turned and led the way without a backward glance. Meg felt a pang of anxiety: Did he let just everyone in like this, without question? Was that safe?

Thank goodness the kitchen looked cleaner than it had the last time she had seen it. There were a couple of plates with crumbs on them sitting next to the sink, but nothing like the moldy chaos she had cleaned up. But that sparsity led her to another worry: Was the man getting enough to eat? There was no sign of pots or pans, and she didn't think she had the right to search through his trash to see if he was surviving on microwave meals. "Where would you like me to put the cake?" Meg asked.

"Oh, anywhere is fine." Douglas waved a hand vaguely. "Unless you'd like to share a piece with me now?"

Whatever his mental state, he seemed to remember the social niceties, probably because he'd been repeating them most of his adult life. "We'd be delighted. Seth, why don't you unwrap it while I find some plates for us?"

As Seth peeled the wrapping off the cake, Meg started opening cupboards, looking for plates. Everything was surprisingly neat, and Meg guessed that social services had stepped up and sorted things for Douglas. That was good. She pulled out three plates and then began hunting for forks in the drawers, plus a knife to cut the cake with.

When they were finally settled around the table, with slices of cake in front of them, Meg asked herself whether it would be better to offer her condolences about Monica or ignore her death altogether. She was relieved when Douglas took the decision from her.

"Monica would be so pleased that people have been helpful to me. You are all so kind."

"We're your neighbors, Douglas," Seth said. "We help each other. I hope you'll let us know if there's anything we can do for you."

"How long were you and Monica married, Douglas?" Meg asked.

"Thirty-some years," he replied proudly. "We were very happy together."

"What brought you to Granford? Do you have family around here?"

"No, no, no family. We never had children, you see, although we would have liked to. We were both only children, but we had each other. We liked to see new places."

Meg noticed that he hadn't actually answered the question. "Where did you live before?"

"Many places, many places."

"This place used to be an active farm," Seth said. "Are you interested in farming?"

Douglas turned his attention to Seth, as if surprised at the question. "No, I don't think so. It was pretty, and quiet. Monica liked the house."

"She certainly made herself part of the community quickly," Meg commented.

"She did like to keep busy. When she could. She wasn't always up to it."

"Was she ill?" Meg asked. It seemed rude to probe about Monica's health, but Douglas seemed not to have any reservations about talking about it, and Meg hoped she might learn something useful. If it wasn't too late.

"Well, no, not ill, exactly. She had a condition, something she'd had since she was a child, and sometimes it flared up. Other times that didn't happen for a long time."

"She certainly seemed full of energy when I talked with her," Meg said.

"Oh, she was fine most of the time. She took good care of me. But I did a lot of the cooking. She'd give me a recipe, and I'd follow the instructions. We made a good team. She would make sure I took my pill, too. The thing was, sometimes she forgot to take her own medications, and I had to remind her. Those men took them away, after . . ."

"You mean the police?"

Douglas nodded. "Yes, the police. But she doesn't need them anymore, does she?"

"I don't think so, Doug," Meg said. "Do you remember what they were?"

"I don't know the name . . . The box was blue." He brightened suddenly. "But I have some here. I told you, sometimes she forgot to take them. When I reminded her she got angry at me, or sometimes she didn't listen. Now and then I had to slip them into her dinner when she wasn't looking. I knew that if she didn't take them, she'd feel really bad."

Meg suddenly felt cold. "Could you show us, Douglas?" she asked carefully.

He stood up. "Let me see if I can find them. I put them somewhere safe." He wandered out into the hall, shuffling along in his worn slippers.

Meg shot Seth a panicky glance. "Are you thinking what I'm thinking?" she asked in a low voice.

"I'm afraid so," Seth replied equally quietly. "And I think we can guess what those pills were."

Douglas came shuffling back, beaming. "Here they are! I told you I kept them safe. Monica always said it was very important to remember to take your medicine." He held out a box, and Meg recognized it immediately.

"Did she get these from her doctor?" Seth asked.

"Oh, yes, she did. She had a very good doctor. But we haven't found one around here yet. I was getting worried that we might run out of her pills, but I made sure she kept getting them." He leaned closer and whispered, "Sometimes I hid them in her food."

"Yes, Douglas, you told us that. You were looking out for her," Meg said sadly. "Would you like to finish your cake?"

Douglas looked down at his plate and seemed surprised to see half his piece of cake there. "Oh, yes, I would like that. It's very good cake. Did you make it?"

"Yes, I did. With apples from my own trees. You've probably driven by my orchard—it's not far from here." She turned to Seth. "Don't you have a phone call to make?"

He looked blankly at her for a moment, and then figured out what she meant. "Yes, I do. Douglas, would you excuse me for a moment? I promised I'd call someone. I'll be right back." He walked out of the kitchen into the front room, and Meg could hear his voice, although she couldn't make out any words.

"Do you take your medicine too, Doug?" Meg asked to distract him.

"Yes, I do. I have a chart, and Monica wants me to check off each time I take my pills, so she can keep track of them. I'm getting kind of low on some of them. I'll need some more soon. Will she be back soon?"

Meg wanted to cry. Whatever lucidity he'd shown only a few minutes earlier had faded, and now he was confused again. Poor, poor man. What was going to happen to him now?

Seth returned quickly, and gave Meg a brief nod before turning to Doug. "Douglas, I asked a friend of ours to join us. His name's Art, and he'll be here in a few minutes. I think you've met him before. Why don't we finish our cake and chat while we wait for him? Do you have any hobbies you enjoy?"

"Oh, yes, I do. I used to like wood carving, but my hands aren't as steady as they once were. Monica thinks I might enjoy painting, even bought me some paints and brushes, but I haven't really tried it yet. I like to cook, though. Do you think I could have the recipe for this cake? It's very good. Is it hard to make?"

"No, Douglas, not at all. I'd be happy to give it to you," Meg said, her heart aching.

And then a car pulled up outside, and Seth went out to greet Art and try to explain what had just happened while Meg calmly went on making conversation about nothing in particular. What had Douglas been like, before the Alzheimer's? Had he and Monica been happy together? Did he have any idea where he was now, and how he'd arrived at this place? And what he'd done to Monica, with the best of intentions? It was all just too sad, and still she smiled and soothed and pretended. And Douglas was happy, for a little longer at least.

A few minutes later Art came in, accompanied by a woman who Meg guessed was from one or another of the local social services agencies—Art must have had her on speed dial. "Seth explained," Art said briefly to Meg, who nodded.

Meg turned back to Doug. "Douglas, this is our friend Art. He wants to talk to you for a little while, if you don't mind."

"I'm glad of the company. Would you like a piece of cake, Art? Meg made it." He smiled at Art, his expression without guile.

Meg couldn't take it anymore. She stood up abruptly and fled to the front door. Outside, she took deep breaths of the cold air, then sank to the granite stoop and fought tears. Seth joined her and wrapped an arm around her, and she turned and buried her face in his coat. "That poor man. He has no idea what he did."

"And if he's lucky he never will."

"Art can find out who her doctor was, before they moved here, right? To confirm what he prescribed?"

"Yes. But does it matter? However much Douglas gave her was too much."

"I'd like to know. I wonder how long Douglas has been going downhill. Did moving to Granford make it worse?"

"I don't think we can know, Meg."

"What happens now?"

"We go home and let the authorities handle it."

"Then take me home."

30

"We need to find some food," Seth said after he'd driven a mile or two.

"Oh. Right. You going to cook? Because I don't really feel like it."

"Not a problem. You want to see if Gran's is open?"

"Hmm. Comfort food, no dishwashing. Worth a try. Is it already dinnertime?"

"Well, it's getting dark, and all we've eaten since breakfast is half a slice of cake. I think we can call it dinnertime."

"Nicky and Brian used to see Monica and Douglas in the restaurant, Nicky told me. That wasn't very long ago. Has he changed so much in a couple of months, or does this thing come and go?"

"I don't know. I've never been close to anyone who's had Alzheimer's or dementia or anything like it."

"Nothing in your family?" When Seth shook his head, she said, "Good genes."

Seth gave her a quick look. "What about your side?"

"Nothing hereditary or degenerative—not to be confused with degenerate. I think there were some shady uncles up the line. Will Art fill us in later?"

"Probably. I don't know if he'll need more detailed information from us, about what Douglas said. I gave him the bare outline about the medications. If he gets jammed up, it might be tomorrow. I don't know when he'll tell Marcus."

"That's okay. I don't have any plans for tomorrow. How are the chicken coop plans coming along?"

"I think we'll be starting on shoring up the foundation this week. Can you handle mortar?"

"Don't know, but I'm game to try."

They pulled into the parking lot at Gran's as the sun slid below the horizon. While there were few other cars in the parking lot, there were lights on inside, and the place looked welcoming. Seth got out of the car and waited for Meg to join him before they walked up the stairs. Inside there were in fact only a couple of other patrons, although it was still early. Nicky came out of the kitchen, drying her hands. "Hey, strangers! Seth, I haven't seen you since the fair, and we didn't get a chance to talk at all. You hungry? I haven't made a special for tonight, but there's plenty of nice hearty stuff, good for a cold night."

"Thanks, Nicky. We'll take whatever you've got," Meg replied gratefully. "We keep forgetting to shop, and I'm scraping the bottom of the freezer about now."

"Then you've come to the right place," Nicky told her. She paused a moment to study Meg's face. "You okay?"

"Yes, just sad. I'll fill you in over dinner, if you've got the time."

Nicky looked around the near-empty room and laughed. "I think my staff can handle the crowds. Sit down, and I'll bring you something to nibble on. Wine?"

"I'm driving," Seth said, "but I think Meg could enjoy a glass."

"I know what you like," Nicky said. "Be right back."

When she'd disappeared back into the kitchen, Meg asked Seth, "How much can we tell her?"

"If it was someone else, I'd say not much. But this is Nicky, and we know she's not a gossip. Plus I think it's unlikely that there will be any charges filed, under the circumstances, so this may all become public sooner rather than later."

"Good. I hate to have to choose my words carefully. I don't really want to think right now."

Nicky returned a few minutes later with a tray laden with warm bread, gooey cheeses, and various small and tasty-looking munchies, as well as a glass of pinot grigio for Meg. "I've got a great mushroom soup, and a country pâté recipe I've been experimenting with. Will that be enough for you? Or do you need some meat to chew on?"

"It sounds great, Nicky," Seth said. "Just keep this bread coming."

"Of course. I love baking bread in weather like this." Nicky dropped into a chair between them. "So, what's got you two so down in the mouth? Something wrong?"

"Not with us, no. It's about Monica's death," Seth said.

Nicky's smile disappeared. "You're going to tell me you two have figured out who killed her? Can you talk about it, or are you sworn to secrecy?"

Meg glanced at Seth, who nodded. "We decided it's okay to talk about it, even though the police haven't quite caught up with all the details, because *nobody* killed her. At least, not intentionally."

"Suicide?" Nicky raised one eyebrow.

"No, not that, either, exactly," Meg told her. "I don't think she would have done that to her husband. We just came from there, and we talked to Douglas. Here's what we believe happened." Meg proceeded to outline the conversations they'd had over the past couple of days, with Art, and with Ginny and Al, and finally with Doug, in that last sad talk.

"Wow, that is complicated. So you said Monica was already taking this colchicine stuff?"

"That's what Douglas told us."

"And Ginny gave her some more, but that wasn't the full dosage, according to her husband."

"Right. But Monica might have upped the dosage if she thought it wasn't working. She was really busy with the fair, and probably under a lot of stress."

"And Douglas was trying to keep on track with her meds and was slipping her extra when he thought she might have forgotten?"

"Exactly. Except his sense of time, or maybe I mean what's past and what's present, is kind of disjointed, so he probably ended up giving her more than she needed. If he didn't see her take her own, he might have believed he was helping her. If you add all this together, the result was an overdose."

"How awful," Nicky said, shaking her head. "I guess the only positive side is that Douglas may never realize what he did."

"True," Meg said. "You said they ate here now and then—what was your impression of him? Brian already told me his."

"He didn't speak much. Monica usually did all the talking, although she tried to include him in any conversation. You know, saying stuff like, 'Isn't that right, dear?' And he'd nod and smile. He was always pleasant. And he had a good appetite. They both did."

A waitress Meg didn't recognize came out and deposited bowls of soup in front of Meg and Seth, and added a new loaf of bread to the table, along with a plate of sliced pâté.

Nicky waited until she was gone, then said, "What happens now?"

"I'm guessing a lot of paperwork," Seth said as Meg dug into her soup. "Art or the state police will track down where the Whitmans came from, if they haven't already, and see if they can identify Monica's doctor, to confirm her medications and why she was taking them. She and her husband may have shared a doctor, or Douglas may have had a different one—he seems physically healthy. Of course we have no idea what their financial situation was. And I can't begin to guess who's going to look after Douglas now. We can't assume he can afford home health visits, and it would be better if someone was monitoring his mental health more closely on a day-to-day basis. Maybe a nursing home."

"Was he a veteran? There's also the VA hospital."

"Something else the police can investigate. I'm afraid it's out of our hands."

"That poor man," Nicky said. "And I'm sorry it landed in your lap."

Meg looked down to realize her bowl was empty, and

she was in fact feeling better. "So are we, believe me. I'm really looking forward to getting back to work in the orchard—something purely physical, and the worst thing I'll have to worry about is insects and the occasional disease. And pruning. And watering. And fertilizing. And picking. And supervising Larry. Have you met Larry?"

Nicky shook her head. "I don't think so. From what you've told me, he doesn't sound like a restaurant type."

"I'd agree with that, but I want to make sure he gets out now and then, makes some local friends. Maybe I'll tell him to deliver our apples to you, and you can chat with him. It's not good for any of us to hole up and avoid people. Has Seth told you that the two of them are going to convert what was once the chicken coop out back into a livable space?"

"Ooh, no. Tell me more," Nicky said, and the talk turned to other topics. Not much later, other patrons started to trickle in, and Nicky stood up. "I'd better get back to business. You want dessert? On the house."

"Sure," Seth answered for both of them.

"No apples, though," Meg added. "I'm just not in the mood."

"Don't worry—I've got a dynamite caramel pecan cheesecake."

When Nicky had left, Meg laid a hand on Seth's. "Thank you."

"For what?"

"Just being here. It's good to know that I can feel sad without having to hide it or make excuses."

"Why would you even think of doing that? You knew Monica. You liked her. It's a shame that she's dead, in such an odd and unnecessary way. I'd worry if you didn't feel sad." He hesitated before going on. "You know the John Donne poem? No man is an island?"

Meg stared at him, then started laughing. "I keep forgetting you went to Amherst and you're 'eddicated.' Yes, I do. What made you think of that?"

"There's a great line in it: 'Any man's death diminishes me, because I am involved in mankind.' I doubt that Donne was thinking of small-town New England, because this country barely existed when he was alive, but I think it applies to us here in Granford, on a smaller scale. Monica should not have died, but she did, and we've all lost something because we're all part of this community."

Meg had to swallow a lump in her throat before she could answer. "I love you, Seth Chapin."

And then the cheesecake arrived and the moment passed. Finally, stuffed to the gills, Seth said, "Ready to go?"

"Definitely. If I think about it, I'm exhausted. But I don't think we have anything to eat for breakfast."

"How about I cadge a loaf of that bread from Nicky? I think we could handle French toast in the morning. I seem to remember a couple of eggs."

"You are brilliant. Go for it."

It was past nine when they finally stumbled into their kitchen, drunk on fatigue rather than alcohol. Even coffee with the cheesecake hadn't helped. Max greeted them happily, tail wagging. "Poor dog," Meg said. "We keep getting held up somewhere else."

"I'll walk him. Why don't you go on upstairs?"

"Deal, but I won't promise to be awake when you get back."

31

Monday morning, Meg thought, without opening her eyes. *Start of a new week. Creeping up on spring and apple blossoms.* If she tried very hard, she could go back to sleep, or at least pull the covers over her head and pretend to sleep. She didn't want to think about the day before and its revelations. She certainly didn't want to talk to any official representatives of the law. She wanted to avoid being responsible for anything, especially those things that affected other people's lives.

It wasn't going to work. She felt Seth's weight settle on the bed, followed quickly by the scent of strong coffee. "No fair," she said. "You're bribing me to wake up."

"In a word, yes. Seems to be working."

"What time is it?" she asked.

"After eight. I promised you French toast, remember?"

"And we're all going to go out and play with the chicken coop. And no doubt our favorite police officers will descend upon us and complain about our interfering with their work."

"At ten," Seth replied.

Meg sat up. "Really? I didn't hear a phone."

"Cell phone. But I think Art and Marcus are coming together, so it's two-for-one."

"Oh joy. I guess I'd better grab a shower, then. You have my permission to start the French toast."

"Yes, ma'am." Seth disappeared quickly down the stairs, leaving the fragrant coffee behind. Did she have any clean clothes? She couldn't remember the last time she had done laundry. Well, the guys would have to take her as she was: Meg Chapin (if that was her new name), slightly grubby crime fighter. She didn't think anybody would pick up the movie option for that one, but the image it called up made her giggle.

Downstairs she and Seth were just sopping up the last of the maple syrup from their plates when Art's car pulled in, slightly ahead of ten o'clock. Seth let him in.

"I'm early, I know," he apologized as he walked in, "but I figured you might need backup."

"Who, us?" Meg said with mock innocence. "All we did was visit our neighbors and chat. It's not our fault that our kindly honest faces convince people to spill all their secrets as soon as we walk in."

"No time to call in the cops, eh? Is there any more of that coffee?" Art asked, sitting down and stifling a grin.

"Always," Seth said, and filled a mug for him.

"Seriously, are we in trouble?" Meg asked.

"No, I can't see why. You have a point, whether or not

you intended it. You're not a professional crime solver. You're nice people who happen to live in the neighborhood. Most people find it easier to talk to someone who isn't wearing a uniform and a badge."

"We didn't go looking for information from anyone, you know," Meg told him. "I really was being neighborly. Ginny's had a hard time lately, so I thought I'd go over and give her a little support, and I wanted to be sure that someone was looking after Doug, after what I saw last time. I was worried about him. That was all."

"And you just happened to find out how Monica Whitman died. I don't know whether you're blessed or cursed with this particular ability."

"I'd gladly hand it over to you if I could. How's Marcus taking it?"

"I kept both of you out of it as much as possible. I said you dropped in on Douglas and found him in a disturbed state, and immediately called me for help. He just happened to explain all the pill business when I walked in."

"That's close enough to the truth, Art," Seth said. "Did you talk with the Morrises?"

"Al and I took a walk through the orchard. Apparently he hasn't come clean to Ginny yet, but he told me about his pill swap. Since it looks like it did no harm, and the state police have the evidence in hand if they choose to look for it, I think I'll skip over that bit. It was Douglas's extra pills that pushed Monica over the top. Poor man. From what I've read, the dosage for that stuff can be tricky."

A state police car pulled in behind Art's car, and Detective William Marcus stepped out, smoothing his already-smooth suit. Seth was ready at the door to let him in. "Detective," he said gravely.

"Chapin," Marcus replied. "Meg. Art."

This conversation is getting off to a great start, Meg thought. "Would you like some coffee?"

"Please. This visit is only semiofficial. I want to make sure that the facts I have are accurate."

"Of course." Meg crossed the kitchen, filled another cup, and set it in front of him. "Everybody, sit down so we can get started." To her surprise, everyone sat. "Do you have any new information, Detective?"

"In fact, I do. We've found where the Whitmans lived prior to their arrival in Granford, and we've tracked down their medical records. Monica Whitman had suffered most of her life from something called Familial Mediterranean Fever. It's a hereditary disease that usually first appears in childhood among people of certain ethnic origins. But it can strike almost anyone, as in this case. Its primary symptoms are joint pains, intermittent fevers, that kind of thing. But it can wax and wane, and sometimes go into remission for long periods. One of the primary treatments is oral or injectable colchicine, which Monica took regularly."

"What about her husband?"

"He was diagnosed with early-onset Alzheimer's in his late fifties. He took early retirement for medical reasons, after the first couple of years."

"Why did they choose Granford?"

"We may never know. As you've no doubt discovered, they had no family here, no personal connections. Maybe they simply wanted to start over, where no one knew them. Maybe Monica thought it would be good for Doug, which didn't prove to be the case."

"Were they all right financially?"

"Yes. He had his pension and medical insurance, and

they'd both inherited nice amounts from relatives, since neither had any siblings. They sold their prior house at a good profit. I don't think you'll find any financial motive in Monica's death. Their wills were up to date—we found them in the house—with provision for the appointment of an administrator if Monica should pass away first. I believe she had no illusions about his capabilities and the likely course of his illness."

"So the WinterFare was her last public effort?" Art asked.

"Most likely. From what limited personal information my staff has collected, she used to be active in various clubs and organizations. She cut back as Douglas's condition worsened." Marcus turned to Meg. "I'd like to hear the details of the confusion with the pills."

Meg debated briefly about playing dumb, but she was the one who'd uncovered it and she felt responsible. "Douglas was telling me about how Monica made him check off on a chart each time he took his own medications. You'll probably find the chart at the house, if you haven't already. He also happened to do a lot of the cooking—apparently he was still comfortable following recipes. He remembered that Monica also took medication, because she'd had this condition as long as he'd known her, and he was concerned that she might forget. So he started adding her own colchicine prescription to her food, although he must have been careful not to put any in his. I'm afraid he didn't remember how often or how much he added, and in the end he put in too much. He showed us his hidden stash of the pills—they weren't with Monica's supply." And that was all she actually knew.

"Yes, Art turned them over to me. No doubt his fingerprints will be on the package."

"Did your lab figure out how much Monica would have taken?"

"They did. It was pharmaceutical grade, mixed with whatever binders are used to form the pills. You can tell Larry that he's in the clear—it's not the kind of chemical he used."

Seth spoke up quickly. "I'll be sure to let him know."

"Will there be any charges filed against anyone?" Meg asked.

"I think not. There is little to be gained from prosecuting Douglas Whitman. He might not remember any of what he said in a few weeks or months."

"What will happen to him?"

"The social services people will look out for him. He can afford decent care, so there should be no problem." Detective Marcus drained his coffee cup and stood up. "I think that's all the questions I have. I'm glad this was cleared up so quickly."

Meg held her breath, wondering if he'd actually go so far as to thank her for her role, but that didn't happen. "So are we, Detective. Oh, do you know where Monica will be buried? Do they have a family plot?"

"Back in Ohio, I believe. As soon as the formalities are completed. Art, thanks for keeping me up to date. Meg, Seth—try to stay out of trouble, will you?"

Meg wondered if she saw a smile as he strode out the door. She thought they deserved one after handing him the solution to Monica's murder on a silver platter, but she was never sure about the detective.

Art stayed behind. Seth asked him, "It is over?"

"All but the paperwork, I'd guess. Good work, you two. You figured it out without anyone trying to shut you up and you handed it over to Marcus without a whimper. You're learning."

"I hope we won't have to go through this again, Art," Meg said. "I only wish there was something more we could have done. If we'd known more about their situation, maybe we could have gotten them help."

"Meg, at the risk of repeating myself, this was not your fault, either one of you. Monica Whitman chose to move here, knowing full well her husband's limitations. She could have reached out, but she chose not to. There was no way she could have reversed the course of her husband's disease, and I'm sure she couldn't have foreseen what he would do out of love. None of us could. I thank you for your help, and I'm pretty sure Marcus would, too. He owes you, even if he won't admit it. Now go about your business, will you? You got something planned, Seth?"

"Yup, we're going to rebuild the chicken coop."

"Good luck with that. Oh, one last question: where did Douglas hide the extra pills?"

Meg almost smiled. "Apparently in his underwear drawer. The state police didn't look too hard there."

"Ah. Thanks, I'll remember that in the future." Art checked his watch. "Gotta go. And if you find another body, will you please call Marcus first?"

"We will. Thanks, Art."

When they were alone again, Meg said, "So it's really over, and we can get back to our normal lives?"

"We can. We will. Let's go build a tiny house."

Recipes

Meg Corey, now Chapin, is often too busy to cook, what with training a new orchard employee and helping out with a new town-wide event—and solving the occasional murder.

Roasted Carrot Soup

This is a recipe that comes from the restaurant Gran's in the heart of Granford. It's easy to make, and it has an eye-popping color!

1 lb carrots, peeled and cut into chunks
½ lb beets, peeled and cut into chunks
1 medium onion, thickly sliced
2 Tbsp good olive oil

4 cups stock (chicken or vegetable)
Salt and freshly ground pepper, to taste

Preheat the oven to 400 degrees F. In a bowl, toss the carrots, beets, and onion with the olive oil, then spread them in a single layer on a large rimmed baking sheet. Roast for about 20 minutes, stirring a couple of times (so they don't stick), until they are tender and beginning to brown around the edges.

Place the cooked vegetables in a large saucepan. Add the stock, cover, and bring to a boil. Simmer over low heat until all the vegetables are tender, about 20 minutes.

Puree the soup in a blender or food processor or with an immersion blender to whatever smoothness you desire. Keep the soup warm in the pan, and season it with the salt and pepper.

Serve in deep bowls. If you want to dress it up, add a dollop of crème fraîche and maybe a sprig of dill. Serve immediately.

Note: in winter you can add other vegetables as well—butternut squash, parsnips, sweet potato—to make it a heartier soup. You can also spice it up with a dash of pepper sauce or chile powder—it's a very versatile recipe!

Almond Cheesecake Pound Cake

No time for baking either, but this recipe makes a single large cake or two loaf cakes, so Meg can pop one in the freezer and pull it out when unexpected company arrives.

3½ cups flour

½ tsp baking powder

½ tsp baking soda

½ tsp salt

1½ cups (3 sticks) unsalted butter, at room
temperature

1 8-oz package cream cheese, at room temperature

2¾ cups granulated sugar

5 eggs

2 tsp vanilla extract

2 tsp almond extract

Preheat the oven to 350 degrees F. Generously butter and flour a 10-inch Bundt pan. (Note: you need a pan that holds about 10 cups. While there's not a lot of baking powder/soda in this recipe, it does rise a bit, and if you try to squeeze into a smaller pan, it may overflow. Don't fill your pan to the top.)

Sift together the flour, baking powder, baking soda, and salt. Set aside.

In a stand mixer set on medium high, cream the butter for 2 minutes. Add the cream cheese and beat for 2 minutes more.

Add the sugar in 3 additions, beating after each addition and scraping down the sides of the bowl. When all the sugar is added, beat for 1 minute more.

Beat in the eggs, one at a time, mixing enough to blend (do not overbeat). Add the vanilla and almond extracts.

Turn the mixer to low and add the flour mixture in 3 additions.

Scrape down the sides of the bowl and spoon the mixture into the baking pan. Smooth the top with a rubber spatula.

Bake for 65–70 minutes in the middle of the oven. (Because it is a dense cake, the outside may begin to brown before the interior is cooked. If you're concerned, cover the top loosely with a piece of foil and/or reduce the heat to 325 degrees F.) The cake is done when a skewer comes out clean and the cake shrinks away a bit from the sides of the pan.

Cool in the pan on a rack for 10 minutes. Turn the cake out on a wire rack and cool completely. (If you want to dress it up, you could add an almond glaze using butter, confectioners' sugar, and almond extract.)

This cake slices neatly and keeps well.

Sautéed Chicken French Style

This is a modern version of a traditional dish—one that Meg can use to impress those guests!

> 4 chicken breasts (note: you can use either boneless,
>   skinless ones, which cook quickly, or bone-in
>   ones, which some people believe add more
>   flavor—just make sure they're cooked through)
> 1 Tbsp vegetable oil
> 2 Tbsp butter
> ½ cup minced shallots
> 1 tsp fresh thyme
> 1 Tbsp minced garlic (about 4 cloves, depending on
>   size)

1 Tbsp flour
¾ cup dry white wine
½ cup chicken broth
½ cup heavy cream
½ tsp fresh lemon juice
Salt and pepper
3 Tbsp fresh parsley

In a large skillet heat the oil over medium-high heat until shimmering. Sautée the chicken until lightly browned, turning once. Set aside.

Reduce the heat, add the butter and let it melt. Add the shallots, thyme, and a half teaspoon of salt, and cook over medium-low heat until the shallots are soft.

Add the garlic and flour and cook for about a minute.

Add the wine, scrape the pan to gather up all those tasty bits that stuck to it, and whisk until there are no lumps. Cook for about a minute longer, until the sauce thickens. Add the broth and stir.

Return the chicken and any juices from it to the pan, dunk both sides in the sauce, cover, and cook until the chicken is done. Remove the chicken to a serving platter and keep warm while you finish the sauce.

Add the cream to the sauce in the skillet, turn the heat up to medium high, and cook until the sauce thickens. Remove from the heat and add the lemon juice. Taste and add salt and pepper if you like. Stir in the parsley.

Pour the sauce over the chicken pieces and serve with rice.